Something in the Water

and Other Stories

Something in the Water

and Other Stories

Douglas Wynne

First Edition
Trade Paperback Edition

ISBN: 978-1-957121-09-3

Editor & Publisher, Joe Morey

Copy editing and interior design by F. J. Bergmann
Author photo by Jen Salt

Weird House Press
Central Point, OR 97502
www.weirdhousepress.com

Publication History

"The Last Chord" first appeared in *Dark Discoveries,* 2013.

"Tracking the Black Book" first appeared in *The Lovecraft eZine,* 2013.

"Rattled" first appeared in *The Gods of H. P. Lovecraft* (JournalStone, 2015).

"The Voyager" first appeared in *The Lovecraft eZine,* 2016.

"Something in the Water" first appeared in *Shadows Over Main Street* (Cutting Block, 2017).

"The White Door" first appeared in *Tales From the Miskatonic University Library* (PS Publishing, 2017).

"The Mouth of the Merrimack" first appeared in *A Secret Guide to Fighting Elder Gods* (Pulse, 2019)

"The Enigma Signal" first appeared in *One of Us* (Bloodshot Books, 2020)

"Contact," "Good Bones," "No Mask" and "Time Out of Mind" are original to this collection.

For Mike Davis, who raised a big tent for the weird carnival

List of Illustrations

Table of Contents

... I beheld the gently undulating form of the Father of Serpents.

Rattled

The myth caught up with me in New York City, returning after years like a dog lost on a family vacation, mangy and battered and possibly rabid. Not to be trusted, and yet, undeniably familiar. It came in a moment of synchronicity, the light of dawn still far off and the light of the skyscrapers scraped thin across the November sky. I was burrowed down in my sleeping bag on the cold ground of Zuccotti Park, listening to bits of conversation and the staggering, syncopated rhythm of the drum circle winding down in the Sacred Space.

After all the years of denial, distortion, and creative recollection, this was the first time I heard the defining event of my childhood, the *final* event of my childhood, framed so succinctly. The words reached me as I drifted in the liminal state between waking and dreaming, the muted pulse of the djembe and shakers lulling me until the phrase struck a chord and jerked me back to wakefulness, images of red rock formations gnawed by the insatiable wind haunting my head.

"You ever hear of the Curse of Yig?"

A small group was huddled around one of the rectangular ground lights that glowed from the granite like the center lines on a highway, the cold white illumination failing to do much to define their faces. I craned my neck toward the group. The speaker was female. I hadn't met her yet, but had maybe seen her working in the library tent. Long beaded braids, aquiline nose, dressed in a pea coat that looked too big for her anorexic frame. She was saying something about how myths weren't meant to be taken literally, but that you could decode any culture's values by them. More of the same pseudo-intellectual blather I'd been hearing all day and now it was going to sing me to sleep, but I swore I'd heard her mention the curse. Or was that just my tired brain slapping a pattern over a rhythmically similar phrase? I'd almost tuned out again and pulled the insulated nylon flap over my ear when she said it again.

"The Curse of Yig. It's a Native American legend from the Snake People. Have you guys heard of the Snake People? No? That's the name the whites gave to the Shoshone and Paiute Indians. They had settlements along the Snake River on the west coast. You guys should read up on the Snake War. It was the deadliest Indian war in the West, but it's mostly been forgotten by history because it was overshadowed by the Civil War."

Someone who sounded like he might be talking around an indrawn hit off a joint interrupted the amateur anthropologist to get her back on track: "What's the curse?"

I silently thanked him.

"I'm getting to it," she said. "I heard about it from a shaman I met in Colorado." The storyteller paused, whether for effect or to take a hit of her own, I couldn't tell. I was lying on my back now, looking up at the light-polluted cloud cover through the little golden leaves of the honey locust trees while I listened.

"Okay, the legend is simple, right? If you kill a snake on sacred ground, you become a snake, or a snake-like creature."

"That's it?"

"Yeah, that's it. Why does everything have to be three acts and explosions?"

"Sacred ground. Isn't all ground sacred to the Indians?"

"Sacred to Yig, the snake god. There are power places scattered over the Earth dedicated to him where ley lines intersect. Places where the kundalini energy of the planet wells up to the surface. In Nepal he's Nagaraja, in Mexico Quetzalcoatl, and in Africa he is known by many names. Anyway, the curse, it's like karma, right? It means that the Indians valued the lowest of the low, creatures literally without a leg to stand on. And if you hurt one, you should expect to find yourself stripped of power and crawling on your belly on the ground among them, yeah? So what I'm saying is: look at any people's myths and you'll see what their values are."

"Yeah, you said that."

"I did. And I'm saying it again man, because you're not fuckin' hearing me. What are the myths of these bankers who prey on families? What myths are the cops digesting when they gather around the Comcast campfire for story time?"

I turned inward after that, sinking down deep in the bag and heating it with my breath as fatigue finally claimed me. The last sound I heard before I drifted off was the languid grainy rattle of maracas from the last percussionist standing in the Sacred Space by the London plane tree.

In the morning I slithered out of my sleeping bag, packed my scant possessions, and headed uptown to the Port Authority where I bought an Amtrak ticket west. In Chicago, I would learn that the police had cracked down on the demonstration right after I left, clearing the park in riot gear. When I read the news I felt a little pang of guilt for checking out early. I'd met some good people at Occupy and I hoped they were okay. I'll admit I've never been especially political, but I've always wanted to find my tribe.

When I reached Omaha, I changed to buses to save money and paid extra for a handgun without a permit at a pawnshop. I barely looked at the thing before rolling it up in my sleeping bag. A simple revolver that looked reliable. Not that I know much about guns. I only knew that it lacked the wicked beauty of the first one I'd ever held in my hands when I was 13 and living in California.

♦

It was a girl that set us apart and a gun that brought us back together, at least for a little while.

Adam and I met on a soccer team when we were seven. The Roughnecks. I played for six seasons and have forgotten most of the teams I was on, but I still remember the orange and black uniforms of the Roughnecks. Adam's dad was the head coach, mine the assistant, and as they became friends we started seeing each other outside of games and practices and spent a lot of time in each other's pools that first summer.

One-on-one soccer on the lawn and board games when it rained. Battleship and an old version of Chutes and Ladders handed down from Adam's grandparents, called Snakes and Ladders. Adam usually won, even in games of chance and if he'd gone on to college, I'm sure he would have climbed the ladder somewhere.

A summer can feel like an age when you're seven years old, and by the time we went back to school it felt like I'd known him forever. We were on different teams the following year, and it wasn't until junior high that we attended the same school. I didn't realize until then that unlike me Adam had plenty of friends. I was more introverted. Well, *bullied* might be a more honest way to put it. And unlike me, Adam had an easy way with girls. Of course at that age, all circuits were firing and it wasn't long before he told me he'd made out with Gina Barbieri, a pert little blonde I knew but didn't find attractive. Blondes weren't really my thing, but I could see why other guys would be into her. Adam didn't go into detail when he told me the score, but it was clear he was bursting to share the achievement.

It was just the latest thing he had done to outpace me, to leave me behind. Over winter break he'd even gone hunting with his grandfather and claimed to have shot a deer. I wasn't sure if I believed him about the kill, but I *had* heard his father talking to mine about the trip before it happened.

A kill.

A kiss.

On the day Adam told me about Gina's tits and tongue, I got some cardboard boxes from the garage and packed up most of the toys that still cluttered my room.

I still don't know if he was just raising the stakes and showing off when he filched the gun from his grandfather's dresser, or if he was trying to repair things between us and bring me in on something risky with him because he sensed how badly I needed it. In any case, I remember the heady rush and the renewed sense of standing at eye level with him when he took it out of his backpack and handed it to me swaddled in a red rag that smelled of oil.

The weight of the bundle surprised me. He hadn't told me what the "surprise" was and I thought maybe he'd brought his BB gun. My parents wouldn't let me have one, and even shooting his would have been good. But the weight in my hand told me this was no BB gun. I looked around the junkyard at the refrigerators and washing machines leaning against uprooted trees amid the fragile lattice of rust-eaten cars. We were alone.

"Go ahead," he said, and bumped my shoulder with his.

I unfolded the fabric, and the nickel plate flared in the sunlight. It was engraved near the grip with a wild horse rearing up. A Colt.

"Is it loaded?"

Adam nodded and I went a little numb in the fingers. This was real.

He had handed me adulthood and it was all silver and black.

Stamped on the short barrel were the words *KING COBRA*.

I met his eyes and I'm sure mine looked too wide, devoid of cool.

He laughed, a lighthearted, breezy sound. "Man, you should have seen Matt's face when I showed him a bullet on the bus," he said. "I don't think he'll be riding you in the locker room after gym anymore."

My face flushed with heat, a mixture of gratitude and embarrassment. I focused on the gun in my hand and felt momentarily lifted off of the ground by a wave of exhilarating fear. *What does he expect of me?*

"What are we gonna do with it?"

Adam laughed again and slapped me on the back. "We're gonna shoot some fuckin' rats, man."

Rats were a huge relief compared to the thought of threatening Matt Fremantle with a loaded gun. They were also better than deer, in my book. I'd honestly felt a little sick at the thought of my friend blowing a hole in a deer, but rats were nasty, disease-ridden vermin. I'd already seen a friend's brother who worked at a pet store feed a rat to a snake one time, and I don't think I could've done that; dangle one from its tail over the fangs. That would almost be the same as crushing one under my shoe. But the gun would take them out in a flash. I could hear them scampering through the junk, see the places where loose scraps of metal and cardboard trembled at their passage. It made my skin crawl.

5

Adam was bouncing his heel on the ground beside me like he did when he was gaming or anticipating something, his knee bobbing in an agitated rhythm, a vestige of the ADHD his parents had medicated into remission. "Get in a shooting stance," he said. "Sight it on the junk pile. You want to be ready *before* you spot one."

I raised the gun, gripped it with both hands, and bisected the trembling trash heap with the sight blade.

I was wired. Was that a scaly tail flicking through a rust hole?

"Feet shoulder-width apart. That's it. Dude, this bitch is a .357. You hit one it's gonna pop like a blood balloon."

A flash of fur.

I saw Adam sliding his hand down Gina's pants.

A deer collapsing in a thicket.

The power to make life. The power to take it. A threshold between us.

A rat scampered across the fuel tank of a tractor chassis and perched there on its haunches, its black fur stark against the blue sky.

I christened it with thunder.

Danny Wormbone. Not a handle I expected a New Age huckster to still be going by almost twenty years later. But there he was in the search results advertising *RUNES, MEDICINE CARDS, SPIRITUAL COUNSELING & RETREATS*. In 1994 my father had probably found him in the Yellow Pages. Now he had a website that might very well be obsolete, and what had once been a "vision quest" was now a "spiritual retreat." I wrote down the phone number. The Greyhound station on Main Street where I had rolled into town still had a few pay phones, but the nearest hotel with an internet kiosk didn't. Apparently they attracted the wrong crowd—people like me, who couldn't keep up with a cell-phone bill.

I hoofed it back to the bus station and made the call before I could think too much about it and change my mind. It rang three times before voicemail picked up. His recorded voice was familiar, if a little more worn down to gravel by years of smoke: "Your call is important to me." That was all he said before the beep, but it was enough to know I had the right guy. I didn't leave a message and was glad he hadn't picked up. The business address I'd jotted on my notepad wasn't located on the strip among the high-end psychics, but here in the old town. I decided to walk.

Would he recognize me when I stepped into his parlor? I didn't think I looked much like I had at 13. Back then he'd said a bunch of stuff about my aura. Told me it was blue. I wondered if he'd see the same energy when I showed up 17 years later. It wasn't likely.

I recognized the symbol painted on the plate glass before I could even read the name. A constellation in white: Ophiuchus, the snake handler, floating in the sky over a crossed feather and staff. The shop was at street level, between a podiatrist and a Mexican restaurant. It looked dark inside, but when I tried the door I found it unlocked and entered to the sound of wind chimes. Of course the first thing to hit me while my eyes adjusted to the cluttered murk was the diffused smell of burning sage.

The proprietor hadn't overlooked the merchandising possibilities. Racks of tie-dyed tapestries printed with tribal motifs, spirit animals, and celestial designs obstructed my view of the shop. Parting a pair of them like curtains, I found my way into a larger area where dim sunlight from the street illuminated a glass countertop through which I glimpsed a variety of quartz crystals and amethyst geodes. Bookshelves flanked the counter, stocked with a sparse collection of New Age and astrological titles interspersed with painted woodcarvings and brass statues: a turquoise wolf, a masked dancing shaman, even a Buddha sitting in lotus position with an awning of hooded cobras over his head to shelter him from the rain. Behind the counter the wall was lined with charts. A medicine pipe hung from a nail by a loop of rawhide. A barstool stood vacant behind the cash register, a knobby walking stick of lustrous black wood leaning in the corner beside it.

Danny Wormbone emerged from the back room through a slit in a tapestry. My first thought was that it couldn't be him, because it looked too much like him. Surely he would have aged more in the intervening years. But he had the same jet-black hair, the same leathery skin, the same sinewy build and that deep hollow I remembered where his throat met his breastbone. The same quick eyes set close to his nose like you see on any wild predator, and the same quiet, gentle demeanor as he moved through the space and settled on the stool as if intent on stirring the air as little as necessary.

I nodded at him. He nodded back, his face as impassive as it had been from the moment it emerged through the curtain, his expression betraying no sign of recognition.

As usual, I was winging it. I still didn't know if I was going to ask if he remembered me or play it like a stranger in search of spiritual counseling.

The moment passed and I browsed the shop in silence. When I looked at the countertop again, Wormbone had produced a small block of wood and was whittling it with a buck knife over a square of canvas littered with shavings.

I approached the counter. I figured I had enough cash to hire him as a guide, but not enough to spend more than a couple of nights in this town before heading on to SoCal where I still had friends. It wouldn't do to have him pencil me in on his calendar like any other walk-in. I'd come a long way to be here, and it was time to get to the point. Probably a lot of people stepped into a shop like that without knowing exactly what they were looking for. I imagine part of his job was getting them to articulate it. I had crossed most of the continent without admitting to myself exactly what I was after. Now I was faced with the only person who could help me. So what was I looking for? Closure? It felt more like I was opening something.

A can of worms.

A grave.

Wormbone remained focused on his carving until finally, wondering if he'd noticed me, I drummed my fingers on the glass countertop. Without looking up from the spiral of blond wood curling around his blade, he said one word. The only word I needed to hear to know he knew me. "*Unukalhai*. Wondered when I'd see you again."

"I want to go back."

"It'll cost you," he said, poking a pupil into the eye of the creature he was carving. I couldn't make out what it was. A crude dragon, maybe.

"I have money."

8

"And I'll take it." He finally looked up and locked his gaze on mine. "But I'm not talking about money."

I'm at my 13th birthday party. I know this because there's a pair of those big number candles on the cake. I don't think my mother ever got those for me, but in the dream, there they are, unlit. The dining room is decorated with nothing but red helium balloons. I think I'm alone at the table. Have I just blown the candles out, or have they not been lit yet? I examine the wicks for ash and find virgin white string. Adam says, "They're blood balloons." He's sitting next to me but somehow I don't see him until he speaks. Each balloon trails a length of ribbon, like the tail of a sperm cell. "Aren't you gonna blow them out?" Adam asks.

I look again and now the candles are lit. But no one is singing. My family isn't here.

I take a breath, make a wish, and blow out the twin flames. The red balloons pop, showering the table, the cake and my hair with scrappy, coagulating splashes of blood and tufts of coarse brown fur.

I had that dream on and off for about a week while the heel of my right hand ached in my sleep from the recoil of the revolver. I'd missed the rat with every shot.

My parents must have discussed the vision quest before my dad presented the idea to me, but it became clear in the first weeks of June as more detail trickled in, that my mother had serious reservations about what my father (having no doubt read too much Carl Jung and Joseph Campbell) thought would make a good substitution for a confirmation or a bar mitzvah. To be honest, so did I. Maybe the same concerns were shared by Adam's mother, Renée. If so, Adam didn't mention it.

"I just hope they don't think they're gonna babysit us the whole time," he said. "It would defeat the whole purpose. I mean, this is supposed to be hardcore, man. Rite of passage, not the fucking Boy Scouts."

9

I agreed fervently, although I knew the only reason my mother hadn't intervened and called the whole thing off was exactly because my dad had been promising her he would shadow me like a scout leader. In my presence he downplayed his role, of course, not wanting to undermine the mystique going in or any sense of accomplishment I might have coming out. But I heard more of their conversations than they realized.

"You can't starve and dehydrate our kid," she said. "And sleep deprivation? If Child Services ever heard about it … Christ, how can this guy operate legally with minors involved?"

"You make it sound so extreme. We'll have water. Absolutely. It's the desert. Do you think I'm crazy? I mean, where did you even get that? I'm not going to neglect him. A little light fasting never killed anyone. It's healthy. Healthier than how he eats most of the time. You know, I'm a little insulted that you don't think I'll intervene if necessary."

She sighed. "It's not you, it's Lee. Or how you two are together. Knowing him, he'll toss your emergency provisions off a cliff just to impress the boys."

"No, he won't."

"And you'll let him, just to prove you're not a wimp."

"Hey, that's not fair. You know I'll take care of Nathan. No harm will come to him."

Everything is vibrating. The striated sandstone formations pulse in bands of blood red, lavender, and bone yellow. The sky stretches and retracts like the skin of a funeral drum with each beat of my heart and under everything, no, *inside* everything, buzzing like the collision of fire-wreathed atoms is the all-pervasive sound of rattles—keratin rings dancing in the tip of a serpent's tail and the world is in thrall to that hypnotic rhythm. A sound as rich as a symphony of cicadas, but I've seen no insects among the sagebrush and mesquite. I'm slicked with sweat and my knees and elbows are skinned from stumbling over rock and I feel like I'm tripping, but I've never tripped, not yet, not until college, I haven't even tried weed yet but Adam has—that was the last thing he tried before me, and it's the last thing he'll ever try before me, but I don't know that yet, and I'm trying to make sense of all this sensory distortion. Can it really be the lack of food and sleep? Is it possible that disturbing the rhythms of the body's needs just a little can screw with your perception this bad, this fast and send you so far out? I'm scared. We got lost. My throat is sore from calling for the men but I'm trying to conserve the last of the water in my canteen and this is not a dream. Not a dream, but still it haunts me. It haunts me for fucking years.

Adam's posture changes when he crests the slope and steps through the arch, leaving a gray handprint in sweat on the limestone. He goes rigid and I swear I can hear his breath stopping in his chest. He steps backward slowly and slips out of the straps of his backpack. He feels for the telescoping shovel that hangs from the pack without ever taking his eyes off what lies beyond the arch, now gliding over the threshold and coiling to strike.

A Mohave green rattlesnake, probably four feet long with black and white rings near the tail. We learned about them in school, so I know it's deaf despite its warning rattle, has heat-sensors between its nostrils and eyes, is notoriously aggressive and possessed of a far more powerful venom than its cousin, the western diamondback—a frequently lethal neurotoxin. Lee has a snakebite kit in his pack but that does us no good unless the men find us, or we find them, and we got ourselves lost on purpose, and I'm praying that they know where we are and are just keeping out of sight, laying low, ignoring our calls to give our trial meaning, to scare us, but my cries have been so desperate that they would have come. They would have come.

The snake winds over itself in a figure eight, its head rising, the rattle erect and vibrating like everything else in this heightened world, a translucent gray blur.

Adam is gripping the shovel, sliding backward, sending pebbles and dust tumbling down the slope toward me and raising the shaft in both hands like a spear, but it's not a shovel, it's a hand spade—too small, too pointed, too close-range. He must be crazy. A square flat blade might take the snake's head off, but this? The blade is triangular like the rattler's head. He would have to move faster than the snake. He would have to have dead aim.

11

I open my mouth to yell *no,* but he stabs the spade down into the dirt, heaving his weight behind it, and I have time to think he's breaking ground on his own grave, but then the snake's head rolls between his hiking shoes, down the slope with the scree. The jaws are still twitching and crying venom, and I jump out of the way of it with an animal vocalization that comes out somewhere between a moan and a yelp, surprising even me with its alien timbre.

But that other sound, the sound under and in the heart of everything, the rattle and hum of cannibal Creation, goes on.

Adam turns to face me, his skin pale against the ruddy sandstone. "Don't touch it," he says. "You know what they say about a severed snake head? It doesn't die until sundown."

The bad shit that happened when I was 13 caught up with me at 31. Or I caught up with it. 1331: tally all the digits and you get 8. Roll it on its side and you get infinity, or a snake winding over on itself. Maybe I never outran any of it, never believed the lies the adults told me back then. The lies they told the police, the school, and each other.

Danny Wormbone hadn't aged much. Maybe that was the Indian blood in him, maybe it was something else. The weather was good for the end of November and he agreed to take me out to the Moapa Paiute lands north of Vegas, the reservation where he had been living when my father called him in 1994. It was early afternoon when we left town in a jeep he kept in a rented garage down the street. He tossed his walking stick in the backseat after my backpack and sleeping bag. I only brought my gear because I had nowhere else to leave it. I wasn't planning on sleeping in the desert.

The jeep smelled of cigarettes. Rock and roll on the radio and a dusty little dream catcher hanging from the rearview. I had paid the old medicine man two hundred dollars for the ride and trail guide, but he wasn't much for talk. He smoked and drove and I watched the city thin out and the silver clouds move in over the Mojave.

Seventeen years ago we had met Wormbone at a picnic area inside Valley of Fire National Park. We came, the four of us, in Adam's dad's SUV and after a final lunch, followed our "spirit guide" to a second site outside the park. He rode a motorcycle with leather fringe saddlebags, but nothing about him besides his braided hair looked particularly Native American. He was dressed in denim, cowboy boots, and sunglasses and asked us if we'd been expecting feathers.

We hiked in silence and I think my dad was wondering if he and Lee were going to get their money's worth. At sunset we arrived at a red rock wall covered with petroglyphs, the rock an almost blackened rust color, the glyphs contrasting in pale salmon: concentric circles, silhouettes of bighorn sheep, spoked wheels, and pairs of zigzagging lines.

Wormbone ran his finger over one of the zigzags. "This is the snake," he said. "Symbol of rebirth. Humans have connected with the energy of rebirth, regeneration, and transformation on this land since prehistoric times. Since long before your tribe or mine ever came here." He took a bottle of red wine from the saddlebag of his motorcycle and a corkscrew from the pocket of his denim jacket. He opened the bottle, lined up five waxed paper cups, and poured.

Without asking our fathers if we could partake, he held his own cup up to the sun in a toast and said, "Join me in the sacrament. This wine, the blood red of the iron earth and the all-sustaining sun, taste it as you absorb the power and glory of this place."

We raised our cups to the sun and drank. The wine tasted bitter.

From another pocket Wormbone produced a silver cigarette lighter adorned with a turquoise stone and held the flame to the end of the cork. He let it burn for a few seconds, then shook it out in the cool evening air. He brushed the hair away from my forehead with his callused fingers and drew something there with the charcoal. I didn't know what it was until he had done the same to Adam: a pair of zigzagging lines like the symbol for Aquarius written vertically.

"Take the serpent as your symbol. The undulating pulse of life, the winding path, the one who sheds his form to be reborn."

He poured the remainder of the wine into the dirt, mounted his bike, and kicked it to life with a roar.

We followed in the car to the next stop where he told us to gather our gear for the hike. He pointed out the ridge and the towering formation that was to be the site of our first camp. In the clear desert air it looked closer than it was. Adam and I set out at a brisk pace and were soon far ahead of the men, but before long we tired and the gap narrowed until Wormbone's staff was scratching the dirt at my heels.

Now here was that sound again, this time ahead of me, as I followed the old shaman up the trail. We had passed by the petroglyphs without so much as a pause to look this time, never mind a pep talk and a toast. The trail was deserted. Most hikers kept to the official park trails, and this one was outside the boundary. I wasn't sure if it was on reservation land or not. We had passed the Moapa Paiute Travel Plaza off of I-15. Fireworks, alcohol, tobacco, and gas. We hadn't stopped. Now, hiking up the ridge, I regretted not asking him to pull in so I could use the bathroom and buy some bottled water. It could have been enlightening to watch him interact with whoever worked there. I wondered what kind of reaction his presence provoked. Respect? Scorn? Fear? Or was he just another New Age snake-oil salesman claiming Indian heritage? Would they even recognize him?

"This is the place," he said, punching the earth with his staff and sweeping his hand over the vast expanse of prismatic sandstone, frozen waves of geologic record lapping at an endless shore. "This is where we made our main camp for the vision quest." His manner and tone implied fulfillment of the job I'd hired him for. But no, we were far from done here.

"Do you still take kids on quests, with the fasting and staying up all night?"

He didn't answer. He traced a spiral in the dust with his staff, scrutinized me, and asked, "You think I'm responsible for what happened to your friend?"

"I don't know."

"His parents took on the risks. They signed a waiver. Yours did, too. Do you think the desert isn't dangerous? Do you think confronting it would mean anything if it wasn't?"

"I don't know what happened to Adam," I said. "But you do, I know you do. I didn't come all the way here to blame you. I just want to know what happened."

"Then you should have gone to his father."

"His father ate a gun a long time ago. And I don't know if his mother ever really knew what happened."

"You boys shouldn't have wandered off on your own."

I scanned the paths that branched off from the ridge. Some wound around sculpted rock formations that resembled faces in profile or the silhouettes of great spiny beasts. Others were lost among the sage and cacti. "This is where you showed us the stars," I said.

Wormbone nodded.

"All that snake-themed mumbo jumbo. Ironic, don't you think?"

His eyes narrowed.

"You pointed out Virgo, Hercules, and the Snake Handler near the horizon. You pointed out the bright star you called the *Heart of the Serpent*—"

"Unukalhai. That's the Arabic name. The double star in the serpent's throat."

"Yeah, you said we were like a double star, Adam and I. Connected by our own invisible gravity, like brothers."

"You were. Anyone could see that. But he burned brighter."

"His parents told everyone he died of a snakebite. But I was there when he killed the snake. It never bit him."

"He should have left it alone."

"So he deserved what happened to him?"

"You don't kill your avatar on a vision quest."

"We were delirious from deprivation and faced with a venomous snake. I think you set us up for that."

"Why would I do that?"

"The Curse of Yig."

Wormbone turned, grinding the end of his staff in the ground, and started back down the trail. "I brought you here, like you asked. You can hitch a ride back to the city from the truck stop, chum."

I drew the gun from under my shirt at the small of my back and cocked the hammer. He spun on me, nostrils flaring.

"I want my money's worth, medicine man. Take me to the arch where it happened."

♦

15

Adam was contorted on the ground beside the severed snake when the men found us. Wormbone hung back while Lee and my dad knelt in the dust and tried to keep him from thrashing. When they finally overpowered him, my dad—pale, sweaty and wide-eyed—asked me what had happened, while Lee curled a finger into his son's mouth to keep him from choking on his own tongue.

Before I could answer, Wormbone asked, "Is he prone to seizures?"

"No," Lee said, never taking his eyes from Adam's bluing face.

"Allergic to bee stings?"

"What? No. Look, it was a snake. He was bitten by a snake."

"Was he?" Wormbone looked at me. He seemed so calm, like we were discussing the weather.

"No," I said. "It didn't bite him. It came after us but he killed it with the spade."

Lee cried out and yanked his finger from Adam's mouth. A ruby ribbon of blood ran down his hand. He stared at it in awe. "Bit me. *Jesus.*"

Adam shook his head in his father's lap, showing his teeth. I could swear they were fangs. We all jumped and shuffled back, all except for Wormbone who held his staff out in front of him, as if it would ward off the threat, and for a second I wondered if he was going to shove the stick in Adam's jaws to give him something to bite down on, like you might do to a dog.

Lee sucked the blood off his finger and dug through his pack, quickly losing patience and dumping the contents in the dirt. Adam hissed at him, and Lee scampered out of range, dragging his fingers through the scattered camping paraphernalia and seizing on a bright yellow plastic box. He popped the lid. A syringe and a set of suction cups spilled out, along with a few alcohol wipes. "Where did it bite him?" he yelled at me. I'd never seen an adult look so scared in my life.

"It *didn't* bite him," I said again, but Lee seemed unable to process the information and by then even I was wondering if I'd seen it wrong, missed something.

"It had to have," my father said. "Did it get him on the leg?"

"I don't know. I ... I didn't see it bite him!"

Lee reached for Adam's exposed calf below his cargo shorts, but Adam kicked dirt at him and kept kicking until he gained some traction and was up on his feet, sprinting up the rise and through the sandstone arch.

The sun was sinking fast, the shadows of the rock formations stretching toward the horizon. My heart was flopping, a fish in a bucket. My eyes stung with sweat. Lee ran through the arch after Adam, and I went to follow, but my father stopped me with a palm to the hollow of my shoulder. "Wait here, Nathan. Just wait for us." He shot a glance at Wormbone and I could see all kinds of calculation in it: not trusting the man to help them restrain Adam, not trusting him to stay with me, and a suspicion that he wouldn't heed instructions anyway. The sound of Lee calling Adam's name echoed in the valley. My dad jogged through the arch, holding his hand out behind him in my direction, his fingers splayed. "Just ... stay back," he said. "Let me go first."

But I followed him through the arch, leaving Wormbone staring at the severed body of the rattler in the blood-gummed sand.

Later there were dogs and a helicopter. The men called 911 from the Travel Plaza and the police came searching for Adam, ready to airlift him to Vegas for anti-venom. But they never found him. Not all of him, anyway. What the dogs found tangled in the brush and cactus needles two days later was tatters of necrotic tissue, gossamer sheaths in the shapes of a boy's limbs, sloughed off and left behind.

It could have been yesterday when I'd last stood here with my father, Lee and Danny Wormbone, except that the season was different: cooler and with fewer yellow flowers in the creosote bushes. And now it was just the two of us. I followed my shadow through the arch. The sun had sunk below the cloud cover in the west, gilding the formations. I felt as if I were passing into a cathedral. The arch marked the pinnacle of the formation we had been climbing. On the other side it began its eastern descent through a series of interconnected open caves, each spilling into the next through terraced slopes of vermiculated red rock, illuminated at intervals where the dusty sunlight spilled through apertures in the sandstone. There were petroglyphs here as well, but they were different, less pictogram and more akin to cuneiform writing.

I worked my jaw and felt a pressure I hadn't been aware of open up in my inner ear. A sound like cicadas poured into my consciousness, an unnerving texture that made my stomach roil and churn.

Wormbone turned to me. I pointed the gun at his chest and jutted my chin toward the descending slopes. He shuffled down ahead of me, jabbing at strategic angles in the rock with his staff for balance. I followed in a crouch, using many of the same footholds, and taking it slower so as not to have need of changing the gun to my left hand. I had no doubt the old medicine man could be swift as a viper if I gave him an opportunity.

"What's that sound," I asked. "Rattlers?"

He paused in his descent and when he answered, his voice echoed in the stone vaults. "Those rattles are to a rattlesnake what a symphony is to a street fiddler, son."

It wasn't much of an answer, but before I could press him further, a new layer of sound emerged from the drone, weaving and winding through the percussive texture with a breathy, sinuous dissonance. A flute.

"Where is that music coming from?" I hoped my voice didn't sound panicked.

He was outpacing me now, passing into the lower bowels of the cave system. He didn't answer.

I asked again. "Who's making that music? Tell me."

His head swiveled toward me, his eyes radiating a jaundiced contempt in the fading light. "My tribe," he said. "Isn't that why you came? For the initiation you never had?"

I sat on the slope and slid down to him, landing in the dust just out of reach of his staff if he chose to swing it. I kept the gun on him all the while, and standing again, I aimed it at his face.

He took a step away.

"No," I said. "Wait." I cupped the heel of my right hand with my left and moved around him in a wide arc, keeping the sight blade aligned to his head, thinking of junkyard rats.

18

"When Adam got away from his father and passed through here ... that wasn't the last time you saw him, was it?"

"No."

"Before, you said I should have gone to Adam's father. When the cops finished questioning us and let you go, that wasn't the last time you saw Lee, either. Was it?"

"No."

"I asked my mother about Adam's parents when I was home from college but she didn't want to talk about them. She said she and my father had a falling-out with them because they'd found religion after losing their son. They'd become fanatical about it, maybe even a little crazy. Was it *your* religion they found? I always assumed Lee would kill you as soon as look at you again after what happened."

"He wanted to at first. But grief can take the fight out of a man. And I had a balm for that."

"A balm? What did you do? Con them into accepting your version of the afterlife? Tell them you could commune with the spirits of the dead? Take advantage of shattered, grieving parents with your mystic bullshit?"

"I didn't have to convince them I could commune with the dead. Their son wasn't dead. I helped them to commune with the living."

"That's a lie. They would have taken him home if he was alive."

"The desert was his home by then, the deep places of the earth for his body and the cold fathoms of the sky for his consciousness, a sine wave undulating in the dark reaches of the night."

"How long did it take you to suck them dry?"

"I asked for nothing. They paid tribute to the Father of Serpents with the carcasses of cats and dogs, which they fed their boy as well. It was a comfort to them, feeding him. They couldn't talk with him in any human tongue by then, but they knew it was him. They knew him by his eyes."

Something massive moved through a tunnel behind me, the sand crunching under its weight.

We had arrived at a level where the curved stone walls were honeycombed with openings. I scanned the arches in the murk and caught glimpses of silhouettes gliding past, the sounds of flute and rattles phasing in and out as they passed, sound merging with echo, substance with shadow.

A quick motion from Wormbone drew my attention back to him. He had raised his walking stick like a javelin and now dashed it at the rock at my feet where it clattered and bounced before the shape of the thing wavered in a scribble of gold light, emerging as a black snake. Wormbone's body dissolved in a twist of oily smoke trailing after it and vanishing up its nostrils.

I sidestepped the snake, slipped on the smooth rock and almost fell. The snake reared up in a coil and hissed. I fired a shot at it, felt the thunder of the gun punch my eardrums, and saw the spray of limestone chips where the bullet drilled into the rock. The snake slithered out of view behind an hourglass pillar as I fired again.

Sweating and trembling with adrenaline, I surveyed the cavernous space around me. Below, the terraced slopes continued their descent through cavities of eroded stone where shadows pulsed like pools of black water lapping against the sand. The chamber around me was relatively wide, with yawning apertures at intervals in the walls. Without pause for deliberation, I lunged through the nearest of these, hoping to find a more direct and open path to the valley floor and the trail back to the jeep.

The chamber was round and high, the walls crawling with glistening sinuous shadows. Here and there ashen appendages reminiscent of human limbs emerged from the chaos of black motion, lit by the green phosphorescence of the central figure, which I first took to be a towering pillar of slime-covered stone. As my eyes adjusted to the darkness, the organic aspects of the form took precedence and I beheld the gently undulating form of the Father of Serpents.

A towering column of armored flesh, the pale ventral scales of the exposed underside bordered by a byzantine matrix of small dark scales that made the monster appear gem-encrusted in its own light. It radiated billowing veils of energy behind which a pair of sinewy arms rose with the graceful fluidity of a conductor drawing an orchestra into the beat preceding a crash. They lashed forward revealing humanoid hands, beaded fingers splayed and tipped with keratin bulbs that rattled as the hands vibrated in a translucent blur. The sound overwhelmed my body and mind, lacerating my brainwaves with virulent interference, paralyzing me in the blazing topaz gaze of Yig.

The creature lowered its head and I felt the baleful scrutiny of those ancient eyes probing my mind from beneath the scaly spikes of an organic crown studded with dying stars. Its forked tongue flickered, a cloven flame, tasting my aura of fear and pheromone.

And then the scrying of my soul ceased and I was released.

I fell to my knees in the darkness, my fingers finding beads of my own sweat in the dust. I crawled backward to the sounds of grotesque motion from the braided perimeter and nearly wept with relief when my groping hand found bare rock to guide me back to the fissure I had entered through.

The light had leeched from the sky and I felt my way through the honeycombed rock on my belly letting gravity and an updraft of sage-scented air guide me down and down to the valley floor.

A spike of pain flared in the webbing of my left hand and I recoiled with a cry as the black king snake, the alter-shape of Wormbone, wound around my forearm and reared up in my face with a hiss. My reaction was reflexive. I shoved the pistol in its mouth, squeezed the trigger, and pissed myself when the roar of the shot decayed in a rain of bone and blood in the darkness.

Moaning, nearly blind and deaf, I rolled and scampered through the hollows until a chute of polished rock swallowed me down and shat me out under the desert stars.

When I was younger I wanted to be a writer someday. I never managed to get it together. Maybe I lacked confidence. Maybe I made excuses. I spent a lot of years drifting, anesthetizing myself, trying to forget what happened that summer. You thought I was trying to find myself, but I was trying to find my tribe.

I may have found them now. And this will be the only story I leave behind.

I'm sorry, Mom and Dad. You should talk to Renée about joining the congregation. It's the oldest religion on Earth.

I took the medicine man's jeep down I-15 like the hordes of hell were on my trail, and I've holed up in a seedy motel on the outskirts of Vegas to set this down.

The skein of shed flesh that I've been depositing in the bathtub is almost the size of a man. Where the heel of my writing hand—my shooting hand—rubs against the paper, it's been worn through to black scales for a while already.

I probably shouldn't have left the valley. I don't know how I'll get back. I may have to travel beside the highway by night and hide in culverts when the sun is up.

I wonder if I will know Adam when I see him, smell him, read his heat signature in the dark. And I wonder if he will still burn brighter.

Something in the Water

If he'd been thirteen, or even twelve, it might have been the other way around, but Tommy Shayne was eleven when the newlyweds came to town, so the first thing he noticed about their car was the raised hood and the second was the lithe white leg jutting out of the passenger window. The leg disappeared from view as Tommy rolled up on the driver's side and resisted the temptation to peer through the window at the thigh that belonged to that calf. There was something playful in the way the lady's white shoe dangled from her toes, but as he passed the car, its own curves regained his attention. It was a Pontiac Bonneville, two-tone green and gleaming in the sun. Tommy, a collector of car magazines, put it at a '58.

The raised hood didn't offer any shade to the man bent over the engine, his tie loosened and his crisp white shirt drenched with sweat at the armpits. His hat lay atop the battery and Tommy could tell from the look on the man's face that he wasn't accustomed to peering beneath the hood of his car, however fine he might keep the paint job.

Tommy coasted his bike around behind the fellow, off the road and onto the crunching gravel. "Afternoon, mister. Nice car."

"Thanks, but it's not running so nice right now. I'm afraid it may have overheated."

"Like everything around here today." Tommy laughed. "Where are you headed?"

The man sighed, turned away from the confounding engine, and looked Tommy over. "New Hampshire. My wife and I are on our honeymoon to the White Mountains."

Tommy looked at the back of the car. "Where are the cans?"

The man smiled. "I think the last one fell off about a mile back." He wiped his hand on a rag and extended it. "I'm Bill Braddock. And the pretty lady riding shotgun is my wife Angela."

"Tommy Shayne, sir."

"And the name of this town we've had the unexpected pleasure to stop in?"

"Dunbury."

"Does Dunbury have a mechanic, Tommy?"

"Mr. Geritson. His garage is just up the road."

"I reckon he has a tow truck?"

"Yes, sir. Want me to go and fetch him for you if he's around?"

"That'd be swell."

Tommy mounted his bike and pointed it toward town just as a black sedan from that direction came up on Mr. Braddock's stalled Bonneville and slowed to a crawl. A round-faced man with ruddy cheeks and tawny hair leaned out the window and raised a chubby hand in a lazy wave. "Need a lift?"

"Well, that's kind of you," Mr. Braddock said. "But I think our young friend here is about to fetch us a tow truck from town."

The red-faced man looked Tommy over, then shot a glance back in the direction from which he'd come. "Dunbury, eh?"

"So I'm told," Mr. Braddock said.

The man in the black sedan rubbed the back of his hand against his chin. "Well, I'm heading to Greenport, which you probably just passed. It wouldn't set you back too many miles to ride with me and send a tow from there. Then, if you need a lift to a hotel, I can help you further. I wouldn't mind."

Mr. Braddock picked his hat up off of the car battery and waved the heat of the engine away from his face with it. "Something wrong with the mechanic in Dunbury?"

The man's eyes widened and he said, "Oh, no. Not that I'm aware of anyway. Just trying to help."

Tommy spoke up. "Mr. Braddock, my parents run the Dunbury Inn. It ain't far from the garage, if you find you need a place to stay."

Mr. Braddock looked indecisive. "I'm sure we'd be in good hands

24

either way. Let me check with the missus."

But before he could, the red-faced man waved him over. Braddock hunched at the window to hear something the Greenporter said in a low voice. Tommy couldn't sift the words through the sound of the idling engine, but Mr. Braddock's brow was furrowed when he stepped away from the one car and leaned into the other to confer with his wife. The red-faced man regarded Tommy darkly.

When Mr. Braddock reemerged, he patted the roof of the Bonneville and said, "She'd like to keep heading north to make the mountains by nightfall if the repairs don't take too long. But we're much obliged for the offer, sir. And son, you'll be the lady's hero if you can ride that bike fast enough to help us make good time."

The man in the black car was already rolling. He gave a curt wave and said, "Suit yourself. But I'd stick to pop and beer in Dunbury."

♦

"Are you planning on having children?" Mama asked over dinner.

"Now, *Sarah*," Papa said shaking a thick dollop of mashed potatoes from the wooden spoon onto his plate. "Don't pry. We've only just met these folks."

"Sorry," she said with a remorseless smile. "I hope you do is all. You seem like you'd make great parents. But it changes everything, having children does."

Papa sighed.

"I remember I was taping crepe paper to a float for the Seashore Festival when my water broke."

"Was that when Tommy came?" Angela Braddock asked.

"No, his brother Michael. Michael's at Town Hall tonight helping with preparations for *this* year's festival."

Papa cut in: "If it takes Geritson more'n a few days to get your fuel pump, you might even get to see the festival for yourselves."

"We've been to Newburyport for Yankee Homecoming," Angela said. "Is it like that?"

"Couldn't tell you," Papa said. "Never been. We have a parade to the seashore and a celebration on the beach. There's food vendors, music—"

"And cotton candy!" Tommy said.

"Even if your car is fixed, you should stay just to see it." Mama said. "We'll give you a good rate on the stay. Won't we, John?"

Papa nodded as he ate.

"It all sounds very nice," Angela said. "If we didn't have a room waiting for us in Conway." She took a sip from her water glass and grimaced, then coughed into her napkin.

Her husband patted her on the back gently. "Wrong pipe?"

She shook her head.

"It's an acquired taste," Papa said.

"Well water?" Mr. Braddock asked. "Sometimes well water has a sulfur taste." He lifted the glass, sniffed it, and grimaced.

"No, it's from the town aquifer," Papa said. "Perfectly good water."

"I'm sorry," Angela said. "The food is wonderful, Mrs. Shayne."

"Call me Sarah, dear."

"We have lemonade, too!" Tommy chimed in. "Would you like that better?"

"If it's not too much trouble …"

Tommy hurried off on the errand, but returning from the kitchen, pitcher in hand, he encountered Mrs. Braddock in the hallway. She gave him a sorry smile, her delicate fingers lightly touching her belly. "Thanks for fetching the lemonade, Tommy, but I'm afraid it might upset my stomach further. I think the heat has gotten the better of me today. I really should go lie down."

While Mama cleaned up after dinner and Papa took his pipe on the porch, Tommy passed the Braddocks' room on the way to his own. Hushed voices infused with an urgent edge drifted under the door, and on a split-second impulse, he detoured to the attic, careful not to step heavy or creak the boards. He crouched with his ear to the vent above their room, baking in the trapped heat of the day and praying that his sweat wouldn't drip through the grate and give him away. He wiped his face with his shirt and listened.

"But the car won't be ready tomorrow," Mr. Braddock said.

"Then we can take a taxi to Greenport. We should've gone with that man on the road. What did he say to you, anyway?"

A sigh. "You won't believe it, but he actually said there's something in the water in Dunbury. Oh, it's just an *expression*. Said Dunbury folk are strange; they shun outsiders. But he couldn't be more wrong about that; the Shaynes couldn't be any kinder. It would be rude to leave now. And who knows what he thought he had to gain by taking us to Greenport."

"Bill, I don't want to be rude either, but something is off in this place. It's been a scorcher of a day, but I've felt *cold* since we got here."

"You're just tired and stressed, dear. You'll feel better tomorrow."

"Are you even listening to me? You didn't taste the water. You had beer."

"What are you suggesting, Angela? That they tried to poison you?"

"Of course not. It's nothing John or Sarah said or did. It's just ... strange things adding up to make me uneasy."

"Well, give me an example."

"You'll say I'm imagining things."

"I won't. I promise."

She sighed. "First it was the women at the soda fountain across the street from the garage. No one said a word to me the whole time I was there. You know me, I tried to make conversation but they just stared."

"That's it?"

"*And* I thought I saw something slimy in one of their water glasses. I tried to put it out of my mind but then when I came up here to lie down tonight, I opened the wrong door. It had to be the old woman's room, the boarder who doesn't take meals with them. She wasn't in the room—thank goodness because I might've screamed. But there was a water glass on the bedside table with a set of dentures in it and I swear to God there was something black and slimy in the water behind the teeth like ... like a *baby eel* or something. And I could feel it watching me. It felt like a mad dog behind a picket fence."

"Are you *sure?*" Mr. Braddock's voice was tinged with revolted fascination.

"We can make some excuse, Bill. We'll never see these people again. Let's just be on our way in the morning, please."

Tommy heard the muffled sound of his mother calling for him and rubbed the grate impressions out of his cheek. Mrs. Braddock had spoken quickly like she needed to spill it all out before she changed her mind. She sounded scared and desperate. And now, as if her fear and bellyache were contagious, Tommy felt queasy. He scampered back down the ladder, wiping the sweat from his brow.

Later, lying in bed, Tommy listened for the sound of his brother's return. Michael would make sense of it all. He'd point out the obvious and make Tommy feel stupid for not seeing it. Michael would dispel the cloying shadows clamoring for space in Tommy's mind in the sweltering summer night. But sleep embraced him before comfort could.

◆

Tommy's next sighting of his older brother wasn't as welcome as he'd expected it to be in the dark watches of the night. He had begun the day by leading the Braddocks—who looked neat and unperturbed, if a little stiff in the hair as if they hadn't showered—to the train station. Their intention was to ride one stop to Beverly for lunch and window shopping while their car was fixed. But when the third train in a row rumbled past the weedy station in a rush of wailing whistle and billowing steam, Mr. Braddock kicked the gravel and asked Tommy to lead them to the best eatery in Dunbury. That was the Fishtale Diner, of course.

No sooner had the waitress clothes-pinned their order of burgers and fries to the string in the kitchen window and set their bottled Cokes on the counter than Michael Shayne pushed through the door and scanned the room, his brow darkening when his gaze settled on his younger brother. He strode across the room and clapped Tommy on the shoulder, swiveling him on his stool, away from the counter.

"There you are. I've been all over town lookin' for you. 'Scuse me, Mr. and Mrs. Braddock, I'm Michael. It's awful kind of you to feed my little brother, but Mama sent me to fetch him with apologies. He never should've imposed on you."

"Oh, it's no imposition at all," Mr. Braddock said. "We wanted to thank him for his roadside assistance."

"All the same, sir, Tommy has chores to do and shouldn't have gone out before they were done. I'll be taking him home, or it'll be my hide. Nice meeting you both."

Michael pulled Tommy off the stool and marched him out the door into the blazing heat.

"You can't go running off with strangers, Tommy. Pa'll whip you."

"They ain't strangers. They're staying at our house."

"Still, you only just met 'em yesterday. They're not from around here and the only thing bigger than your appetite is your mouth."

"What's that supposed to mean?"

Michael glanced around. "It means you're liable to go and say something that Ma and Pa wouldn't approve of. They've always said it's delicate business dealing with out-of-towners."

"Well I don't know why it should be. They seem awful nice. I figured if I showed them around, it might put them at ease and they'd stay longer. That'd be good for business, right?"

Michael ruffled Tommy's hair as they walked, then pulled his hand away and theatrically shook off the sweat. "I guess your heart's in the right place, but running out the door yelling over your shoulder doesn't cut it. You been told a hundred times you need to check first before doing anything with guests. And what do you mean about putting them at ease, anyway? You have some reason to think they're not?"

They had left the center of town and were passing under the shade trees that lined Prospect Street. Tommy stepped off the sidewalk to kick a crushed can down the road. It clattered away to a satisfying distance and he sprinted after it for a follow-up.

"I'm talking to you, squirt. You kick that thing one more time and I'll kick your keister all the way home. What are they uneasy about?"

Tommy slumped his shoulders and waited for Michael to catch up. "Someone told 'em the Dunbury water's bad and Angela—I mean Mrs. Braddock—didn't feel well last night. *I* think she has a case of nerves 'cause she's on her honeymoon, but she also thought the water tasted bad, and she was bothered about the ladies at the soda fountain giving her the silent treatment."

"Boy, she must really confide in you. The water, huh?"

Tommy nodded. They had stopped walking at the corner of Athol and Main and Tommy's eyes drifted up to the rusty water tower on Ward Hill.

"You ever hear those rumors?" Tommy asked.

Michael shrugged and started across the street. "Everybody has," he said over his shoulder.

"So there's something to it?" Tommy trotted to keep up. His brother seemed suddenly determined to get home at a brisker pace.

Tommy caught up at the next corner and tugged Michael's shirt, turning him around.

"All the kids who play ball on the hill have heard the tower groaning. And I know you helped the men do something up there that night when it got real bad. What is it, Michael? Tell me."

Michael looked at the tower and his eye twitched. "I can't talk about it."

"It's about the women, isn't it? How they're different?"

"Tommy ... you'll find out when the time is right. At the festival if Pa doesn't talk to you sooner. You can wait a day, can't you?"

"Why at the festival?"

"You were too young last time so you probably don't remember. Just have a little patience. You'll find out when the time is right, like everybody does."

"Michael?"

"Yeah, squirt?"

"I'm scared."

♦

On Saturday morning, Tommy was tasked with washing the pickup truck to get it ready for the parade. He thought his father might check in to critique his work, but Papa took Mr. Braddock to Geritson's garage to check on the Bonneville while Mama took Mrs. Braddock to church to watch her ladies' choir practice and pick up some things that needed polishing for the festival.

Tommy contemplated the gray soapy water in the bucket with suspicion.

It was the only water he had ever known, beside the briny ocean, and it looked to him like water always had. He'd bathed in it from infancy, been baptized in it, and quenched his thirst with it every day of his life. If it had a smell he could barely detect it.

The truck was dry and shining in the evening sun when the ladies returned home. The men had come back with the Bonneville about an hour prior and were smoking on the porch when the women walked up carrying silk hatboxes by the strings.

When they reached the steps, Mr. Braddock rose from his rocking chair and swept his arm in a grand gesture toward the car parked in front of the inn. "Your chariot awaits, my dear. And the White Mountains beckon."

Watching from the side of the house on his way to dump the bucket of suds, Tommy thought Mrs. Braddock looked pleased, but not as relieved as he'd expected.

"That's wonderful," she said.

"I haven't packed our luggage yet," Mr. Braddock said. "But with the late sunset, we still might make it before dark."

"Don't be foolish," Mamma said. "You must stay for dinner."

"Actually," Angela said, lacing her fingers together and swiveling on her heel, "I wondered if we might stay for the festival tomorrow."

Mr. Braddock took the hatbox from her and set it on the porch. Placing his hand at the small of her back, he led her around the other side of the house, his voice growing faint as he began: "Possibly we could, but we've already paid a deposit in Conway, and time is ticking...."

Tommy jogged down the corridor of shade between the house and the hedges and was concealed by the azalea bushes before the couple reached the backyard.

"... thought you wanted to leave here as soon as possible."

"Perhaps I was jumping at shadows. It's been an emotional week. A wonderful week, but suddenly we'd gone from being overwhelmed with friends and family to being alone in a strange town. Maybe I was overly sensitive."

They stopped walking when they reached the crabapple tree. The fallen fruit lay scattered and decaying in a pungent pulp at their feet. Bill Braddock touched his wife's chin and tilted it upward to look into her eyes. "What's changed?"

"Sarah says the festival is not to be missed, and it's only one more day. Maybe providence stranded us here so we'd have the chance to add something special to our trip. And the ladies' choir, Bill—they were *magnificent*."

"I thought the Dunbury women were giving you the silent treatment."

"I was mistaken. The church is a strange denomination. Many of the women take a vow of silence later in life. It's a peculiar custom, I know. But no more odd than how the Amish live. So you see it was nothing personal. Sarah explained it to me. And Bill, you should hear them sing. You should go to the festival just to hear them sing. It's majestic and sublime, like all the peaks and valleys of the deep blue sea."

He brushed a lock of golden hair from her temple, leaned in and kissed her on the mouth, lingering for a long moment.

In the bushes, Tommy held his breath.

Mr. Braddock jerked and pushed his wife away, unlocking his mouth from hers with a mangled moan. He wiped his hand across his lips and it came away bloody. "Jesus Christ!" he spat, and buckled over retching at the ground between his feet.

She watched him, her arm extended in his direction, delicate fingers splayed and reaching for but not touching him.

"What the hell is in your mouth?"

She brought her fingers to her lips, pinched her tongue and pulled it out. It had a dark gray pallor, almost blue, and it kept coming and coming, far longer than it should be able, curling around her fingers. Tommy was seized with the need to urinate, but he couldn't look away. Bill Braddock's back was up against the tree now, his heels grinding pulped crabapples into the earth, his face contorted with horror. Tommy had the feeling the man might scurry up into the boughs to get away from his wife, or break and run, like he should be doing right now. But both man and boy remained paralyzed in place.

Angela removed her tongue and offered it to her husband. It wriggled and pulsed on her porcelain palm. Tommy couldn't make out the details across the yard, but it looked like an eel or a giant grub. After displaying the thing, she sucked it back in and Tommy realized that she needed it to speak.

"It's the town's gift," she said. "It's alive, Bill. At first I thought it was a canker sore, but it ate my tongue while I slept and made a nest from the roots. I was terrified at first, but it sucked the fear right out of me. And I'll be able to sing like them soon—the oldest, most beautiful song. What a lullaby for our babies that will be."

Tommy tossed and turned in the hot night. He drifted in and out of a disquieting dream in which his mother served a cauldron of wriggling creatures at the big table. He opened his mouth to scream, but what came out was a flowing stream of glossolalia like the alien syllables he'd heard a southern preacher gibbering on a radio station that crackled in and out in the sweltering Chevy when they'd taken that trip to Florida to visit his great-grandmother.

He woke glazed in sweat, heart racing, breath hitching in his chest, and ran his tongue over his teeth. He sat up and touched his tongue, shivered with relief when it didn't bite his finger. He kicked off the tangled sheet and shuffled out of bed, following the faint aroma of tobacco to his bedroom window.

The moon was almost full. By its light he could read the hands of his bedside clock: 2:40.

It was too late for his parents to be up, and apart from Mrs. Ruess the Braddocks were the only boarders in residence. He put his ear to the screen and listened, but heard no voices from the porch below. The smoke didn't smell like Papa's and Tommy imagined that Bill Braddock was probably down there riding out a sleepless night. He pulled a T-shirt on over his boxer shorts and crept down the stairs, avoiding the creaky boards with a practiced step.

He opened the screen door to the porch gently and took a seat beside Bill Braddock, who gave no sign of recognizing his presence. The man reminded Tommy of the seated pose manikins he'd seen at Osgood's, his eyes fixed on some distant point in the night, his cigarette dwindling under a long plug of ash on the arm of the chair, threatening to burn his fingers.

Tommy cleared his throat. Mr. Braddock knocked off the ash and took a drag.

"Are you okay, sir?" Tommy asked.

Braddock squinted and shook his head slowly, his eyes still fixed ahead through the thinning pall of smoke.

"You have trouble sleeping? I know I sure did. Had a nightmare wake me up."

No reply.

"At least it's cooler out here," Tommy said.

Small talk wasn't going to reach this guy. His state reminded Tommy of what they called shellshock in the movies. Tommy drew a deep breath and tried a different tack. "I saw you under the crabapple tree today. When Mrs. Braddock kissed you."

That got his attention. His eyes swiveled and locked on Tommy. "Do you know what happened to her? Do you know what's going on in this town?"

"No sir."

"Bullshit. You were born and raised here. We never wanted any trouble. Never meant to pry into anyone's secrets. Now ... I can't even lie in that bed beside her. I should have listened to the good Samaritan on the road, but you ... you were so willing to help." His voice took on a steely edge. "Did you lay a trap for us, boy?"

"*No,* sir. I swear I didn't! I don't know what happened to Mrs. Braddock. I swear to God, I don't. But I'm ascairt of it too."

Tommy felt his lip trembling and tried to keep from crying in front of the man. He recovered and finished: "And I'm afraid to ask my folks about it in case they're in on a wicked secret. It's making me sick, sir. It truly is."

Braddock crushed his cigarette in the glass ashtray on the arm of his chair and drew another from the pack of Pall Malls poking out of his shirt pocket. His eyes returned to the horizon as he squinted and lit the cigarette, and Tommy finally recognized the focus of the man's gaze: the town water tower silhouetted against the lowering moon.

"Something in the water," Braddock murmured. "Something ..."

"It groans," Tommy said.

"Huh?"

"The water tower. Sometimes it's quiet and sometimes it groans. I heard it groaning some days ago. I think it's to do with the festival."

34

Mr. Braddock considered this for a long moment and then asked, "How does it groan, Tommy? Like metal stretching or like an animal?"

"Uh ... to me it sounds like a voice, like a whale song I heard on a phonograph, mixed with something deeper like a mad elephant might make. But it's kinda sad, too."

Mr. Braddock's face glowed red in the light of the cigarette cherry and the deep shadows of his brow made his face look fierce. "That .22 shotgun your Pa keeps on pegs over the hearth ... Do you know where to find shells for it?"

Tommy felt like he'd swallowed an ice cube, but he nodded. "There's a box in the bottom drawer of his toolbox."

Mr. Braddock leaned forward and stamped out his smoke. His breath smelled like gin, tobacco and something sour when he spoke. Tommy thought it might be the gut-eating smell of fear itself. "If you want to help me put an end to this wickedness, son, you go and fetch them."

♦

The moon dissolved in a sea of haze over Ward Hill, a picture of perfect stillness in the deep night but for the shapes of man and boy ascending the dome to the water tower at the summit. The boy carried a rifle, the man a gas can. As the pair approached the tower, their pace flagged under the weight of the unearthly din emanating from the tank. The town seemed as distant to them as the moon in that moment, just a scattering of yellow pools of light in the gloom below. A dog barked from a far-off yard, its warnings almost drowned by the knee-buckling groans issuing from the rust-stained tank.

Tommy stopped walking, planted the stock of his father's shotgun in the dirt at his feet, and holding it by the barrel, gazed up at the hemisphere of rivet-studded metal.

"It's bigger than it looks from down there, but it doesn't look big enough to hold water for the whole town," he said.

"It doesn't," Mr. Braddock replied. "If Dunbury's like most towns, you have a reservoir and a filtering station. Most of the water in your pipes comes from the reservoir pump houses, but some of it gets pumped up into this tank every day. When there's a peak in use—

Douglas Wynne

like every morning when most folks are running showers and making breakfast—the tower provides the extra water to fill the demand. It's also there in case an emergency knocks out power for the pumps. That's why it's high up on stilts. The hill helps, too. It adds pressure so gravity can carry the water through the system."

"How do you know all that?"

"I'm an architect. I had to learn about utilities in college."

"Oh. Are you going to build your own house, now that you're married?"

Tommy could see Mr. Braddock's Adam's apple bob as he swallowed. "I don't know if that's in the cards anymore, Tommy."

"So ... did you decide which you want to do?"

"I need to see what's in there, first. You don't have to climb up with me. But I need to see the thing that poisoned my bride. I know it's not just some sort of bacteria. Whatever's in there, it might be *spawning* microorganisms, but it's not small. Nothing small makes a racket like that."

Tommy nodded.

"Well, I'm going to put an end to it." Braddock wrapped a rag from his pocket around a stick he'd picked up at the base of the hill and tied it tight, then unscrewed the cap on the gas can and sloshed some fuel onto the cotton. The sharp odor of the fumes flooded Tommy's sinuses and he swooned.

"A torch? What about the flashlight?"

"Beasts don't like fire. It'll give me a gander at the inside of the tank and keep whatever's in there at bay. Then I can decide if I want to shoot it, drain the tank, or incinerate it."

Braddock slid the barrel of the rifle through his belt like a sword and climbed with the unlit torch in his mouth. Tommy thought he looked like a pirate boarding a ship. When he reached the steel-grate platform that ringed the circumference of the tank, he produced a coil of twine, tied one end around the railing, and dropped the rest down. Tommy tied it to the handle of the gas can and snapped off a salute to the tower. Braddock hauled the can up and set it down on the grate before biting the torch again and climbing the second stretch of ladder to the hatch on the conical roof.

36

The groaning had not ceased entirely, but it had quieted, as if whatever lived in the tank were listening to the footsteps on the rungs. Before he had time to reconsider, Tommy grabbed hold of the bars and climbed to the platform. He didn't know what he could do if Mr. Braddock needed help, but at least up here it would take less time to come to his aid.

A whooshing sound filled the air above Tommy's head, accompanied by a flare of yellow light. Braddock had lit the torch. Tommy craned his neck, but the bulk of the water tank obstructed his view. The squeal of stubborn hinges sang out and he knew the hatch was open.

The silence that followed was excruciating. All groans, metallic and organic, had ceased and now the light faded as Braddock lowered the torch into the hole.

Tommy wondered how high the water level was inside. If it went down every morning, was it replenished to its highest point by this hour of the night? He didn't know if that was good or bad.

A wavering moan drifted down from the peak. It had to be Braddock's voice, but it had the timbre of a child's cry of fear. Heart pounding, Tommy started up the second ladder but paused when he didn't find Braddock's feet on the rungs above him. Cool dread seeped under his skin.

Water sloshed in the tank with a thrash and clang and he almost let go, almost plummeted to the ground below.

"Mr. Braddock?"

Legs shaking wildly, Tommy completed the climb and found Braddock crouched on the roof, in the dark, the rifle in his white-knuckled hand aimed into the hole. He shot Tommy a terrified glance, and in that flicker of an instant when his eyes were diverted, something black and sinuous whipped out of the hatch, wrapped around the barrel of the gun, and pulled the man into the tank with a splash and a yelp that echoed for half a second, then went mute.

Tommy scurried down to the platform and stood frozen, staring at the tank, listening.

Silence.

"Mr. Braddock?" His voice was barely strong enough to travel to his own ears, never mind those of the man inside the tank, in the

Something massive struck the metal shell from within …

water. A long moment passed in which the only sound was the baying of that distant dog, now mournful and anxious. Tommy took a step toward the tank, his shoe dragging on the scaffolding grate. He placed his hand on the cold rusty metal and then pressed his ear against it.

Something massive struck the metal shell from within, ringing the tank like a bell and Tommy jumped, flailed, and clutched at the railing behind him. The clang had been so loud he marveled at the absence of an outward bulging dent. He looked at the gas can beside his feet. Mr. Braddock couldn't be alive in there, but something malevolent surely was. Tommy couldn't believe what he was contemplating doing. Did he have the moxie to set fire to the tower? It would be a beacon to the whole town. Until now he had been a stealthy accomplice to an adult, but to carry on without Braddock …

His eyes pricked on the verge of tears. His breath rasped in short, shallow cycles.

Then he remembered that the lighter was in Mr. Braddock's pocket with his cigarettes. He couldn't light the fuel even if he wanted to. The realization that the last option was out of reach flooded him with relief. He moved to untie the rope connecting the gas can to the railing but remembered there would be no returning his father's rifle to the pegs over the hearth, either. Best to let all of the missing goods go missing with Mr. Braddock. Best to get down the ladder and down the hill with wings on his heels.

♦

On Festival Day, Tommy woke from a paltry stretch of restless sleep and plodded to the bathroom. By force of habit he put toothpaste on his brush and ran the sink, but before he'd put his brush under the tap, he detected a pinkish hue in the stream and shut it off as his heart fell through his feet.

He dressed without showering, dragged a comb across his cowlick, and gave up when it wouldn't yield. He could hear the bustle of breakfast down in the dining room and girded himself for the interrogation that would await him if his father had noticed any signs of his complicity in Mr. Braddock's disappearance. Tommy lingered at the top of the stairs, listening, and was surprised to find that none of the voices below carried urgency or worry. He descended the steps with a dreamlike slowness, his hand dragging on the bannister, and stood in the kitchen doorway. The ladies were having toast and tea while Michael chased his scrambled eggs and bacon with black coffee.

"I thought you'd never wake," his mother said. "Take a seat and have a bite. Quickly now, we have a big day ahead and can't be late."

"Where's Papa and Mr. Braddock?"

"Your father ate early and took the truck for parade setup. Mr. Braddock's probably gone for a stroll. I'm sure he'll be back soon if he wants to join us for the festival."

Was that a look of caution Michael shot at Mama?

Angela Braddock, who had been staring into her teacup as if she could divine the future in it, now raised it and took a sip. Tommy thought of the water that had been boiled to make the brew and suppressed a shudder.

The parade rolled through town under a robin's egg blue sky, the cars and pickup trucks trailing black streamers and bearing effigies of the Gods enswathed in clouds of pungent incense. Even the vehicles that lacked elaborate decorations were emblazoned with thorny sigils soaped on the windows. Michael drove the family Chevy with Mama in the shotgun seat. Tommy sat in the back next to Mrs. Braddock, who hadn't spoken all morning, although at times he thought he detected a faint, mournful melody from her direction, hummed softly through closed lips. They cruised down Main Street at the tail end of the procession, then turned onto the four-mile stretch of unnamed road that meandered past derelict cottages, bait shops, and wind-lashed crab grass to the dunes of Dunbury Beach.

The salt air was humid and brisk. The canvas food tents rippled and snapped in the ocean breeze but held their ground by virtue of deep stakes. Tommy could taste the aromas of fried dough and spiced calamari on that wind, mingling with the darker scents of incense plumes rising from iron braziers placed at intervals along the shore.

At low tide the beach was a vast stretch of smooth, damp sand reaching down to the languid surf, littered here and there with empty lobster traps and kelp-encrusted rope, but mostly clean, groomed by the sea, and cool under bare feet. The children ran and splashed and screamed. A paper kite in the shape of Dagon swooped, climbed and dove, inscribing circles and barbs in the sky at the end of a length of twine, like the script of some arcane alphabet. The seagulls kept their distance, despite the fragrant promise of scraps, and no sails shone on the horizon.

At dusk, the women's choir gathered at the waterline in their black frocks, their heads adorned with the dazzling silver diadems they had kept concealed in their silk hat boxes until the appointed hour. Tommy's father appeared behind him and clapped him on the back. "Listen well, son. You won't hear this music again for some years," he said and gave Tommy's shoulder a squeeze before continuing down the beach to take his place with the other husbands. Tommy looked around for Mrs. Braddock. He didn't find her in the gathering crowd, but when he turned to look up the beach, his brother was looming over him.

"Looking for Mr. Braddock?" Michael asked.

Tommy shook his head.

"Didn't think so. I saw you two on Ward Hill last night. Don't worry, I told Pa about Bill, but not his little helper."

"Michael?"

"Yeah?"

"What's gonna happen?"

"It's part of growing up, that's all. You learn things you didn't need to know before."

"Like what?"

"Just remember that Ma loves you, even if she can't tell you the same as before."

"Is she taking the vow?"

"Already has. Now all that's left is the offering."

Tommy looked at the bonfires and thought about scenes of human sacrifice he'd seen in comics. "What's the offering?"

"They give their voices to the sea. It's an honor for every family that has a lady in the choir. No one knows why the water chooses a woman to be a host, but you should be proud of Mama. Mrs. Ruess, too. That's two from our own house, and Mrs. Braddock'll be next. Maybe she'll decide to stay with us."

Now Tommy spotted Angela Braddock at the other end of the horseshoe crowd, her hair whipping in the wind. "If she was chosen, why isn't she in the choir?"

"Her turn will come next time, probably. How long the gestation takes is different for every woman; how much time the passenger needs to soak up their dark feelings. I thought it might never happen for Mrs. Ruess. But Angela will need time to learn the songs, too." Michael looked at Tommy severely. "Good thing for you that fool didn't get lucky last night. We're all blessed in our home and don't you forget it."

The women sang and Tommy's arms broke out in gooseflesh. Something immense and mottled rolled in the churning water beyond the sandbar. They sang and their song was as beautiful as it was mournful; a lilting, yearning melody that stirred the air with its dark currents, and yet, Tommy felt that it was shot through with a trembling blue light at its upper reaches, and a green phosphorescence in its minor key depths. The tide rolled in as they sang, and the waves dressed their black frocks with a lace of foam. They joined hands and waded in to the edge of the drop. Tommy remembered the first time he'd slipped off of it into the deeper water. The shortest of the women were up to their necks when the song reached its final cadence and lingered on a long, disquieting chord.

And in the dimming of the day, the choir bowed to the rising moon and gave their borrowed tongues back to the water.

The Last Chord

Ifound the haunted guitar in a bus driver's garage. The bus driver was dead, had been for about a year, and his daughter Terry Sadowski was finally going through his stuff to clear it out and sell the house. She'd known he had a few guitars stashed away from the rock tours he drove in the seventies, had even heard the story of how he'd come by them, but it wasn't until she saw me on TV appraising some instruments for an episode of *Rock 'n' Roll Detectives* that she realized the Stratocaster might be worth more than the house.

I didn't take her phone call myself, and I didn't have high hopes for authenticity—I spend most of my appraisal time looking at junk—but the house wasn't too far out on Long Island, only about a twenty-minute drive from my shop in Greenwich Village, so I found time to head out on a Sunday afternoon and take a look.

Lo and behold, the first thing I saw when Terry led me into the living room was a black-and-white photo of her father with Cane Sinclair, standing in front of what looked like a school bus finger painted by King Kong on acid. That was when my heart started picking up the tempo and I wished I had a better poker face. When it comes to Sinclair, I'm not just an appraiser. Hell, I'll admit it—the word *fan* isn't even strong enough. I'm a disciple.

It shouldn't have been me who found it. I'm sorry for that. If it had been someone less versed in the man's music, someone who couldn't play it, then that black Strat might have gone straight into a glass case and the world would never need to know how the song ends. But

43

maybe I never had a choice, and everything in my life, from the first time I heard him on the radio as a kid, has led me to this.

I had a briefcase full of photographs with me for comparing the wood grain and the paint scuffs, the hardware, and even that ghost of a bloodstain that had stubbornly refused to ever come out of the white pick guard. I flipped through the 8x10s mostly for Terry's benefit so she'd feel she was getting something for the fee, but I didn't need photos. I knew. As soon as I popped the latches and lifted the lid, I knew this was it: Cane Sinclair's 1966 black Stratocaster, the guitar he had called his soul mate.

"Tell me again how your father came by it." I was kneeling over the case, brushing my fingertips across the strings. I didn't dare pick it up, but I couldn't take my eyes off it.

I sensed her shifting her weight from one foot to the other behind me, folding her arms, to recite the oft-told tale. "He was driving Cane and the band on a little East Coast promo tour. Just a few dates to promote a single. He had dropped Cane off at an airfield where a Cessna was supposed to hop him over the Long Island Sound to a radio gig in Connecticut. That was the plane that crashed and killed him. A few of the electric guitars were left behind on the bus."

"Because Sinclair only needed his acoustic for the radio show he never made it to."

"Uh-huh. My dad was devastated like everyone—more so, because he thought of the band like family. People used to say the CIA made it happen, but Dad never believed that, even with all the near misses they had on that damned bus. Anyway, he didn't even check the cargo bay for a couple of months after Cane's death, and when he did, when he realized what he had, he called Mrs. Sinclair a couple of times, but she never took his calls. I'm sure it was a difficult time for her, what with the press, and the, uh ..."

"Time she spent in the clinic?"

"Yeah, that. It got harder to reach anyone at the compound after that, and the guitars just sat here. I'm not sure if the others belonged to Cane or his band, but everybody knows this one."

"So it never left this garage in *forty-two years?*"

"No sir."

"Okay. First thing you need to do is put it in a secure environment with temp and humidity control."

She put her hand over her mouth to stifle a squeak of giddy laughter, then got hold of herself and said, "Mr. Brodie, are you saying you're gonna verify that this is …"

"Yeah. This is Dahlia. Congratulations."

♦

If the guitar had gone to auction the Sadowskis might have made more money at the block, but they probably would have had to give a good chunk of it to Cane's widow anyway. And if it didn't even make it to auction, if Terry and her husband had to fight for it in court, they would have been seriously outgunned. I think Terry knew that, but I also think she cared about what her father would have wanted—for the guitar to finally find its way home after all those years. So when Myra Sinclair made a private offer within an hour of my public announcement, Terry and her husband accepted. I'd been storing the guitar in my vault for them, and when the deal was done, Myra Sinclair's people called and asked me to personally deliver it to the Sinclair ranch in California. I bought a seat for Dahlia on a 747, and flew out to L.A.

Most people think of the Appalachians when they think of Cane Sinclair because he grew up there and referenced the region so much in his music. But the fact is, he had left upstate New York for good by the summer of 1967, moved to California and bought the piece of land that he would dub "New Jerusalem"—a sprawling studio complex nestled in the Santa Monica hills. That's where he was working on a new album in fits and starts right up until he died, and it's where his wife Myra still lives today.

Conjure Man, Root Worker, Hoodoo Priest, Hex Doctor. All of those titles have been placed on Sinclair at one time or another. There are even college courses that seriously examine the question of whether or not the lyrics to "Deluge" prophesied assassinations of John and Bobby Kennedy and MLK. I'll admit that I've considered the notion myself. But nothing could have prepared me for what came into my life with that guitar.

45

I was expecting just a driver to pick me up at LAX, but when I found the placard in the crowd with my name on it, I noticed that Myra had also sent a security officer: a crew-cut man in a navy-blue blazer, wearing shades and probably a shoulder holster. Neither man offered to take the guitar case from me, but they fell in around me as I walked, and ushered me to a black town car. Now, I've handled some high-profile items in my time, but this felt different. Riding through the hills, I started feeling guilty and a little afraid. Not unlike a man carrying a suitcase full of money. A man who has skimmed some off the top.

I played it.

There you have it—a confession in writing. On the first night I had the guitar in my possession I played it. This was back at my shop on 8th Avenue after meeting with Terry, after photographing the instrument and logging it into my ledger.

I played one of Sinclair's songs on it. Don't think I did so lightly. Terry had told me that her father had no ability whatsoever on the guitar, so I knew the odds were good that the last man who had strummed a chord on the thing before me was Sinclair. I struggled with the temptation, and it felt a little like stepping into a dead man's shoes, or maybe more like bedding a dead man's wife, transgressing on the sanctity of something for the first time. It felt a little wrong because of how much reverence I had for him, and it was irresistible for the same reason.

Walking up to the studio door at New Jerusalem with the case in my hand, the conjoined scents of sweet lilac and bitter jimson weed wafting up around me every time the sea breeze shifted, I welled up with guilt. Sinclair told *Playboy* in 1970 that Dahlia was his soul mate. Watching my armed escort type a passcode into the box beside the door, I knew that when I met Myra Sinclair face to face, I would lie about what I'd done.

In the quiet and dark of my shop, the help gone for the day, the cream-blue light of a neon sign smeared across the whitewashed brick wall like a divination of dawn, I had inserted a cable plug into Dahlia's jack, strapped her on, flicked the power switch on an old Fender tube amp, and strummed a chord. The sound was warm and deep. I dug my tender fingers into the strings knowing that the sweat of a legend had corroded all of the treble out of them over the decades.

I've never been a songwriter. I tried when I was younger, but figured out quick that I lack the knack. And yet, with Dahlia in my hands, I could hear something new emerging and diverging from my well-worn Sinclair riffs. It was something Sinclair had never written, but undeniably his. It was as if the guitar had taken hold of me and was showing me how to play it.

When the plate-glass door of the studio swung open and my reflection slid sideways toward the dunes, I was relieved to find not Myra Sinclair but a member of the staff greeting my guilty face: a slender man about my age with close-cropped graying hair and bright blue eyes framed by Buddy Holly glasses.

He shook my hand as I stepped over the threshold. "Hi, Cal. I'm Jake Campbell, chief engineer."

My security escort had done an about-face and was headed back to the car. Jake waved me in. "Don't worry, your bags will be delivered to your room." He pointed at a coffee bar in the foyer. "Can I get you anything before I show you to the studio? Coffee ... tea ... something cold? Myra will be joining us in the control room in a moment."

"No, thanks. *Jake Campbell* ... why does your name sound so familiar?"

His poker face was better than mine, and he let me tick through it on my own.

"Got it. You engineered that last Billy Moon album in the nineties, right? That one that, uh ..." He was nodding, but not smiling. "Well, excuse me for stating the obvious, but that was one helluva shitstorm, huh?"

Now he smiled. "You could say that. Yeah."

"Shame what happened to him...." This was getting awkward. I'm usually better than this in professional situations, but my shame about the guitar, combined with my surprise at meeting the guy, had thrown me off. I flailed around for a conversational footing. "I can see why Mrs. Sinclair would have scooped you up—composure, discretion ... Anyway ..."

"Studio's this way."

He led me down the hall to a control room that looked like it hadn't been touched since 1971. Guitars leaned against stuffed chairs and couches, legal pads with amp settings and lyrics scrawled over them in a familiar handwriting that raised the hair on the nape of my neck lay scattered atop effect processor racks. Even the cigarette butts heaped in glass ashtrays under lamps that looked old enough to belong at a yard sale but not quite old enough for an antique shop—and the way the ashes had compressed—suggested a session in progress, but with a clock that had stopped ticking long ago. I had an idea, but it was crazy, so I decided to let Campbell walk me through it. "Is someone recording here?"

"No."

I waved my hand at the place, at the obvious evidence of work.

"The control room is just as Cane Sinclair left it."

My eyebrows told him to go on.

"My position here has more in common with a museum curator than a recording engineer. I keep the machines tuned up, and when Myra wants to hear some of Cane's unfinished music, I mix it for her. The console, that's my domain. I'm allowed to change settings as needed when we do the occasional vault release for a boxed set or something. But the guitars, the lyrics, and everything out there …" He gestured to the live room beyond the glass where a piano, a guitar amp, and some mics were waiting for overdubs that would never happen. "I don't touch it."

I pointed at an ashtray.

"Yeah, they're his."

"You're telling me those ashes have been here since 1970."

"Yeah."

"It's a *shrine*."

"Please don't touch anything, but have a seat." He rolled a chair over to me and spun it around. "Sorry for the inhospitable rules."

I sat down and laid the guitar case flat at my feet. We both stared at it in silence. Thankfully, it couldn't have been more than a minute before Myra Sinclair appeared at the glass door and entered to the sound of hissing hydraulic hinges.

It took me a moment to reconcile the woman in the room with the one I knew from photos and film. She had the same haircut—the same black bangs, no doubt dyed now—and her figure was as slender as ever, but I hadn't been expecting the deep lines etched into her face around hazel eyes that were a revelation because I had only ever seen her wearing her iconic sunglasses. She was dressed in blue jeans and a long black blouse that hugged her hips like a skirt with several layers of scarves blooming at the neckline. She squeezed my hand lightly, and settled into a black leather couch.

I noticed that her eyes never left mine, never once flitted to the guitar case at my feet. The expression on her face was neutral, could have passed for a smile in some noncommittal way. "Thank you for coming, Mr. Brodie."

"Cal, please."

"And call me Myra." She folded her fingers around her knee and said, "You're certain that this is Dahlia?"

My stomach dropped half a floor, like the elevator in the Brooklyn apartment I used to rent. "You must have read my report before you spent the money.... I mean my reputation *is* at stake."

"Of course. But you know there have been some impressive replicas over the years. I'd just like to hear you say it."

"*Yes,*" I almost whispered the word, then cleared my throat and opened the case. "The places where the black paint is worn through to reveal the factory sunburst finish all match up, the rosewood grain on the fret board is as telltale as a fingerprint, and the pick guard under UV light reveals—"

"You played it." Now she smiled. It brought no warmth.

"No, Ma'am."

"You did, you played it." Her voice had a playful pitch to it, if a fishhook can be considered playful to a fish. "Don't lie."

I looked at the guitar.

"Did she give you a song?"

A chill passed through my shoulders, and I nodded.

"Cane used to say that old guitars sometimes have the ghosts of songs in them waiting for willing fingers to find them. What did it sound like?"

"Just a chord progression. It sounded like one of his. But I'm a fan, so ..."

"Don't belittle it, Cal. I dreamed that you would come here and play it. I didn't know who you were, but I've dreamed of you for years."

I wasn't sure what to say to that. I looked at Campbell, but he was stoic and appeared to be waiting for some cue from his boss. Maybe he was used to this sort of talk.

"Aren't you going to play it for me?" Myra asked. Now she was looking at the guitar, and there was something new in her eyes, like the way you might look at an atomic bomb.

"I'm not much of a player," I said.

"How much do you suppose Cane was paid to play at the Royal Albert Hall?"

"A lot."

"I'll pay you the same amount to play me a few bars of Dahlia's song."

She didn't have to wait for a reply; she knew it was way more than I could turn down. She nodded at Jake, and he pulled his chair up to the console.

Dahlia's song. It was a crazy idea. And yet I knew I wasn't a songwriter, but here I was with a song. Or a fragment of one. "I'm afraid you'll be disappointed," I said.

"You said it sounds like Cane's music, so how could I be?"

"It's pretty dark. Minor."

"Do you know the meaning of the name *Dahlia?* It means 'dweller in the valley.' As in, *Yea, though I walk through the shadow of the valley of death.*"

Jake had threaded a master tape onto the machine and was rewinding it.

"What are you doing?" I asked him with an edge in my voice from the fear of little red RECORD lights.

"Nothing yet. Just being prepared. Relax." He tapped the STOP key, rose from his chair, and plugged a cable into the battered Stratocaster in my lap. He switched on an amp and handed me a pick—no doubt last handled by Sinclair.

50

I strummed an open chord to confirm that she was still in tune. Then I spun the volume knob up, took a deep breath, and played through the scrap of music that had come to me that night in the shop. I didn't know how to finish it, so I just let the last chord hang in the air with all of its unresolved tension. It was an E-flat diminished chord, and I only know that because I looked it up.

When the notes had faded into silence and the reverb springs in the amp ceased ringing, Jake pressed the PLAY button on the multitrack machine, and Cane Sinclair and his band spilled out of the monitor speakers, hot and wet like bourbon, playing the same song, but with words. The tune lurched along rough and ragged until the chorus climbed to an apocalyptic coda near the end.

Well I planted a seed
Now it's time for me to go
Them clouds are gonna bleed
But for now, they're movin' slow....

The vocal trailed off, the band unraveled, and I could hear Sinclair's husky speaking voice, off axis of the mic, saying, "S'all I got boys. Dunno how it ends."

Jake stopped the tape. The silence in the room was loud, but in my mind I could hear more: another line of lyric floating over the missing diminished chord Dahlia had given me, and then a final cadence. I felt like my anchor to reality had broken free of its chain.

I looked at Myra and she said what I couldn't. "It's the same song; the one Cain was writing when he died, and the one you're writing now. Do you know how it ends, Cal?"

I shook my head. "Not really, no. Probably a lot of chords could go there."

"What about the words?"

I laughed. "I'm a fan and all, and a bit of a guitar player, but a poet I am not."

"I didn't accuse you of being a poet. You know what I think you are? A conduit."

"For what?"

"Maybe Dahlia is the artist and *you're* the instrument."

"You think what? Cane's *spirit* is haunting the guitar, trying to finish his last song?"

"Don't you?"

I looked at Jake. He examined his fingernails. I noticed a long smooth scar running down his forearm.

Myra stood up and said, "Jake will show you to your room. Keep Dahlia with you. Change the strings, do a setup, get her ready for recording. And sleep on that song. In the morning Jake will record whatever you have." She held up a hand to stave off my protest. "Strictly for my edification, don't worry, we won't be releasing it. You'll still make your flight, and I'll send you home well fed and well paid. Do we have a deal?"

"I can't promise anything."

"I'm not asking you to. Just sleep on it."

◆

My room was what a realtor might have described as "rustic luxury." There was a river rock fireplace and a lot of Mexican textiles, a large flat screen TV mounted like an onyx gem in the east-facing cedar plank wall, and a larger picture window in the west. Rows of recessed shelves were well stocked with liquor and a comprehensive collection of Sinclair CDs, DVDs, and biographies.

I should have been tired, but I felt restless, nervous. I sat on the bed and gazed out the window. The Malibu sun was descending beyond the sage-speckled hills toward the dark blue Pacific in the distance. My body was still on New York time, and I knew I'd need to sleep soon. I considered the guitar case and decided it would be best to do the maintenance now, before slipping under the sheets with a DVD on the screen and a Scotch on the nightstand. With Dahlia in good shape, I could leave in the morning. No one could force me to write a song.

Jake had jotted a three-digit extension number on a pad beside the phone with instructions to call him at any hour if I had an idea for the song, so he could record it before it evaporated. Well, slim chance of that, it was already circling around in my head like a litany. I already knew how it ended. I had what Myra wanted, but I didn't know what it meant, or why it frightened me. I even had the last few lines of lyrics.

Well I planted a seed
Now it's time for me to go
Them clouds are gonna bleed
Gabriel's horn is gonna blow
Where they gonna feed?
Don't you know?
Welcome to the show

I could hear the whole thing vividly, in Sinclair's familiar tones.

There was a desk in front the window, its surface bare except for a leather tool case and a fresh pack of strings. I draped a Mexican blanket over the desktop, laid the guitar down on it, and set to work: wiped it down, replaced the strings, adjusted the truss rod, and pricked my finger on the sharp steel point of the G string. A bead of dark blood welled up and dripped onto the fret board where the dry rosewood drank it right up. I put my finger in my mouth and heard a faint harmonic sigh ringing off of the strings, like a sigh of pleasure after a thirst has been quenched.

The pad of paper with Jake's number on it was paired with a pen on the bedside table. I knew I could write the lyrics and chords on it, but I didn't want to. I know how this sounds, and it wasn't the first time I've been pricked by a string, but I felt like Dahlia had bit me. I could sense her impatience, her anger that I wouldn't play her. How long had she waited in her little velvet-lined coffin with the song?

I poured myself that Scotch, and scanned the familiar spines on the media shelves. A memory teased the edges of my mind, like a shape under a sheet. My gaze was drawn back to the guitar, to the dim stain on the white celluloid pick guard where a fan's blood had splashed it at the Hanson's Field protest concert in 1968. Everyone over thirty knows the story—the clash between the protesters and the police in riot gear at the perimeter of the nuke plant. The newspaper photos of the massacre are flash-burned into my generation's memory, and the official story, the story told by the police and the press with lockstep wording, about how the rolls of

... "opening the door of judgment with the black axe."

razor wire were picked up by the storm and raked across the crowd, has never been questioned.

There were other stories, though, nestled in the pages of some of those Sinclair biographies, and quoted in ones and zeroes on those DVDs. Heard in passing, they sound like evidence of the psychedelic delirium that defined the era, but taken together the eyewitness accounts paint a chilling picture. You'd have to believe in mass hallucination, *shared* hallucination, to discount them.

Bassist Jerry Newcastle gives the most complete version, in the film *Mark of Cane*. He's still wearing a paisley shirt, but his hair is shorter these days. Looking beyond the camera, he says:

"Cane always talked about the spirit fish, called 'em the Qliphoth. Some of the hardcore fans used to send me mail about this stuff after he died, theories from Kabbalah and shit. Anyway, Cane, he said the fish were like hungry ghosts that fed on negative emotions. Like anger and fear and hate. Said it was part of the circle of life and we were helping people to purge those negative vibes. Cane used to put something in the fog juice for the light show, some kinda hoodoo powder so we could, you know, see them. Sounds crazy, right? I swear it looked like a shoal of silver piranhas feeding on the crowd. But they were just spirits, right? Most people didn't even know they were there. At Hanson's Field, though, they were real. They could cut you; they could bite. Flesh, not fantasy. They were getting stronger."

Newcastle rubs his arm and looks away.

It's the weirdest moment I've seen in a Sinclair documentary. The film goes on to talk about the drug culture. Sinclair's influence on it and vice versa.

The books hold other clues. Cane's music was always apocalyptic, but it got darker and more violent toward the end of his life. He's been called the godfather of heavy metal, and when his native scene in rural New York went all peace and love with Woodstock, some of his mystically minded peers hinted that they'd meant to use that festival to banish something dark unleashed by Sinclair on the left coast the previous year. In his published poetry, there's an oblique reference to "opening the door of judgment with the black axe." Is that Dahlia?

The black Strat? I've often gotten the sense from his late-era lyrics that he thought the world was beyond redemption and in need of cleansing by a second flood. Tonight I wonder what might swim in that ethereal tide.

I think Myra wants me to end it. Not just the song, but maybe the world. Is that crazy? I wonder. I know how it goes. I can't get the tune out of my head. The black axe in the closet is calling me to take it up and play the tune … and God help me, *I want to.*

It's like an itch, like a sexual urge. Part of me needs to hear it, to channel it, to birth it into the world.

After the Scotch I must have dozed off. The DVD was looping through the menu screen when I came to, and Dahlia was in the bed with me, tangled in the sheets, her curves looking more like a woman's than ever, but I don't remember taking her out of the case.

I swung my legs over the side of the bed, and picked the guitar up to put it away. But with the body in my lap and the neck in my left hand, my fingers just curled around in the shape of a chord. I tried to slide my hand off of the thing, but I could feel some kind of magnetic pull. I watched in horror as my fingertips were sliced open by strings turned to razor wire, my blood splashing out onto Dahlia, the sheets, the floor. I could hear my blood pattering on the polished wood, could smell the iron in the air.

Then another sound: tapping on glass, like birds at the window, but when I turned my head to look at the window, it was like looking into an aquarium. Silver fish with needle teeth crowded the glass. A wave of cloud surged over them and the window shattered, raining glass on the bed. I curled my body inward and away from the tsunami, tucked my chin to my chest, and watched as the Qliphoth swarmed to the red ribbons of blood trailing from my fingers. That's when I woke up.

The DVD menu looped, reflected in the unbroken window. No blood on the sheets, just a lot of sweat.

Dahlia is in her case in the closet, and I'm writing this account on my laptop at the desk. I called Jake Campbell. He must have been waiting up for the call because he answered on the first ring. It's three a.m. and the rest of the ranch must be sleeping, but I wonder about Myra. The moon hangs low, and I can see silver-washed thunderheads over the ocean, getting closer. Their shapes don't look quite right for clouds. More like dense flocks of starlings, or shoals of fish. They'll make landfall before dawn.

I told Jake that I might know how it ends, and he surprised me by saying, "Me too."

"The song?"

"No," he said, "The whole fucking mess."

"You mean the world?" I laughed. Nerves.

"Listen, Cal. It's a cold night for the valley. Bad weather's brewing. You might want to warm that room up. Do you need any wood for the fireplace?"

I looked at the closet. The song in my skull was so loud it almost drowned out what he was telling me.

"No. There's enough here."

"Good. Goodnight, Cal."

"I'll never work again, you know. If I do this."

"I understand. The price of action is high. The price of inaction may be higher."

"How did you get that scar on your arm, Jake ... fishing?"

"No. Old war wound from the Billy Moon sessions."

"Well, if you're ever in New York again, look me up. We'll have a drink."

"Deal. Listen, Cal, you can dial nine for an outside line. You might want to have a cab meet you at the end of the lane before the ranch wakes up."

He hung up.

It's getting hard to write this with the music so loud it feels like the room should be shaking, that same coda going around and around like Hell's own calliope. I'm going to save this file to the cloud, shut the laptop down, and pack my things now. I might use some of the books on the shelf to get the fire going. Then I'll find out if I can take

Dahlia out of her case and lay her down in a bed of flames without my fingers betraying me and reaching for that goddamned lost chord.

Good Bones

Whether the morning sickness affected her perception of the house, or the house made her feel sick, Meghan Pelham didn't know.

A little off, she thought. *It looks a little off.*

At a glance, it was typical of Arkham's historic riverfront district—a three-story Georgian colonial with a steeply pitched saltbox roof, five gables, a central chimney, gray clapboard siding, and diamond-paned casement windows. Her first thought was that it must be dark inside with such small windows, and that was disappointing, but it wasn't the idea of a gloomy interior that unsettled her—it was something about the angles of the place.

A little off. A little asymmetrical.

As if the measuring tapes used to build it counted feet in increments of thirteen inches. Did they use measuring tapes in the 1600s? She had no idea. Meghan was an English teacher, not an architect, but her eye rebelled against the proportions of the place.

"What is it?" Paul asked. "What does that look mean?"

She shifted her eyes from the house to her husband in the driver's seat of their Honda. They were going to need a bigger car soon for the stroller, pack-and-play, and God only knew what else. And it was all going to cost money. She should be thrilled that he'd found a crazy deal on a condo to save them from pissing away most of their income on rent.

"*What* look?" But she knew she'd been staring at it slack-jawed.

"The face you make when you can't even."

Meghan jabbed a finger at the stereo, cutting off a reporter in the middle of a story about the insurrection. The Fighting Diamondbacks militia had just seized control of the New Hampshire State House, and she felt a brief pang of guilt at muting the report—if Boston fell, WBUR would be silenced by powers more permanent than her finger—but she couldn't stand to hear another word about it right now. Combined with the architectural dissonance of the house, the unsettling news was just too much.

She took a deep breath in the silence. "I'm sure it's lovely inside, but … do you not see how *off* it looks?"

"Off? Off how?"

"Never mind. Maybe the hormones are inflaming my aesthetic revulsion or something."

"Hey now," Paul said in a teasing tone, "don't blame everything on hormones. That's sexist."

Meghan scoffed. "Hormones got me into this mess. I'll blame them all I like. Come on, let's go. Introduce me to this genius teacher of yours."

As if summoned by the mention, an older man—tall, thin, and dressed in a plaid shirt and khakis—appeared on the porch and gave them a wave.

"That him?"

Paul smiled. "Speak of the devil."

Meghan tripped on the porch steps. At seven months, she was used to carrying the extra forward weight, but the stair didn't meet her foot at the accustomed height and Paul caught her arm just in time.

"Sorry, they may not be up to code," the tall man said. "Place is too old for that, but you get used to it. You must be Meghan."

"No, this is the other woman I knocked up," Paul joked. The professor gained a point in Meghan's ledger for not taking the bait.

"Pleased to meet you, Professor Wolejko. Paul raves about your class."

"Well, Paul is a talented mathematician. I'll get him sorted out on the Haar integral yet. And the pleasure is mine, but please call me Vlad."

"Meg is a teacher herself. Elementary English."

"That's wonderful. Your child will excel in both hemispheres of the brain! Tell me, do they still teach children to write in cursive with all of the typing they do now?"

Meghan nodded. "We cover it. Mostly for signing their names."

"Ah. An endangered art. Though I'm afraid many subjects are these days."

Meghan nodded, taking the hint that while he might not be looking to talk politics, the professor was likely as alarmed as she was at the recent attacks on the science and history curriculums gaining steam across the country.

"I'm not facing the same pressures as some of my colleagues," she said. "Not yet, anyway. But the way things are headed ..."

"Indeed. We live in troubling times. But this house has stood long enough to have witnessed other witch hunts. I hope you'll find it to be a refuge from all that."

He led them through the front door to a central staircase. On the left was pair of closed doors. On the right, an open sitting room. Movement caught Meghan's eye across the sitting room and she turned to find her own reflection looking back at her from a wide mirror painted in a gold marbled pattern.

"The first floor is my unit," Vlad said. "I use a lot of mirrors to throw the light around and brighten the place up. You'll find I've done the same on the third floor, where windows are scarce with the pitched roof."

He gripped the polished banister and spoke as they climbed. "The house was built in 1687. It stood for over two hundred and forty years before the roof was damaged by a gale in 1931. By then the walls were rotting, but the foundation was still strong. Workmen razed it down to the beams. The owner—he lived in the first-floor unit and rented out the others as a boarding house—sold the property to a professor Upham from Miskatonic."

"*Hiram* Upham?" Paul asked. "The math professor who published those controversial papers about higher dimensions?"

Wolejko chuckled. "You're certainly up on your esoteric math history. Yes, the same. Though, the papers that damaged his

... the house had been built on principles of sacred geometry ...

reputation are now thought to be based on the work of a student he was enamored with, a Walter Gilman, who also resided here for a time. I suppose you could say we belong to a lineage of eccentric calculators who have occupied this space. Anyway … where was I? Oh yes, when Professor Upham bought the structure, it was a mere skeleton of a house, but he insisted on a period-perfect reconstruction. This may have had more to do with his academic interests than with the historical value of the house. He speculated that the house had been built on principles of sacred geometry, so it was important to him that the essential proportions be preserved. Something to do with measurements of ancient ruins documented by one of his colleagues on a recent expedition to Antarctica. Anyhow, now you have some trivia for dinner parties, but I've gone on quite a tangent. The point is that the place has good bones. They're the original bones, built to withstand the ravages of time. The triple casement windows, while not original, are from another house of the period. I couldn't bear to replace them with modern glass; it would have felt like sacrilege."

"They are very quaint," Meghan said. "Pretty, I mean. But I can see why you've resorted to mirrors to stretch the light."

"Indeed. They're almost enough. The other concession I've made to the modern is a pair of skylight domes on the third floor, as you'll soon see."

Meghan was winded before they'd reached the first landing. Paul offered a hand that did nothing to lessen the burden but at least showed empathy for her ordeal. They paused for a brief rest on the second floor, where the professor told them the current tenant, a chemistry major, would be moving out after graduation the following month. "I don't have anyone lined up yet, so if you decide to take the third floor and find that you need more room, we could discuss a deal for both units."

Paul met this with polite, non-committal noises.

"Who knows how fast your little family may grow," the professor said, elbowing him in the ribs.

"Not *that* fast," Meghan said, embarking on the second climb and eager to be done with it.

The dark wood wainscoting and eggshell walls seemed almost monochromatic in the vacant third floor unit. There were sparse furnishings—a kitchen table in a dining area and a loveseat in the living room. She could easily imagine how their desks would fit beneath the skylights, which—she had to admit—was an attraction.

"Mind if I sit?" she asked, pointing at the faded blue and gold floral print loveseat.

"By all means."

Meghan settled in to give her feet a rest. She pinched the neck of her tee-shirt and fluffed it. "Is it just me and climb or is it hot in here?"

"It is a bit stuffy," Paul said.

"I'll crack a window and get you a glass of iced tea," Vlad said. "I left a pitcher in the fridge up here, anticipating your walkthrough."

"That sounds nice. Thank you." Meghan leaned back and took the place in while Paul roamed the living area, gazing through each of the thick windows, probably looking down on their tired car and doing math of the simple budget balancing variety.

The professor returned with two chiming glasses. He placed them on an end table beside the loveseat. At the first sip of the cold drink, the baby kicked. Meghan buckled forward and put a hand to her stomach.

"Is it all right?" the old man asked with alarm.

"It's not the tea. The baby kicked. Sometimes he reacts to cold drinks."

"Ah, it's a boy then. Do you have a name picked out?"

"We have a few we can't agree on," Paul said.

"Then go with Vlad!"

They all laughed, but Meghan found that despite the refreshment she was feeling more disoriented than when she'd first sat down. "No offense," she said, "but I'm afraid it would remind me of Dracula."

"Or Putin," Paul chimed in.

"Unfortunate associations, both. My birth name was Ladislas. My parents were Polish immigrants. They thought I might fit in better if they chose an anglicized version of my grandfather's name, which was Vladislov. But how many boys named Ladislas have you met? When I enrolled in the university, I changed it to Vlad."

"That's interesting," Paul said. "I've been lobbying for *my* grandfather's name: Robert. But Meg says everyone will end up calling him Bob."

"She's probably right."

The professor lingered near the sofa, smiling nervously. Meghan sensed what he was too shy to ask and forced herself to smile. He was being polite, and she couldn't blame *him* for the fact that she was feeling unwell.

"Do you want to feel him kick? He might not do it again, but ..."

He nodded reverently and extended his hand. She took it in hers and guided it to the spot on her belly where she'd last felt the kick, noticing a tangle of white scar tissue on the inside of his wrist as she did so. He smiled in anticipation and Paul leaned in to watch. No sooner had the man's hand touched the curve of her belly through her shirt than the baby began thrashing wildly. Meghan let out a surprised laugh, then recoiled, suddenly afraid the outburst was inspired by distress rather than excitement.

"I think he must like me," Vlad said.

Paul murmured agreement but seemed to sense the discomfort on Meghan's face. "Are you okay, hon?"

"I'm sorry," she sighed. "But I really don't feel so good."

"Are you in pain?" Paul asked, setting his glass down on the table. "Maybe we should go. Can you manage the stairs, or should we wait it out?"

"Not pain, just nausea. I've had it since the car but it's getting worse."

"Why didn't you say anything?"

"I thought it would pass. I think I just need to rest."

"Of course," the professor said. "The bed is made up with clean sheets. Let me show you."

If they'd been touring a unit on the first floor, Meghan was sure she would have preferred to go straight to the car, but the stairs were intimidating so soon after she'd climbed them. It wasn't so much the physical exertion as the disorientation that came from what she would swear were off-kilter angles. Maybe it was her. Maybe her inner ear was thrown out of balance by the pregnancy. Was that a thing that happened? She had no idea. All she knew was that she felt like she'd arrived here by way of an M.C. Escher sketch, and it was getting hard to keep her eyes open, as if her body were shutting down as a stress defense mechanism.

Vlad extended his hand to help her up from the sofa. She waved it away with a forced smile, pushed herself off by the heels of her hands, and followed him to the garret bedroom.

She was surprised to find a four-poster bed complete with silk curtains in the small, barren room. The steep angles of the roof gave the feeling of being in a boat. For a moment, the scuffed floorboards seemed to rock beneath her feet, and she must have swayed because her host steadied her with a light touch and guided her to the bed. Paul watched from the doorway as she kicked off her sandals (her feet were too swollen for her shoes lately) and tucked her feet up under her, her head resting on a cool pillow that brought a measure of instant relief.

"There now. That's better, isn't it? You just take all the time you need to recuperate."

"Thank you. I just need a moment. I'm sure it will pass."

"The bathroom is the next door on the right. Give a holler if you need anything else."

She assured him that she would and the men departed, leaving the door closed but not latched behind them. She could hear the low murmur of their sympathetic commiseration moving down the hall.

The baby had settled again. Now that she was resting, her heart followed suit. She looked around the room, taking note of the lighter squares on the walls where a previous tenant had hung pictures. It needed a fresh coat of paint, but that was a ritual she enjoyed undertaking in a new apartment—making it new, making it hers.

Was she really considering living here? She didn't know. It was impossible to separate her feelings about the place from the reactions her body was having—and impossible to separate either from the quiet terror she'd lived with since learning she was pregnant. People always said you should trust your gut, but was it still trustworthy while it had a tenant?

Her gaze landed on a steeply angled wall that seemed to have no relation to the gambrel roof. It was set with a small door that suggested a closet or crawlspace, fitted with an undersized antique knob of filigreed silver. Her stomach lurched at the sight.

She could feel the motivation to investigate the room draining from her body now that she was prone, but she couldn't resist the pull of the silver knob. It beckoned to her in a way that felt absolutely magnetic. And it wasn't just curiosity at what might lie behind the oddly proportioned door in the oddly angled section of wall. The sensation was more gravitational than that. It seemed that the entire room pitched toward that spot. She felt a peculiar certainty that a marble dropped on the floor would roll straight at that door and pass through the gap at the bottom.

And then, as if thinking it had made it manifest, there *was* a marble on the floor, bouncing high and slow, then fast and low until it settled and rolled toward the black gap. It was violet, the marble, and when it passed beneath the door it glowed from within, casting an aura over the shadowed floor. Her mind traveled with it, a passenger pulled along into the darkness. She expected to find dust bunnies or a dustpan and broom in what surely could not be a large space. Instead, the violet sphere bounced down a series of steps. With each drop, she felt a sickly sweet plunge, and now she saw that the spaces she traversed were not small steps like the ones she'd climbed to reach the third floor of the house but the terraced slopes of a mountainside.

At first she perceived everything through a thick haze: The line of the far horizon where the spiraling towers of a great city corkscrewed into the sky. A sea of swirling vapors nestled in the foothills, seething with the languid motion of great, gray tentacles. A pack of small brown creatures, their hides shining in the pewter light of the veiled sun as they migrated with the synchronized geometry of a flock of birds across an amber plain.

Through all of this, she did not inhabit the violet sphere but felt herself to be pulled along behind it, her consciousness tied to the object by an invisible cord. When she focused on it again, she found that it was no longer a sphere but a faceted polyhedron tumbling across the alien sky.

In time, she and her guide came to rest atop a watchtower situated between the lake of vapor and the distant city. Her body had the same shape here as in the material world, but she felt it to be more like an avatar, a mere container for consciousness and whatever noble gas enabled her to float and fly. But as she settled onto the flagstones atop the tower, she nonetheless felt weight and solidity counteracting her buoyancy, which was accompanied by an instinct to gird herself against the dizzying height. Her fingers wrapped tight around a balustrade made of some exotic green alloy. She held tight to it as she surveyed the landscape stretching out below, her astral hair floating around her head as though teased more by electrical currents than the winds of a high place.

At once terrifying and exhilarating, she felt that the experience must surely be a dream—that she had fallen off into deep sleep the moment she'd laid down on the bed and was still dreaming even now, her lucidity doing nothing to break the spell.

At her back was a square structure of white brick set with an iron door. She could hear voices beyond it, the muted rhythms of speech reaching her phantom ears through the metal. Though she could not make out the words, she knew from the cadences that these were the voices of her husband and his teacher. She pressed her ear against the cold iron and found that the voices came into sharper focus. They had moved on from expressions of sympathy for her to a discussion of some arcane theorem.

Listening, she placed her hand on the door. A bolt clicked inside the stone structure and the door swung open on groaning hinges. Inside the squat structure, a corridor extended horizontally, farther than any space that could be contained atop the watchtower. Rooms branched off on either side, alternately lit by sunlight, moonlight, and candlelight. The shadows of the two men spilled out of a sunlit doorframe, their voices echoing down the hall. But then, from a closer doorway, Vlad stepped into view, detached from the version of himself that was carrying on a conversation with Paul in another room. He approached her with a knowing smile on his face.

"So you've found me. I knew you would. I wanted to have a private word with you while Paul is occupied."

"But isn't he talking with you?"

"Yes. When I was a boy, I learned the trick of being in more than one place at a time. Also more than one time at a place."

"I don't understand. Where else are you?"

"Part of me is always here, on the borderland of Elysia. Another part of me is always in this house as it was before it came to ruin, on the threshold of sacrifice in a sloping attic room. Part of me is in the kitchen sketching out an equation for your husband on the little blackboard over the countertop." He rubbed the scar on his left wrist with the thumb of his right hand, his eyes far away. "And part of me is buried at Hangman's Hill, where the chanted hymns carry across the river from the little island of standing stones on this night, Walpurgis night, and set my tiny bones buzzing in the earth. Can you hear it?"

Now that he had asked, she noticed what had been there all along—a droning rhythm threshing the air about them, faint but strong.

"I do," she whispered.

"We could step through one of these doorways and set foot on the soft grass of that island. We could move among the revelers in the sacred circle and add our voices to the never-ending song. But breath is not enough. Voice is not enough to nourish the Black Man. Even blood is not enough. I know, because mine was spilled in his bowl when I was two years of age—too young to sign my name in his book. He took me into the folds of the cosmos then, his glittering garment. I had fallen out of my body into a wedge of the velvet void. I lived here for many years, nursed and tended to by the familiar he appointed to my rearing, one of the Jenkins. When I returned to the physical world, I was a grown man and my birth mother had passed away in her grief. My spiritual mother, Keziah Mason, was killed on the night of my severance, strangled by a man so tormented that he shunned eternity for misery, madness, and death."

"You're not making sense, professor. None of this makes sense because I'm dreaming. Everyone talks about food cravings, but they don't tell you about the crazy dreams you'll have when you're pregnant."

He laughed, a sound like rusted chimes. "Denial takes so much effort, child. Wouldn't it be better to surrender to the gift you've been offered?"

"What gift is that?"

"Freedom from fear."

"What fear?"

"You know."

"I don't."

"How can you not? Your fear is so loud, even I can hear it."

Something brushed against Meghan's calf. She recoiled from it but was too transfixed by the professor's words to look down.

"Fear of what?" she asked again, needing to hear it confirmed. Needing to know that he had a deeper insight into the turmoil she'd lived with since learning of the pregnancy than her husband did.

"That your baby will die young of the same genetic osteosarcoma that claimed your brother. You saw what that loss did to your mother."

"How could you know that? Did Paul tell you?" She wanted to deny the reality of the entire conversation, to rationalize that of course he could know her private thoughts if he were a figment of her dreaming mind. But that *was* denial talking. She knew the exchange was real.

"Have *you* confided in your husband?"

"He knows my brother died of bone cancer."

"But he doesn't know your burden. The white terror of it in your heart. The fear that you will outlive your child. Or the other fear, twined around the first: the insanity of bringing a child into a world like this. Even if the boy is healthy, what turmoil will you be thrusting him into? Civil war. Societal collapse. Ecological disaster."

Meghan swallowed. He could see right through her.

"I can offer protection. From both fates."

"Don't lie to me. Not about that." For all that he frightened her, she could not let the false promise go unchallenged.

"You stand here light years from your body, surveying an alien world, and you doubt my power?"

"This is a dream."

"And your waking life is a nightmare."

"How? How would you protect my baby?"

"There are regenerative effects that come with time spent outside of time. Whole bodies can be grown in the light of Elysia. New bones. Not to mention the obvious shelter from more violent threats. A place

70

to disappear when the Diamondbacks roll down the street with their guns and flags, demanding you swear an oath."

The furry thing rubbed against her leg again and this time she looked down. It was one of the sleek, brown creatures she'd seen migrating across the plain. She couldn't make out the details of its face from her higher vantage, but its paws scratched at the floorboards in a familiar and incongruous way—like tiny humanoid hands, nimble and leathery.

A clopping sound reached her ears, and when she looked up from the little creature at her feet, Vlad was at the far end of the hall, following a tall black man in a long coat who moved with a loping gait. The professor beckoned to her with a wave of his hand. He passed through an archway, and the rat thing scampered after.

Meghan followed, passing into darkness. She tracked the clopping sound of the black man's footsteps, striving to catch up with the professor, her only hope of finding her way back to Paul. But those odd footsteps were increasingly soaked in the echo of a vast and growing distance. She reached out with her hand in front of her face, groping for obstacles in the absolute darkness, and her fingers grazed a delicate beaded chain. She pulled it, clicking on a light bulb.

Meghan was in a closet. The filament in the bulb glowed like a frozen fragment of lightning, searing her eyes but casting so little light that the objects on the shelves surrounding her appeared mossy and indistinct, barely revealed in the scant illumination. Ahead of her was the inside of the small door she'd seen from the bed before her mind had spilled out of her body and followed the violet sphere through the crack.

She tried the handle and found it locked. Turning to retreat the way she'd come, she found no passage, only shelves of linen and a stack of water-damaged file boxes. She lifted the dusty lid of the topmost box and peered inside, a gentle rain of mouse droppings trickling to the floor as she did so. There were sheaves of crumbling yellowed papers tied together with string and an object at the back of the box: a small sculpture cast from oxidized metal. She removed the sculpture and held it up to the light, turning it over in her hand and examining the shape. It resembled a pinecone with two starfish shapes—one

71

radiating from each end of the thing—and a pair of fan-like wings sprouting from the center. The metal was colder to the touch than she felt it ought to be, given the stuffy, overheated atmosphere at the top of the house. She felt repulsed by the object as if touching it for too long might somehow poison her and harm the baby. She tucked it back into the box, closed the lid, and rattled the doorknob again.

Still trapped.

She could feel her heart rate accelerating. The baby hadn't kicked since she'd lain on the bed. It worried her that he was so motionless in the midst of her stress. She put her ear to the door and listened for the sound of the men's voices. How had she become trapped in here? Would they hear her if she screamed? Had the old man drugged her drink?

She knew she should scream to get Paul's attention but before she'd finished drawing the breath to do so the images she'd seen while rifling through the papers finally struck her, igniting a curiosity that drew her back to the boxes again.

One of the bundles was a stack of newspapers. Through a film of dust she read the front page of the *Arkham Gazette* dated April 29, 1929 with the headline **Kidnapping At Orne's Gangway**. Meghan held the paper up to the light and scanned the story, her breath going shallow in the stale air of the cramped space, the smell of mold from the papers constricting her throat.

The story gave the report of a laundry worker named Anastasia Wolejko, whose child had gone missing on Walpurgis night. The journalist's tone struck a delicate balance between disdain for the immigrant woman's superstitious fears and enough sensationalist encouragement of them to sell newspapers. Mrs. Wolejko was described as hysterically fixated on a witch cult rumored to be active in the Miskatonic river valley. She claimed repeated sightings of a rat-like creature she called Brown Jenkin, which she believed had marked her two-year-old child, Ladislas, for sacrifice. The article ended with the implication that the woman's boyfriend might have had a hand in the disappearance for reasons having nothing to do with witchcraft. But it wasn't the story's lurid suggestions that were troubling to Meghan's agitated mind; it was the math. The dates. The professor had made a point of telling her his birth name, and in an oblique way had led her to this closet. Was it some kind of sick joke? An attempt to terrify a pregnant woman he'd only just met? What would be the point of that?

The next sheaf of papers she examined were handwritten in a cramped, archaic style that she could barely decipher, heavily ornamented with esoteric diagrams. A treatise that seemed to alternate between a rambling confession and a dissertation on some occult relationship between genealogy and geometry.

Something furry brushed up against Meghan's ankle in the darkness and the light flickered out like an extinguished flame. She felt faint, dizzy. Violet particles swarmed in her optic nerve as she slid down the wall to slump on a stack of boxes.

The darkness pulsed, swelling and fading.

She saw herself propped up on white pillows, sunlight streaming through the sheer white curtains around the four-poster bed, nursing her healthy newborn. A dream within a dream? A premonition of the future?

A small voice whispered in her ear: A bargain, a bewitchment, a balm.

She jerked awake to find herself sitting amid moldy newspapers in the dark, nursing a tiny, bearded chimpanzee with the body and tail of a rat, visible only by a wedge of sour light seeping through the crack under the door.

Meghan screamed and the creature's claws cut her breast as it skittered up her shoulder and launched itself into the dark.

♦

When she regained consciousness the doorknob was rattling in its socket. She fumbled with it in the dark and the door swung open, spilling her out onto the floor at Paul's feet, her eyes blinking at the brightness of the room.

"Oh, God, Meg, are you okay? What were you doing in the closet? We heard you scream. Oh Jesus, you have blood on you. Are you hurt?"

She curled her knees to her chest and touched her shirt, feeling vulnerable, exposed, and disoriented. She could see the professor's shoes a few feet away, black leather loafers with a short heel that made her think of the clopping sound she'd heard in those impossible corridors between the walls, and the tall black man whose step had sounded like that of an animal with hooves. She couldn't bear to lift her eyes above Vlad's knees, fearful that if she met his gaze something would pass between them. Some knowledge. Some confirmation that what she'd experienced wasn't a dream or a delirium.

"Do you have bandages?" Paul asked. "Or a paper towel?"

"Of course."

Meghan watched the leather shoes pivot and retreat from the room. When they were gone, she sat up with Paul's help and examined her chest. Her shirt and bra were punctured with holes small enough to have been made by the teeth of a rodent. Blood stains bloomed around the holes.

"What did this to you?" Paul looked pale, queasy.

"There was something in the closet. I think it bit me."

"You don't know what it was? Did you go in there looking for it?" He stared at the patch of darkness, the stacks of papers and boxes, as if afraid something might leap out at them.

"I don't know. Maybe? Maybe I heard something in there and got trapped checking? I thought I was dreaming. I think it was a rat." She whispered this last, not wanting the landlord to hear.

Paul helped her to her feet and guided her to the corner of the bed. Then he returned to the closet, found the chain for the light bulb, and clicked it on. The space was cluttered but too small to offer many hiding places for an animal. He appeared to be mustering the nerve to poke around when Vlad returned with a first-aid kit. He placed it on the nightstand and set about dousing a sterile bandage with hydrogen peroxide. "Here, hold this to your wound while I open a bandage. I'm so ashamed this happened. A family of rats got in through the eaves while the top unit was vacant. I thought I'd caught them all. This is so embarrassing."

"Where did it go?" Paul was stooped over, peering into the cramped closet. "I didn't see it leave when the door flew open."

"We must have missed it in our concern for your poor wife."

But Meghan didn't believe it was a rat. And she didn't believe it had exited the closet in any direction other than through a crack between worlds. A gap one might slip through for shelter against the ravages of time. It was a feature of the house the professor hadn't advertised to his bright, rational math student, but she was beginning to see it as a feature after all. He'd been willing to show it, but only in a private aside, mind to mind. Because he knew she would understand its value.

She studied Vlad's hand as he passed her a Band-Aid. Earlier, the scar on his wrist had drawn her attention, making her wonder if it was a tangle of hesitation marks. Now she focused on the rest of his hand. It showed some signs of aging, but there was no way she was looking at the hand of a man in his nineties, which he would have to be if he was the child abducted in 1929. She steeled herself to meet his gaze, knowing that he'd arranged for her to find the evidence of his identity. He'd wanted her to understand that a child who could pass in and out of time and space might live a span of eons, aging only when he wanted to. Such a child might outlive his own children, never mind his parents

Vlad himself had slipped back into Arkham from the foothills of heaven, back into a physical body, long after his grieving mother had passed. He'd embarked on his academic career after even Miskatonic University had forgotten his name. What had been the price of that longevity? Allegiance to the Black Man? A signature in his book? If so, wasn't that a small price to pay? Meghan didn't know if she even believed in the soul, but the roving gangs of armed men overtaking the country certainly did, and wouldn't an oath of allegiance to them carry a heavier price?

She reached under her shirt and pressed the Band-Aid to the stinging wound, wondering if she'd already sealed the pact by allowing the creature to feed on her blood. Had she encouraged it? Accepted its offer? Succumbed to its spell? She didn't know. She only knew the stress and sickness that plagued her were lifting like a heavy fog burned off by the sun. She felt more calm and clear-headed than she had in months.

Vlad patted her free hand where it rested on her knee. "You must be shaken by the experience. I feel just awful about it."

"I'll be okay."

"I still don't understand how you passed out in a closet," Paul said. "Should we go to the hospital? What if it was rabid?"

"I'll be okay," Meghan said, rising from the bed cautiously but finding the dizziness was gone. The professor ushered her back to the sofa in the living room.

"Rats carry bacteria but seldom rabies," the professor reassured his student. "The most important thing is to keep the scratch free of infection."

The tension in Paul's posture seemed to dissipate as he let go of the notion of rushing his wife to the car for a trip to the emergency room. He rubbed his face and said, "Maybe I will take you up on that White Russian."

"A wise choice." Vlad retreated to the kitchenette where Meghan could hear him fiddling with bottles and ice. "You know what else would be a wise choice?" he said, reappearing with the milky beverage.

"What's that?" Paul took the drink and sat down beside Meghan, placing a comforting hand between her shoulder blades while their host refilled her glass of tea from the pitcher.

"Mason. For the baby. It's traditional yet timeless."

Paul tilted his head and grinned. "That does have a ring to it."

Meghan considered the name, nodding slowly. "That could grow on me."

"With an English teacher for a mother, he'd be writing it in no time. In cursive, even!"

In the Black Man's book, Meghan thought. *For the gift of eternal life and shelter from the storm.* The notion warmed her and she laughed.

She raised her glass. "What do you say, honey? To Mason and our new home?"

"Really? You don't need time to think about it?"

She looked around the apartment, imagining their future. "No. I'm charmed."

Paul shrugged and raised his glass. "To Mason and our new home."

The Voyager

Brooks scanned the radio for some rock 'n' roll and got an earful of commercials, auto-tuned voices, and static instead. He had read somewhere that radio static was the sound of residual radiation from the Big Bang, the sound of creation breaking through all day and all night between the car salesmen, drum machines, and weather reports. He turned it off and cleared his throat.

He wanted answers, but as he was the low man on the totem pole at SPECTRA, no one was offering him any. He wanted to know what was in the aluminum attaché case in the trunk and he wanted to know what was in the head of the diver sitting beside him in the passenger's seat. What made him tick? Three days of silence was getting on Brooks' nerves. Were all divers this cagey or had he just been dealt Mr. Personality from the deck by the dumb luck of the shuffle?

They were headed to New Hampshire, having tracked down the ride operator via a drunk and disorderly citation in Florida and a vehicle registration in Massachusetts. Like most carnies, the guy's tax filings were scant. It had taken a while to find him, but it made sense that he would end up not far from where he'd worked years ago—most people did sooner or later, even carnies. With their quarry more or less pinned down, Brooks had the feeling that events would accelerate following the interview, the opportunity for small talk receding like a hitchhiker in the mirror.

"I've been thinking about what you do, Durham. At first I couldn't get my head around it, but seeing as you don't talk sports, I've had plenty of time to mull it over and I finally came up with an analogy: you're kinda like the bomb squad. Am I right?"

The diver might have raised an eyebrow a millimeter or so. It was hard to tell.

"Except that you can't send in a robot first," Brooks said. "You've got nothing to prod stuff with but your own mind."

Brooks kept his eyes on the road, but this time the diver turned to look at him.

"It's gotta take a special kind of person right? To do that. I mean I don't know exactly what you do.... But I know I couldn't defuse bombs. Too much tension. Give me a chase or a firefight over that any day."

The silence welled up around them again, nothing but the sound of tar patches in the road drumming an endless rhythm: *thumpthump ... thumpthump ... thumpthump*

"Are you always this Zen, or do you blow off steam when you clock out?"

The diver's voice came out phlegmy when he finally spoke. "If you've ever talked down a guy with a gun, you've defused a bomb."

Brooks tapped his fingers against the wheel, keeping rhythm to absent music. He knew it *wasn't* the same but it took him a minute to articulate how. "When I'm facing off against a madman with a gun, it ain't like I'm worried I'm gonna catch his madness."

The diver stared at the island of hilly grass that divided the highway and Brooks had the feeling that he was studying the trees, searching for a glimpse of something in the shadows of the foliage. He took up the burden of conversation himself again. "I mean I kind of get what you're saying—cops, military, agents ... we all take risks. But risking your life is different from risking your sanity."

Still looking at the trees, the diver said, "Have you served? In the military."

"No."

"Well, war is not sane. Most soldiers think they're risking life and limb when they're really risking their sanity."

"So you've served? You've been to war?"

thumpthump ... thumpthump ... thumpthump

"We're driving to war right now."

When Durham did not elaborate, Brooks turned the radio back up: Blue Oyster Cult.

Dimension divers were a queer breed.

Off the highway they took Route 1 north through Salisbury into Seabrook, past boarded up gas stations, failed shops with sun-bleached realtor signs, and newly minted big-box stores until winding east they came to the shore. The cheap motels and fried-clam stands stood desolate. As the low structures gave way to mud flats, an early March wind buffeted the car, sending eddies of sand twisting across the road, and battering the phragmites reeds. But the wind failed to stir the upper regions of the atmosphere where ribbed clouds in hues of dirty ice loomed over the iron sea.

The royal-blue beach house was incongruous with the colorless landscape. They parked on the side of the road and Brooks had to force the driver's side door against the wind to get out. He squinted into the dust and climbed the peeling porch, aware of Durham coming up behind him. Hardware on a flagpole chimed a staccato distress signal. Brooks rapped his knuckles against the frame of the screen door.

The inner door opened and the operator appeared, matching his Florida mugshot: a diminutive olive-skinned man with thinning hair and several days' growth of salt-and-pepper stubble.

"Mr. Grossman?"

The man nodded.

"I'm Agent Jason Brooks. We spoke on the phone. This is my ... associate, Alan Durham."

Grossman grunted and ambled away from the door. Brooks shot a glance at Durham, then followed. The place was dark and cluttered. They found Grossman settled into a scuffed leather easy chair behind a coffee table upon which a puzzle of Van Gogh's *Starry Night* was creeping into existence from the corners. He gestured at a stained sofa littered with newspapers but made no move to clear it off. Instead he slid a puzzle piece from the pile with a gnarled finger and moved it around the empty space in the center of the table like the planchette of a Ouija board. Brooks transferred the papers to the floor and sat down, while Durham lingered in the hall, shoulder to the wall, as if he were uncommitted to staying.

The place smelled of sour milk and stale cigarettes. Grossman lit one and waved the pack at Brooks, who declined. "I'd offer you boys coffee, but the machine's broke." He took a drag and blew it at the ceiling. "So you want to know about the ride, huh? This about the Nolan kid again? Did something turn up?"

Brooks leaned forward, swatted at the crease of his trouser leg, and idly poked through the scattered puzzle pieces. "You operated the Voyager from 2011 to 2013, is that right?"

"Yeah."

"And you were the operator on November 19, 2013. The night of Jack Nolan's disappearance?"

"I think you know that already, or you wouldn't be here."

"In the time that you worked for Destination Amusements—and thinking back to your job interview and training—did you ever meet Gustav Zann?"

"No, sir, I did not. He was gone before I was hired."

"Gone where? Did anyone ever tell you?"

"People said he fell off the map. Most popular theory on the midway was he went back to Switzerland. But you should talk to Fat Barry, who managed the park. That was before my time."

"Listen, you're not in any kind of trouble. I needed to verify that we're talking to the right man, but I'm not going to retread the same ground the cops did back in '13. You told them you don't remember seeing Nolan strapped into the ride and I'm guessing you haven't recovered any new memories in the time since?"

Grossman shook his head.

"We're not police, Mr. Grossman. We're not FBI either. And we could give a shit what drugs you may have bought, sold, or used while working at Cosmic Park. Even while operating the ride ..."

Durham shifted slightly in the hall, but Brooks ignored him and continued, "What we'd like to know is if you ever saw anything ... *strange* while operating the Voyager."

"Strange."

"I don't mean *suspicious* or out of the ordinary. I'm talking *out of this world* strange."

Grossman uttered a dry laugh. He stamped his butt out in a cardboard foil ashtray. "The Voyager was strange, all right. Yeah, you could say that."

Brooks waited for him to continue. He counted the clangs of the flagpole.

Finally, Grossman said, "I only tried Cat 9 once, and never while running a ride. That's what you want to know, right?"

"That's not what I asked, but why only once?"

"Once was enough. Besides, any employee caught with the stuff would have been fired."

"That seems a little draconian for a carnival."

"Fat Barry didn't care if you did other stuff when you weren't operating. Cat 9, though … that shit was a problem for the park."

"Why is that?"

Grossman shrugged. "Kids who took it always won big at the games. It took a while to see the connection, but the cats always cleaned house. People on TV say the name comes from some kinda cable, that it was about being wired, but back when it first caught on, everybody knew it was a reference to nine lives. Nothing could hurt you on Cat 9." He snorted. "'Cept maybe *Cat 9*. I know some drugs that make you *feel* like nothing can hurt you, but on Cat you see the world around you at weird angles. You see the spaces *between* spaces. Like the *opposite* of impaired. Shit, you could slip through the eye of a needle on it."

"You saw something strange when you took it?" Durham asked.

Grossman shifted in his chair, and looked out the grimy window where the curtains were parted. Brooks followed his gaze. The concrete dome of the nuclear power plant cut a lonely figure against the flat landscape. "I thought you were here to talk about the Voyager, not what I did with my free time."

"You're the one who brought it up," Brooks said.

"Why you want me to tell you what you already know? All the Cat users who rode the Voyager ended up in rubber rooms. All except for Jack Nolan. You've probably visited some of them already."

81

It was true, they had. Brooks snapped a puzzle piece into place and pressed down on the flaking cardboard. "You just said you didn't see Jack Nolan on the ride."

Grossman's eyes narrowed with a new thought. "He didn't turn up *alive,* did he? After all these years?"

"No. Still missing. Maybe he's in Switzerland, too, eh? He'd be twenty-two now."

Beyond the curtains stray shafts of sunlight broke through the cloud cover and glanced over the concrete dome and the marshes. Silver flashes twinkled in cavities of mud and tall grass. The tide was going out.

Durham had wandered over to the window. Now he peered through the glass and said, "Is that what brought you back to New Hampshire? The plant? I bet you sleep better near it after all that time operating the Voyager. Bet you'd sleep best of all in a trailer at Cosmic Park, if we didn't have it barricaded. Did you ever try to go back?"

Grossman stared at the fragments of fractured night on the coffee table.

"Maybe you were afraid," Durham said. "And who could blame you?"

Grossman tried a puzzle piece, turned it, tried it elsewhere, tossed it back on the heap.

"Maybe you're afraid now," Durham said in a tone that conjured a ripple of gooseflesh on Brooks' arms. There was real empathy in that tone, not counterfeit cop compassion. "Afraid a couple of strangers will think you're crazy, or worse—that *you'll* think you're crazy if you say it out loud. But I think I know what you saw in the Voyager on that night in November. You told the police you didn't see Jack Nolan, that he wasn't on your ride. And every day since then you've told yourself he wasn't there. But he *was* there, and then he *wasn't.* You saw him and then you didn't. Jack's friends say he was bug-eyed on Cat 9. Highest dose ever. So I'll tell you what happened: after winning more stuffed dragons and pandas than he could carry, after absolutely killing it at Star Darts and the shooting gallery and the ring toss, and passing the trophies off to little kids and pretty girls, he got on the Voyager.

"His friends didn't. They knew better, they'd heard the stories. One of them tried to hold him back and ripped his flannel shirtsleeve—I think maybe you saw that part. But that night Jack Nolan could see around corners, he could see the moon and stars at oblique angles, and he wanted to go. He wanted to visit those spaces. He walked up the ramp and you tore his ticket and he pulled the restraining harness down. You turned the key and pressed the button and the Voyager began its rotations: arcing out and up, climbing the night, sweeping over the fairgrounds, tracing parabolic pentagrams in streaks of light. Motors thrumming, magnets humming, screams twisted by G-force. And then he was gone. His shoulder harness still locked down, like the seat was never occupied. And that's what you decided: that he was never there. You thought Jack the Cat would be the next teen up and off to the state mental hospital, but he slipped off to somewhere ... else."

Brooks tried to read the expression on Grossman's face. The operator's jaw had gone slack, his eyes wide. "How do you know all that? You say you're not FBI. So what's SPECTRA, anyway?"

Brooks rattled off the answer: "Special Physics Emergent Counter-Terror Recon Agency."

"The hell does that mean?"

Brooks shrugged.

"I know all that," Durham said, "because I've seen the equations—the chalkboards and notebooks that Zann left behind."

"What do you need me for? Wait, you think Zann was a *terrorist?*" Grossman's eyes shunted back and forth between the two agents.

"No," Brooks said. "He was well respected at CERN for almost a decade. He never would have been cleared to work on the LHC if he had terror ties. But he was banished from the scientific community for fringe ideas. How else does a Nobel laureate end up working for a carnival, disguising a dimension-diving accelerator as a thrill ride just to see if it works?"

Grossman held his trembling, oil-stained thumb and forefinger an inch apart. "I understand about this much of what you're saying. So let's have it: what do you want from me? What do I need to do to never have to talk about that night again?"

Brooks looked at Durham. The diver squatted beside the easy chair. "Gustav Zann designed a very peculiar key for the Voyager," Durham said, and presented his hand, palm up. He had a musician's fingers, Brooks thought as they uncurled, or maybe a magician's.

The stale air seemed to congeal for a few heartbeats. Then Grossman tugged at the neck of his T-shirt, reached in and produced what looked like an obsidian shaft notched with Braille and hieroglyphics suspended from a beaded chain. He slipped the chain over his head, hesitated, and then dropped it into Durham's palm.

"Why did you keep it?" Durham asked.

Grossman took another cigarette from the pack and set it on his lip. It stuck there and bobbed when he spoke. "I saw Mrs. Nolan on TV back then. I thought maybe the day would come when I'd get up the nerve to run the ride on Cat. Try to find her boy."

Durham pocketed the key.

"Is that what you're gonna do?" Grossman asked, "Bring him back?"

Durham didn't answer. He nodded at Brooks and headed down the hall toward the door.

"Thank you for your time, Mr. Grossman," Brooks said and tossed a piece he hadn't found a home for into the void at the center of the puzzle.

♦

Behind the wheel again, sand streaming over the road in white wisps, Brooks asked, "Where to now? Back to Boston?"

Durham turned the black shaft over in his fingers, mesmerized by its intricacies. Finally, he said, "Too much paperwork."

♦

The ruins of Cosmic Park covered just under two miles of lakeshore property in Ashbrook, New Hampshire, all of it fenced off with chain link, electricity, and razor wire in 2014 when the investigation of Gustav Zann confirmed that the pine-shrouded grounds were home to a crown jewel of weird physics. For eighteen months SPECTRA had offered lucrative salaries through back channels in an effort to skim the shallow end of the talent pool surrounding the Large Hadron Collider.

But the Voyager refused to give up its secrets intact. And so the project languished, the theoreticians were let go, and the bureaucrats backed up their computers and left the Quonset huts behind. On to other case files, even though Voyager's was never officially closed.

The only points the physicists and occultists had agreed upon were that the passenger pods somehow crossed a dimensional barrier when they reached full acceleration, that the crossing was accomplished by the angles the pods traversed, and that these angles were derived from a geometric figure: an oblique pentacle that the occultists recognized from their grimoires. But without the black key the Voyager project eventually fell to lesser minds—a handful of field agents hunting down leads on the whereabouts of Gustav Zann and Sam Grossman. So Brooks had been surprised when Durham, a diver with higher clearance, had approached him with the tip that ultimately led to the operator.

Brooks showed his ID at the checkpoint, brought the car through the gate, and turned onto the gravel road that snaked to the park. The lake flashed through the trees and he stole glances at Durham. Brooks wondered if the information leading to Grossman had really come from web searches and inter-agency connect-the-dots, or if the diver had found Grossman and the strange black key in some subliminal realm that he dipped into off the books, piecing together the digital breadcrumb trail later to satisfy Brooks and anyone who needed answers after the fact.

As they approached the lake, gravel crunching under the tires, chassis rocking over roots and potholes, Durham stared at his phone. He had been thumbing through it and had frozen on a photo of a woman and pair of boys.

"You might want to slow down and think this through," Brooks said. "Maybe we should bring that key to HQ."

Durham blacked the phone out and slipped it into his pocket. When he looked up, Brooks saw a desperate desire in his eyes to agree to this more cautious plan, to turn the car around and take the winding path through bureaucracy, through days, weeks, maybe months of testing with crash dummies wired to the gills with cameras and radiation sensors.

"They'll end up sending me in anyway, sooner or later. I prefer not to wait."

"Do you really think he's still in there? Alive? You think Jack Nolan went through a door that closed behind him, and he's still sitting there on the other side waiting for someone to open it?" Brooks scoffed. "All these years ... without food, water ..."

"The laws of Earth don't apply," Durham said. "To *us* it's been years. To him ... maybe minutes."

"You have a wife and kids," Brooks said. "You should be taking every precaution."

"*Brooks*," Durham snapped. "If one of my boys disappeared into the Voyager, do you think I'd be taking every precaution then? Do you think I'd let a day go by once I had the key? Would *you* if he was yours? When people are trapped in a burning building, do you think the fire truck goes back to the station first?"

Brooks nodded. He had brought the car to a crawl while they talked. Now he put his foot down on the accelerator and climbed the road with purpose.

♦

It seemed strange to Brooks, surreal even, that a globe-spanning investigation spearheaded by an agency operating beyond the oversight of taxpayers and powered by deep pockets of laundered money should reach its climax with two men parking in a muddy field, firing up a gas generator, and climbing the entrance ramp of an amusement park ride in the dusk of a Thursday evening in March. Astronauts with no mission control and no fanfare.

The platform was overgrown with crabgrass, the nearby structures stricken with occult graffiti from the era between the closing of the park and its occupation by SPECTRA. Hardened puddles of red and black candle wax still littered the platform in places, reminders of the rumored ritual activity by members of the Starry Wisdom Church that had led the agency to the site in the first place. A warm breeze fluttered Brooks' tie, an early hint of spring despite the last remaining mounds of snow scattered about the grounds.

The Voyager was a sprawling construction of purple-painted steel, studded with light bulbs and threaded with hydraulic pistons and flexible cable enclosures. It looked like a slumbering monster against the pink wash of sunset and the black spires of the pines—its many-jointed limbs resembled the tentacles of a robotic squid, each ending in a great three-pronged claw of passenger pods.

Brooks' gaze settled on the one black vinyl seat marked with an X in yellow spray-paint—the seat from which Jack Nolan had vanished, according to his friends.

Durham knelt on the platform beside the marked pod and unsnapped the clasps of his aluminum attaché case. Over his shoulder Brooks could see a jet-injector gun and a set of glass vials tucked snugly in compartments cut out of a brick of black foam rubber. It brought the reality of the situation home to him. He looked at the control stand—little more than a wooden podium with a button and a ball-shaft shifter beneath an awning airbrushed with galaxies and nebula clouds at the nexus of the mechanical arms.

"We should have brought the operator along," Brooks said.

"Why?"

"Because who's going to inject you with the abort drug if you need to pull out? I can't ride the pod with you if I'm on the controls."

Durham focused his eyes on the vial he was screwing in. "This is in-house Cat 9, designed for a shorter duration and intensity, a threshold dose. I'll be surfacing before you know it."

"How long?"

"Minutes, not hours."

"How many minutes?"

Durham set the injector down on the case lid and concentrated on unbuttoning his shirtsleeve with what Brooks surmised was more than the requisite level of attention. Avoiding eye contact. "Relax. It's recon. I'm just poking my head under the surface for a look around this time. Then we'll know if we can devise an extraction."

"We should have brought the operator."

Durham picked up the injector and checked his watch. Brooks drew a sharp breath to tell him to stop, wait, think it through, but the sound of his inhalation rushing between his teeth spliced into the hiss of the device's exhalation into the diver's arm.

Brooks sighed and kicked a candle stub off of the platform.

Durham set the injector back in the case and strode toward the passenger pod with Brooks at his heels.

"Wait." Brooks put a hand on Durham's shoulder. "I don't even know how to operate the thing."

"Nothing to it. Hit the button. Once it's moving, click the shifter up through the three speeds. The flashing lights on the arms will change color when it's time to kick it up to the next stage."

"That's it?"

"That's it," Durham said, pulling the safety harness down over his torso until he felt it lock. "Built to be run by a carny. You aren't color blind, are you?"

"No."

"Then just follow the changing lights through the cycle: up to speed and back down."

Durham pressed the cold black shaft of the key into Brooks' hand.

Brooks held the diver's gaze. "Is there anything you want me to tell—"

"She knows."

Brooks went to the control podium where the arms of the machine converged. He could see Durham's face in profile, staring up at the sky. Brooks found a steel bezel with a slot in its eye and pushed the key into it slowly, wondering if the orientation of the hieroglyphic impressions mattered. But it didn't resist or jam. Quite the contrary: the channel seemed to suck the key in with magnetic force.

The red START button illuminated. He wished there was a STOP button beside it and wondered if hitting it a second time after a premature downshifting would abort the ride. You couldn't make a carnival ride with no kill switch, could you? Would cycling down too fast damage it? His hand felt clammy on the shifter. Durham was more concerned with getting in than out, and Brooks didn't like it.

His index finger hovered above the button. He punched it. The machine engaged gracefully, arms rising slowly and gliding away from the ground without the slightest hint of a mechanical lurch. It was as if the thing were alive and waking from a long sleep. The many-jointed steel arms uncoiled soundlessly, and yet a subsonic vibration thrummed in his feet, testicles, eyeballs, shaking the desiccated leaves that still clung to the trees like dusty bells, shaking the fine white filaments on nearby reeds to set the Earth's ears ringing, the stars trembling.

And then the world was moving around him. No, he was moving against the orbit of the passenger pods, and looking down he saw that the control tier he stood at was rising and rotating, bringing him up with it atop a circular platform. His altitude kept pace with Durham's pod, and it soon came into view again, crossing his line of sight. Durham's face looked bloodless. Then the lights came on, bathing it in a cold blue sheen.

Brooks took a deep breath and pushed the throttle out of the neutral rut into the first speed position. The limb of the machine from which Durham's pod hung swung out in an arc away from the nexus where Brooks remained perched, feeling his stomach follow in the smear of blue light.

He dragged his palms across his chest to dry them on his shirt, and gripped the sides of the control box. Another improbably sinuous steel arm drifted into view bearing another trio of pods. These spun off along a different trajectory, passing over his head in a rush of air.

Full dark had descended on the park, the only light cast by the myriad rows of blue bulbs now shifting to orange. Brooks nudged the shifter into second position.

No music played, but the Voyager was a symphony of limbs, spirals within spirals expanding and retracting, tracing trails of light through the darkness in a pattern so fluid that it seemed impossible it could be motivated by a mechanical heart, transmitted through gears and pistons. Rather, the motion of the machine was like the billowing of tendrils in an ocean current, the undulations of flames in a wind. He was mesmerized in the eye of the vortex.

He tried to track Durham's pod, but lost it—one ball among many at the whim of a master juggler. Only, the juggler, Zann, had left the carnival long ago. Had he preceded Jack Nolan through the veil? Had he designed the drug as well as the ride?

A face sped out of the darkness at him and his heartbeat tripped at the sudden sight: Durham, his mouth a black tunnel, his eyes all whites as he gazed up into the recesses of his own skull. And gone again—a streak of orange light morphing to violet.

Brooks followed the pod with his gaze, tracking it like the prize cup in a shell game. He threw the shifter into third speed, rocketing the pod into a zone where it became almost impossible to follow and making him wish that he too had partaken of the drug for the speed it would bestow upon the flitting of his eyes and the sparking of his synapses.

The platform on which he stood had reached its full height; its corkscrewing had ceased, but he continued to turn on his heels, following, he realized, a human vocal drone; a dreadful whine that seemed to require no replenishing breath to carry for all eternity.

There: the manned pod screamed into view a mere yard from his face and the body beneath the safety harness was no longer a body but a cutout in the shape of a man through which the cancerous rays of distant stars pulsed through a range of unearthly colors. It sped past, and the purple bulbs turned back to orange, and Brooks shifted the Voyager down and remembered to breathe and felt the platform rotating beneath him, winding him back down to the ground. Blue lights. And down to first position. The sprawling robotic limbs retracted, slowed, descended. The charged air relaxed, and it was over even as the universe continued to spin around his dizzy head.

He knelt at the podium, rested his forehead against the cold metal of the control box, opened his eyes and caught sight of the black nub of the key.

He pulled it out.

Climbing to his feet, he scanned the machine's now dormant anatomy and found Durham, once again a man, slumped in his harness, chin to chest.

Brooks ran to the pod. He slapped a nervous tattoo against Durham's cheek, got no response, laid his palm on the man's forehead and tugged an eyelid up with his thumb: all pupil, shot through with sharp spokes of violet light stretching from some vast depth. Brooks recoiled at the sight. He undid the harness and pushed it up. Durham slumped forward into his arms. Brooks lifted the diver out of the pod and laid him down on the coarse grass.

He checked for a pulse and found it, put his ear to Durham's nose and detected shallow breath. He slapped the man's cheek again and again, whispering to himself, "*Come on, come* on come on COME ON! WAKE UP, YOU SON OF A BITCH! *DURHAM!*"

The diver's eyelashes fluttered. He drew a shuddering breath, hitched and gasped. His eyes shot open, riveted to the sky. "Saw him," he said.

"Who? Nolan?"

"… *eeeeeEEEEE … aliiive …*"

"He's alive?"

"*Eeeeeaten* … alive. It's still … eating him alive."

"What is, Durham? What's eating him alive?"

Durham laughed, wheezed, hyperventilated.

"Calm down," Brooks said. "Try to calm down."

Durham's crazy eyes focused on Brooks now, the spokes of violet light converging to a pinpoint. He could hardly bear it. "Ripping his atoms apart with teeth like shards of broken stars … but he's alive. He'll always be alive."

A peal of hysterical laughter fell out of the diver's mouth and set Brooks' skin crawling. The sound mocked everything good and sane in the world, and all Brooks could think of doing in response was to draw his piece and mute that godforsaken sound, to snuff out Durham's ninth life because there was something irrefutable in that laugh, something that bore witness to chaos and embraced it.

Brooks put the gun out of his mind and focused on the memory of Durham gazing at his phone. The photo of the man's family. He clutched the memory like an amulet against the laughter. Because if he let that laughter spill under his defenses and take hold of him, he might start laughing, too. And he might never stop.

... climbed like a tree frog down the side of the house ...

The Mouth of the Merrimack

Shane Rundell rode his bike to the job that night, pumping the pedals in short bursts, then coasting long stretches of Water Street, winding past the Joppa flats and over the bridge to Plum Island. He knew the house, though he'd never been there before—knew it as soon as Mr. Williamson described it over the chatter of students funneling out of AP History. It was a modest colonial facing the ocean at the mouth of the Merrimack, distinguished from the crowd of cedar-shingle beach shacks by its pink clapboard siding, octagonal cupola, and iron widow's walk.

Shane had noticed the house on kayaking trips he'd taken around the island, though it had never been his destination until today. And he'd never seen it quite like this—set against the gray trim of a cloudbank as the sky drained of color, an aquamarine glow shifting behind the leaded glass panes of the cupola, as if someone had left a lava lamp cooking up there. Mr. Williamson didn't strike Shane as the lava lamp type—less than ever when he answered the door in a tuxedo.

The effect was startling. In the classroom, the history teacher was partial to rumpled plaid shirts and corduroys, but there was no denying that he cleaned up nicely; the sharp attire lending an air of sophistication to a freshly trimmed salt-and-pepper beard. It was Shane's first time babysitting for the Williamsons, and the tux added an aspect of the surreal to the brief tour Mr. Williamson gave him while his wife did her hair and makeup.

"Jonah, say hello to Shane. Shane is one of my students. He's going to be your babysitter tonight while Mama and I have our date."

"I'm not a baby," Jonah said without looking up from the sketchpad in his lap. He sat at the center of a glossy pine plank floor, hunched over his art, colored pencils scattered like kindling around him.

The teacher cracked an asymmetrical smile at Shane as if to say *See what you're in for?*

And because a single correction to his statement wasn't enough, a female voice carried down the hall, curled with teasing melodic admonishment. "It's not a date night, darling. You're getting a medal."

"You are?" Shane tucked his head back as if blown on the wind of the man's achievement.

"It's nothing. They're giving me a jewel—a *pin*—for service to the Masonic lodge. I'm not the only one receiving the honor tonight. Phoebe just wants to remind me that it doesn't get me off the hook for a *real* date this month, even though we're doing a harbor cruise with cocktails afterward." He waved a hand at the broad step at the foot of a flight of stairs. "You can set your bag down there. Kitchen's this way. Phoebe already prepared Jonah's supper. You'll find it in a casserole dish in the fridge. Just needs to be reheated. The microwave settings are right here."

Mr. Williamson tapped a notepad on the gold-flecked marble slab that topped the kitchen island. "She's so organized. Opposites attract, right?"

Shane laughed, following the man through a series of rooms that juxtaposed roughhewn beams with stylish modern embellishments.

"I'm afraid we don't have much of a home entertainment system to keep you occupied. But there's a stereo with some vinyl and plenty of books. Did you bring your homework?"

"Yeah. Got my notes for the local history paper. Figured I'd bang out a first draft. *If* Jonah lets me, of course."

"Good man. You should be able to get some work done after you tuck him in. Bedtime is eight-thirty. His toothbrush already has paste on it up in the upstairs bathroom. And if you read to him, it won't take long before he's out like a light. Lullabies work too, but that's Phoebe's department. Jonah loves music almost as much as drawing. I'm sure he'll play his recorder for you. He can't resist a fresh audience."

94

Mr. Williamson turned to face Shane, tucked his hands in his pockets, and rocked on the heels of his shiny black shoes, his Masonic lapel pins glinting gold in the lamplight. They'd arrived at the second-floor balcony overlooking Jonah in the living room, the top sheet of his sketchpad covered in a furious tangle of turquoise and violet. "Any questions?"

"None that I can think of. It's a beautiful house. I've always noticed it because of the widow's walk."

Mr. Williamson smiled and nodded. "When I inherited the place, I had grand ideas about making an observatory out of the cupola. But really it's just a place to keep my telescope and flask for stargazing on clear winter nights."

Shane raised his eyebrows and looked around, letting the unspoken question hang between them: *How do you get up there?*

Mr. Williamson indicated a cherry-stained door with a scrimshaw knob. "It used to be an open ceiling and staircase for ventilation through the cupola, but when Jonah was born, I had a contractor close it off so we don't have to worry about finding him climbing around on the roof. It's the only room in the house that we keep locked." He clapped Shane on the shoulder. "If we weren't short on time, I'd take you up for a look at the sunset. Maybe next time."

Mrs. Williamson stepped into view below, one arm in a black frock coat. "Cal, we're going to be late." She was a tall, pretty woman, her gray-streaked dark hair and red lipstick a stark contrast to her vellum skin.

"Coming," he said, rounding the balustrade and trotting down the creaking stairs. "Do we really need coats?"

His wife shrugged, slipping into the other sleeve of hers. "*You* might be fine, but I'm wearing one. It's always chilly on the water at night."

Shane descended the stairs and examined a bookshelf while Mrs. Williamson bent to kiss her son on the forehead.

"Last chance for questions," she said to Shane, rising and plucking lint from her lapel.

"I think I'm good. Have fun."

"Cal gave you the supper instructions and cell numbers?"

"He did."

95

"Well then, we're off. We'll be home before the horses turn back to mice."

♦

When the car had turned out of the driveway, Shane turned toward the sound of ripping paper rising over the crunch of tires on gravel. Jonah sat among paper scraps scribbled with color.

"Aw, what'd you do that for? You ripped up your artwork?"

The boy nodded, staring at a blank space on the floor as if he could see through it.

"Why? I wanted to see it." But Shane knew why. Jonah was venting anger at his parents leaving him with a stranger for the night. A typical and harmless act of destruction for a boy his age.

"It was sucky," Jonah said.

"Language, buddy."

"It wasn't like what I see in my dreams."

Shane laughed and resisted the urge to tousle the kid's hair. "Well, ain't that the eternal struggle of the artist? You wanna play a game?"

Jonah shrugged.

"It's a little early for your supper, so let's play something. What do you have around here?"

"Cards."

"Perfect. Go get 'em."

Jonah fetched a deck from under the lid of a piano bench beside an upright in the corner. Shaking the cards from the box, Shane was taken aback to find it was an antique French tarot deck, the grunge-speckled artwork and gilded edges dulled with age. The uncoated cards smelled of mildew and myrrh, their texture like dried skins between his fingers.

One card caught his eye as he shuffled through them—a man falling from a tower into a roiling sea, a crudely painted black barracuda opening its jaws to devour him. A bolt of lightning threaded down from a cloud above to strike what looked like a stone idol in the tower window. Another card depicted a devil with the forelegs of a goat joined to the scaly, curling tail of a fish. Shane quickly dropped the cards back into the box.

"We can't play with these, Jonah. Do you have a regular deck with … you know, hearts and clubs and stuff?"

Jonah went to the kitchen and returned with a cheap pack of Bicycle playing cards.

"What games do you know?" Shane asked, idly shuffling the deck. "Got a favorite?"

"Goldfish."

"You mean *Go Fish?* Okay, cool."

They sat on the floor amid the shredded papers and played while the house grew dark. Shane's phone chimed with a text, but he only spared it a glance to make sure it wasn't Mr. Williamson. When Jonah finally won a round, Shane decided it was a good time to call it quits and feed him. He rose from the floor with a cramp in his leg and fumbled with the beaded chain dangling from a stained-glass lamp on a nearby end table. The room lit up a buttery shade of yellow.

Shane read the message on his phone while Jonah put the cards away. It was from Kelly, his girlfriend—though he was still getting used to calling her that.

> **KL:** *Hey nerd. R U really babysitting on a Friday night instead of taking me out?*
> **SR:** *I'm making money so I CAN take you out. Tomorrow.*
> **KL:** *Which house is it? I'll visit you.*
> **SR:** *Don't. Please. It's my first time. If the kid tells, I'll lose the gig.*
> **KL:** *Your loss. I'm \m/.*

Shane snorted at the homemade emoji for devil horns. Kelly was boldest when she knew she couldn't have him.

> **KL:** *What time do you put him to bed?*
> **SR:** *Seriously. Save it for tomorrow. Gotta go feed him now <3*

Jonah was sitting at the dining room table, humming under his breath, when Shane placed a grilled cheese and a glass of iced tea in front of him. The kid wrinkled his nose at the food. "What's this?"

"The dish your mom left for you went bad, so I fixed you something else. Sorry, I'm not much of a chef, but you have to eat something."

"I don't want this. I want what Mama made. I want my Friday supper."

Shane sighed. "I don't know how it went bad in the fridge, but I couldn't feed it to you. Trust me, you wouldn't want it. It was rancid."

Jonah pushed the plate away, slid off his chair, and headed for the kitchen.

"Where are you going?"

"I'm getting my supper."

"You can't. It's in the trash."

But the kid was already gone. Shane scrambled after him, noting the rattle of the silverware drawer and the creak of the trashcan lid yawning open. He found Jonah lifting a chunky spoonful of the putrid mush out of the trash: chunks of shellfish in a curdled sauce, trailing strips of green-black noodles that looked like kelp.

"Oh, God. Give me that." Shane seized the child's wrist and wrenched the dripping spoon away.

Jonah flashed his dirty teeth in defiance.

"Stop! Just … you can't eat out of the trash. That food will make you sick, Jonah. You don't like grilled cheese? Fine. Just tell me what you'll eat, and I'll make it."

Jonah burst past Shane. He bounded across the living room and up the stairs with the loping gait of an animal. The sound of his bedroom door slamming shut reverberated from the second floor balcony.

Shane heaved a sigh of frustration, then plodded into the living room. He plucked his knapsack from the staircase and carried it to the kitchen, where he settled down to unpack his notebooks and pick at the grilled cheese while he let the kid cool off. He was just beginning to find his focus when it was shattered by a knock at the door. Kelly stood on the stoop, her curled fists jammed into the pockets of a light hoodie, her foster mom's grimy Saturn parked askew on the gravel behind her.

"Kelly. I told you … I'm working."

She ignored the admonishment, stepping past him into the house. "Thanks for inviting me in. It's fucking frigid out there. I thought it was supposed to be spring."

"How did you find the house?"

"Your bike gave it away. In the future, when you're avoiding me, you might want to stow that somewhere."

"Keep your voice down. The kid's upstairs. And I'm not avoiding you." Shane, trying not to be annoyed, reminded himself that Kelly had abandonment issues. Her mother had committed suicide when she was eleven, just a little older than Jonah was now. She'd never known her father. And she'd never been big on rules about where she couldn't go or what she couldn't do. Shane still marveled that he was dating her. If she'd been in his class at Newburyport High, they'd never have connected. He was far too nerdy and straight-laced for her.

But they'd met as lifeguards last summer at Salisbury Beach, where the Harbor Schools program for at-risk youth placed her after paying for her Red Cross certification. Truth be told, he was slightly embarrassed that she was visiting him at a babysitting gig, but he was only taking jobs like this one to get through the off season until the beaches opened. Some parents were weird about hiring a male sitter, but his CPR certification usually sealed the deal. And the money was good.

"Is he asleep?" Kelly asked.

"No. He's just pissed at me about his dinner. I'll have to coax him out soon and get him to eat something before bed."

Kelly plunked down into an empty chair at the scuffed farmhouse table, her gaze roaming over Shane's library books, notes, and laptop. "Homework? On a Friday night? You are hopeless."

Shane resigned himself to sitting with her for a moment before giving her the heave-ho. Maybe, if she felt reassured that he'd rather be with her—and would be tomorrow after putting a little cash in his pocket—she'd leave of her own accord before Jonah saw her.

"We're going out tomorrow, and I don't want it hanging over my head on Sunday."

She picked up a book and knitted her brow at the cover art. "This is homework? Looks like Dungeons and Dragons. Are you sure I didn't crash your secret geek club?" She tossed the book on the table—a sea monster dripping black ichor glared up from the cover.

"It's for a local history paper. Find some obscure fact about the town and research it. I'm doing H. P. Lovecraft, the horror author?" Kelly liked horror movies, but the name brought no flicker of recognition to her cold green eyes.

"*Lovecraft?* What did he write, the Kama Sutra?"

"He was a pulp horror writer in the 1920s. Newburyport features in one of his longest stories. The character visits the library and the historical society and learns about a cult of like … fish people. They moved it—the historical society—but I visited the house where it is now on High Street, and the one where it used to be when Lovecraft visited. Turns out he was inspired to write the story by a train ride he took to Newburyport back before the town got a facelift. Back then it was like a shantytown. The Towle silver factory was the only industry besides fishing. The rest of Water Street was just rotting shacks."

Kelly yawned theatrically.

"Well it's way more interesting than most local history. At least I get to read a horror story and write about how this racist, sex-phobic dude was fascinated by human/amphibian crossbreeding, right? Give me some points for style at least."

"So, it's like mermaid porn?"

"Would that make it cooler to you?"

Kelly planted her elbows on the table, raked clawed fingers through her hair, and shook her head in dismay. "What am I doing with you?"

Shane dangled his pen over his notebook, looking for the last line he'd transferred to the laptop. But it was no use. He couldn't concentrate with her sitting there bored, restless, and all kinds of hot in that pink halter top. He needed to get her out of here, needed to work on coaxing Jonah out of his room and back to the kitchen where they could negotiate a meal.

As if reading his mind, Kelly sat up, sniffed the air, and frowned. "Did something die in here?"

"It's the food I threw out. It went bad."

She wandered into the living room, waving a hand in front of her face. Seeing the paper scraps on the floor, she knelt and sifted through them, assembling the shredded drawing like a jigsaw puzzle.

Shane closed his laptop lid in resignation and flipped random kitchen cabinet doors looking for cereal or peanut butter, anything he could offer the kid. He found a can of tuna and set it on the counter.

When he came up behind Kelly to see if he could get her to leave, his throat constricted at the sight of the reconstructed drawing on the floor. In a riot of ocean blue, mossy green, and shadow black, it depicted the ruins of a sunken city. Cartoon fish swam between cyclopean columns rising from winding terraces. It was an unsettling combination of a child's crude effort and a veracity of detail that might be almost accidental—his brain interpreting scribbles and random white spaces as barnacles and wavering fronds of kelp.

"How old is he?" Kelly asked.

"Eleven."

"He's gifted, huh?"

"I guess. I think he might be on the spectrum. I don't know."

The hollow sound of a flute floated down over the balcony railing, mournful and faint, with a minor note that reminded Shane of soundtracks from movies set in Egypt or Persia. The melody and technique were crude, not unlike the drawing, with flourishes that could have been discordant accidents or an intentionally unnerving tune.

Kelly touched the hollow of her throat and laughed. "Well, *that's* creepy as shit."

"I need to feed him, Kel. You can't be here when I do." His eyes lingered on the drawing as he spoke to her. Something about the style was vaguely reminiscent of the tarot cards he'd seen earlier.

Kelly looked up at the second floor railing, her eyes following the haunting tune. "Where's the door to the widow's walk?"

"If I don't get fired tonight I'll show you next time. Anyway, it's locked."

"Ooh, a secret room? I bet I can find it," she sang, springing from the floor and prancing up the stairs on tiptoes. Shane fumbled to his feet and gave chase, almost shouting after her, but catching himself.

The flute melody haunted the upper hall as Kelly crept along the row of doors. When she reached Jonah's bedroom, Shane waved his hands, brushing the air at his waist in a *leave it alone* gesture. With a glint of mischief in her eyes, Kelly scurried to the narrow cherry door with the scrimshaw handle. Shane could see now that the design etched into it was a giant squid. He watched as she rattled the unmoving knob.

"Okay, you found it," Shane whispered. "You win. Now let's go."

Kelly was up on her toes, feeling along the upper edge of the lacquered trim. When her hand came down, it held something the pewter color of a thunderhead. She slotted it into the key plate before he could move to snatch it from her. The door clicked open and swung inward, and she turned a broad smile on him, bobbing her upper body with pantomimed laughter.

"How did you know the key was there?"

She answered with a *Do you even know me?* expression of mock scorn. "Where do you put something you don't want a kid to find?"

The sound of Jonah's flute had ceased. Was he listening to their hushed exchange, or just pausing between tunes? Shane reached past Kelly and seized the knob, intending to pull the door shut, but as he did so, Jonah's door clicked open. Shane pushed Kelly through and closed the door to the cupola before hurrying to Jonah's bedroom.

"Mama?" Jonah said through the gap between door and frame, his face out of view.

"No, buddy, your mom and dad are still out. It's just me."

"Then who were you talking to?"

"Nobody. It's just me. Hey, I'm sorry about your dinner. What can I get you to eat? You must be hungry."

No reply. But the door remained open.

"You like tuna? Can I make you a tuna sandwich?" The casserole had been seafood, so Shane was hopeful this suggestion might score, but now the door did swing shut with a slow creak. At least the kid hadn't slammed it in his face. A moment later, the flute melody resumed. He put his hand on the knob and found it locked. For a moment, he debated knocking, mustering a firm tone, and threatening to call the boy's parents if he didn't open the door and come out to eat. But the sound of the mournful melody gradually took the wind out of Shane's sails. He decided that as long as he could hear the flute, he knew what Jonah was doing, and that was good enough for now.

He turned to the door he'd pushed Kelly through. She'd taken the key with her, but—to his great relief—the ivory knob turned in his hand when he tried it. He slipped through and closed the door carefully behind him.

Looking around, he was surprised to find not a staircase leading directly to the cupola, but rather a small room lined with bookshelves, a leather armchair on a Persian carpet in the center, and an iron spiral staircase ascending to the octagonal glass room above.

Kelly sat perched on the ledge, her legs swinging idly, the cherry of a joint burning in the shadow that fell across her face, her form dusky beside the silhouette of the telescope. She hadn't turned on a lamp, and the light had drained from the sky. Candlelight lapping at her throat played a trick that made it look like she had a scar he'd never noticed before. The effect was unsettling.

"I thought you'd never come," she said, her voice a laconic drawl.

Shane felt a flash of anger and struggled to contain it. How had he lost all control of the evening? He climbed the spiral stairs to her level and glared at her. "Seriously? You're smoking in my teacher's house. In his private room that's supposed to be locked. You're leaving the smell of weed in the one forbidden room of the house where I'm getting paid to watch a kid?"

"Oh, will you just chill? It's not mine. I found the dude's stash. The place already smells like it. He'll never know." She offered him the joint, but he waved it away and she tilted her head with an expression of … was that sympathy? It was hard to tell in the dark, but then the green glow he'd seen from the driveway traced a sine wave across her jawline, frosting the ends of her hair.

"You could use a hit, Shane. You're wound so tight tonight."

He looked past her for the source of the illumination. A statue of a woman carved from what looked like a block of granite squatted on a pedestal beside the antique brass telescope. Or was it a woman? The curves glimmered with a phosphorescent glow, different lines shifting in and out of prominence—some human, others serpentine. A hybrid of the erotic and the grotesque, equal parts woman and dragon.

"I thought it was a lava lamp from outside."

Kelly nodded "It's beautiful," she said, and exhaled a plume of smoke. "How does it do that?"

"It's chemical," Shane said absently, climbing the remaining stairs and approaching the statue. He was dimly aware of the panoramic view of the island through the windows of the cupola—the waves sweeping the beach below, the moon rising from a cloudbank, the white embers of Salisbury Beach scattered in the distance. But the stone figure drew his focus like a magnet. As he stepped closer to the pedestal on which it was perched, he felt a tightening in his sternum, as if he were passing through some kind of magnetic field or invisible current in the air. When he tried to push through it, his body rejected its proximity to idol, his bladder sending urgent signals and his skin prickling with gooseflesh, every sense urging flight.

"It's like something out of that book you were reading," Kelly said.

"Yeah." Shane moved back toward the stairs.

"This teacher you're sitting for, is he the one who told you to read Loveshaft?"

Shane forced his gaze from the idol, focused it on Kelly. She looked so ambivalent. Was she really not feeling the palpable malevolence radiating from that thing? "I found the Lovecraft/Newburyport connection on my own," he said. "Mr. Williamson didn't tell me to read anything. Why?"

She leaned forward into the light, eyebrows raised, the joint hanging from her upturned hand. "Because he's obviously into this, like, fish-worship stuff you were ranting about earlier."

Shane blinked. "I wasn't ranting."

Just like that, she'd yanked him from the borderland of a trance back into their dysfunctional dynamic. Sometimes he really couldn't remember why they were dating except that it was incredible when they *stopped* talking. "It's just a statue," Shane said.

Kelly laughed and jutted her chin toward the book-lined chamber at the bottom of the iron stairs. "Check out teacher's desk."

He followed her gaze to the source of the wavering light: a fat candle burning on the desk beside an open book, a massive leather-bound tome too big to be shelved. Even from his high vantage on the stairs, Shane could make out the rough lines of a woodblock illustration nested among the text. He descended, approaching the book like a sleepwalker, the illustration coming into focus with each reluctant step. It depicted the same coral terraces as the drawing Jonah had made with his pencils. Something vast lurked in the silt-clouded water beyond the towering columns. A shape reminiscent of the idol that glowed and pulsed like a psychic beacon at the peak of the house. The caption under the illustration read: *Pth'thya-l'yi, she that dwells amidst wonder and glory in Y'ha-nthlei.*

Shane projected a smile that didn't quite reach his eyes. "He's a scholar. There's probably all kinds of weird stuff in these books. You're not freaked out, are you?"

Kelly scoffed. "No, but you look like you are. I actually think mermaid porn is kinda hot."

Shane climbed the stairs again. Something nagged at him, something that had nothing to do with the unsettling illustration or the bad energy of the statue. Not a presence, but an absence. Kelly, her legs still draped over the edge, leaned back on her elbows and unbuttoned her jeans. Shane climbed past her, ignoring the invitation. He reached the top step and continued past the statue, making a deliberate effort not to look at it. His eyes were drawn to the shoreline below where waves darkened the sand in retreating cycles, leaving strands of ruddy seaweed behind.

Something pale clambered over the grassy dunes, flopping toward the water. It was the size of a dog, and for a moment Shane thought it must be a harbor seal, its pelt bleached by moonlight. But then he caught the shadow shapes of vertebrae down the creature's back. His gut rolled over as he identified the absence that had been nagging at him. There'd been no sound from Jonah's flute for … how long?

He tilted the telescope toward the figure as it reached the surf and felt Kelly's hands on his hips as he bent to peer into the eyepiece. Her slender fingers slipped around his waist from behind. Shane's pulse throbbed in his carotid artery, propelled more by what he saw than what he felt.

The naked figure lunging for the waves was Jonah.

"Oh, my God." Shane reeled around, knocking the telescope over and fumbling past Kelly. He was halfway down the stairs when she leaned over the railing and called after him, "Is that the kid you're supposed to be watching?"

Shane careened across the little library, thinking as he went that he should put out the candle—it was beside a book, probably a rare one, and Kelly was too messed up to be trusted in here with an open flame— but there was no time. He had to get to the waterline before Jonah did.

The door to Jonah's bedroom was wide open when Shane flew past it. He turned his head without slowing, just on the off chance he might see the boy in there, sitting on the bed with his flute or sketch pad, but the room was empty. He tore down the stairs and slipped when he hit the polished floor, then managed to regain his balance and avoid a wipeout. The front door was open, a gaping maw of terrible possibilities, inviting the salted night air into the house and setting the curtains to shiver at its kiss.

Shane leaped across the threshold and hit the sand running.

From the cupola, Kelly watched Jonah wade into the surf. He lurched with an awkward gait against the force of the waves, but also from the transformation of his bones, his limbs flapping and elongating as the water rolled over and around him, the brine awakening something amphibious that had slumbered until now under his skin. He moved fast despite his ungainly transient form. When the water reached his waist, he stooped and dove into the foam of an incoming wave, the fins that had sprouted on his calves and spine slicing the water and vanishing under the moon-frosted foam.

Shane splashed into the spot where the boy had been only seconds ago and was knocked backward by the next wave. He managed to stand, staggering against the weight of his wet clothes, and swiveled his head, searching the dark water, treading deeper toward the shelf where the bottom dropped off. He must have spotted a sign of Jonah because he dove through a wave and swam along a vector that spoke of clear purpose.

Kelly couldn't see what he moved toward, but she knew he wouldn't miss. He was a good lifeguard. She'd seen him lock in on drowning people in worse conditions than these. She picked up the fallen telescope and set it on its feet, but squinting into the brass eyepiece, she found only wavering shadows.

She was resigned to abandon the device when Shane's head popped above the grainy surface of the water. Had he tried to rescue Jonah from below? No, he'd been pulled under, and no sooner had he gulped a breath of air than it happened again. When he came up the second time, it was for just long enough to expel what remained of his breath in a ragged scream, thrashing against a predator she couldn't see until it pulled him under for the last time.

Kelly pressed her cold hands to her throat as the icy headlights of a car splashed over the house below.

●

Calvin Williamson saw the front door hanging open before he'd turned off the car. He touched his wife's hand as she reached for the seatbelt release. "Wait here. I'll be right back." There was concern in Phoebe's eyes, but also trust. He snuffed the headlights, climbed out of the car, and headed for the beach.

He found Jonah crouched over the ravaged body he'd dragged away from the reach of the breakers. It almost looked as if he were trying to perform CPR on Shane—a black irony, considering the babysitter's training. The hallmarks of a Deep One were receding from Jonah's flesh, withdrawing now that he'd been out of the water for a few minutes. Only his shark teeth were still prominent, stained as if he'd been caught gorging himself on cherry pie. His gill flaps and vestigial fins were already hidden, as they would remain until his molting next fall.

Calvin felt a pang of regret. He'd liked Shane, and hadn't wanted things to turn out like this. Not yet, anyway. The boy was a bright student. Calvin had hoped that he might at least have the chance to appreciate the hidden wonders of their town and its place in a secret history before the end of his brief span. But weren't all lives brief for folk who hadn't got out of the idea of dying? Who hadn't learned to breed it out of their bloodlines?

At his father's approach, Jonah looked up, his head slung low between his shoulders like a dog that had made a meal of something forbidden while its master was away.

"It's okay," Calvin said. "It's hard to resist the call of the sea."

"He threw my supper in the trash, Papa." A witness on the beach would have thought the words an incoherent gurgle, but Calvin Williamson was practiced at interpreting his son's vocalizations in the between state.

"You had to feed. Your mama would have been upset if you went to bed without supper."

The squeal of an unoiled hinge carried on the breeze and Calvin, recognizing it, followed the roofline of his house to the silhouette of a girl perched at the railing of the widow's walk. The aquamarine aura of the idol delineated her face, pulsing from the cradle of her arms, and Calvin hailed her. "Sister," he said in the old tongue, "do you wish to feast?"

By the time she'd returned the idol to its pedestal, her transformation was complete. Kelly L'Orne, Childe of the Deep, curled her batrachian fingers around the railing, climbed like a tree frog down the side of the house, and crawled through the tall beach grass and over the dunes. When she reached the body, she rose up on her hind legs and fanned her gills in a wet sigh of grief. Jonah slinked away, back toward the house and his mother.

"He would never have been one of us," Calvin said. "You know that."

Kelly blinked, translucent membranes sliding lazily over her bulbous eyes. They caught the moonlight with a tremulous shimmer.

"I'm sorry." Calvin tugged at his bow tie, pulled the black silk from his collar and stuffed it in his pocket. "If you're not going to feast, you should change. You can help me get his bicycle and backpack off the island. Leave them where they'll be found. Upriver, between here and his home. I'll dive with the remains down to the reef."

"Let me," she said, and before he could argue she'd knelt and slid her green-spotted arms under the dead boy's knees and neck, her fins slicing grooves in the sand. She lifted him with a gentle strength she could never have exhibited in her human form.

Calvin nodded, scanned the horizon for boat lights, then turned to follow his son over the dunes. When he looked again at the water, he saw her wading through the foam, guiding the floating corpse along a road that would lead to the moon, if silvered waves were white bricks.

"Give my regards to your grandmother," he said, though he knew his words would die on the wind.

No Mask

They say you can't change anyone's mind anymore. Well, I'm living proof that's not true. I know I haven't posted on this journal in ages. I never meant to give it up in favor of social media, it just sort of happened that way. Probably because there was more engagement on the social sites, but they also ended up making me a little crazy.

Anyway, I don't know if anyone will read this but I want to record my story for posterity while my thoughts are still coherent. *For posterity.* Is that pretentious? It feels weird knowing that my first audience for this post will probably be the police. Friends and family might see it if it isn't deleted right away, and then maybe strangers if someone archives it, spreads it around, gets it to go viral? What a funny word for the time in which we're living. But I'll admit that's what I'm hoping for—that this post will get around after I'm gone, maybe inspire others to seek out what I found.

tl;dr: If you're locked down at home and marinating in your own fear and anxiety, you're afraid of the wrong things. I'm here to tell you that it's going to be okay. The king is coming, and everything is going to be better than okay. It's going to be glorious.

I know I sound like a Jesus freak or something, and I used to turn my nose up at those people too. I thought they were brainwashed. And maybe they are. Maybe I am. But I'm thinking about that word in a new way. You wash something to clean the dirt out of it. To purify it. Sometimes it does feel like what I've seen washed all of the fear, anxiety, and misconception right out of my mind. All of the personal pain and grasping at things that were never going to make me happy, never solve my problems, or give me the clear-eyed confidence that comes from seeing the true nature of reality.

Hear me out. But maybe get a cup of tea first. This is going to be a long one.

♦

It was November 23rd when Mark got the invitation on Facebook. Like most people, we'd been housebound since March, pretty much living the same day over and over again on endless repeat. Working from home on our computers, video chatting with family occasionally, even trying the rare and unsatisfying Zoom happy hour. Case numbers had leveled off after a big spike in September, but everyone was bracing for a surge after Thanksgiving, with high death numbers to follow two weeks later. You know the pattern. So it felt profoundly weird to get an invitation to a public event.

We live in Boston and used to get them all the time. Too many, to be honest. I work in publishing and Mark used to play in bands, so we have a lot of friends in the arts scene. Before 2020, on any given weekend we were bound to feel guilty about skipping someone's gig, gallery opening, or poetry reading. Most of those events had moved online, but this one made a point of stating that masks would be required, so it stood out. There wasn't a venue listed at first, just a creepy and intriguing graphic with a date and the words *DETAILS TO COME*.

The event was posted by a page called The Yellow Sign. It had been shared by Mark's friend, Jack Scott, an old bandmate who'd traded his drumsticks for paintbrushes. Jack had managed to remain a struggling artist in his thirties while Mark's second act had taken a divergent trajectory through a series of increasingly boring jobs and nicer places to live. My own work is only slightly more creative— writing marketing plans for nonfiction titles, and I think we both felt a little honored that our friends who still live in the city hadn't written us off entirely. They still invited us to things, still wanted us to be a part of the scene, even after we'd moved out to Arlington.

We were watching Netflix when the alert came through. It annoys me when Mark checks his phone while we're watching something together. He usually tries to be discreet about it, but this time he paused the show, stared at his screen, and whispered, "No fucking way." Then he passed it to me.

It took me a second to sort out what I was looking at, and when I did I thought his reaction was to the idea of a live performance while the virus was raging in the city. A vaguely esoteric font proclaimed *MASKS REQUIRED: PROVIDED AT THE DOOR.*

The banner image might have been one of Jack's paintings. It had his surrealist style written all over it—a horned figure in tattered yellow robes and a porcelain mask with a single eye hole, hovering before a sickly green sky studded with black stars.

"Yeah, no thanks," I said after a cursory glance and tried to hand the phone back to him. He wouldn't take it.

"*What?* What am I missing?"

"Did you even read the title?"

I hadn't. I was annoyed that he'd paused the show and had only looked long enough to see that it was a live event invite from Jack. On second glance, I saw that it was a performance of a play, and not just any play, but Mark's weird obsession: *The King In Yellow.*

"This is that urban legend thing you've been talking about since our first date?" To be fair, he only talked about it occasionally when he had more than his usual two drinks in him and a conversation gave him a segue. It had been a while since I'd heard the details, but I had no doubt they were still sharp in his mind, just waiting to be dusted off.

"Urban legend." He scoffed. "That makes it sound like a rumor."

"At least I didn't say 'conspiracy theory,'" I teased.

He took a deep enough breath that I knew I was in for a mouthful. "Just because I believe there are still mysteries in the universe and that—radical idea—the government is capable of deception doesn't make me a conspiracy theorist. Okay? I am not in the same boat as the microchip anti-vaxxers. Don't put me in that boat."

"I'm not. But if there's anything we should've learned from the past year besides maybe that deforestation and wet markets are a bad idea, it's that social media is a cesspool of disinformation that needs to be vetted."

"Zoey, I've been following this story since before social media was a thing. You know that. There's something to it."

"Maybe there is. But you know how memes work. People hijack a viral idea just to get clicks and likes and bodies showing up at their event. And the last thing I'm doing during a pandemic is going to a public indoor event in November just because it was branded with the trappings of your obsession. I mean, Jack probably got the idea from you in the first place, right? It's not the real play, if that even ever existed in the first place. It's a hoax. A stunt."

This little tirade met with silence and by the time I ran out of steam I realized he was seriously considering going, whether I liked it or not.

"You're not thinking of going."

I feel like I should mention that I don't usually tell him what he can and can't do and I feel like a bitch transcribing my memory of the conversation right now because I'm not like that. But you have to remember we were cooped up with cabin fever going on eight months. We were more than a little edgy by then, and it scared me that he might do something reckless when a vaccine was right around the corner and we only needed to hang on a little bit longer.

I know my generation isn't exactly known for taking the risk seriously, but I've always consumed a lot of news. Real news. Stories written by journalists who fact check and print retractions when they get something wrong. Stories sourced by experts with professional credentials, not some dude on Instagram. And with the extra time on my hands, I was doing a lot more reading than usual, so I knew all about the prevalence of long-term complications, even in young people. It just seemed unnecessary to take chances for convenience or entertainment. But I also knew that the sacrifices suited my introverted personality to begin with and that it was harder on other people. I knew it was harder on Mark. And nine months in, even I was going a little crazy and wanting to get out and blow off some steam. Everybody was. That was exactly why someone would put together a bad idea like this—a live performance of a play, probably in some cramped loft in Cambridge, where masks weren't going to make a difference.

"It's masked," he said lamely, as if that settled it. He and I were mostly on the same page about this, but I could see he was going to talk himself into thinking this one exception was okay, even though we both knew it was about more than masks. It was about ventilation and how much time you spent in a space. I thought I could argue the details.

"You don't even know where they're doing it. It just says details to come. Probably because it would violate all of the state's restrictions."

Maybe it wouldn't even happen, I remember thinking, and I was getting into a fight with him over nothing.

"They private-message you the location after you RSVP," he said. "But not until the night of the show. It's always like that."

I felt an actual chill when he said that. It seems so strange to me now, looking back on that person, afraid of all the wrong things, but that's who I was. It's important to establish that.

"Wait.... You've received one of these invitations before?"

"No." His eyebrows scrunched. "If I had I would've gone. I've seen other people posting about them in private chats."

I must have groaned at this. I don't remember, but I remember the look he gave me. "So they don't publicize the location. Why is that? Because they'd get hit with a fine for violating capacity during the pandemic?"

"No," he said, the single syllable dripping with condescension, "it's because the play is more dangerous than the pandemic. Don't you remember anything I've told you about it?"

"Oh, I remember plenty. Let me make sure I've got it right: there's a covert agency called SPECTRA that has an entire division dedicated to tracking down and destroying illicit editions of a banned book the government has never acknowledged the existence of, and they do this because of some crazy stuff that happened in France in the late 1800s. And because they don't want to arouse interest in this book that apparently causes people to go insane, they never make a public spectacle of confiscating or destroying it. They just break into your house when you're sleeping or not at home and quietly remove it from your hiding place that they know all about because of their superpowers of surveillance. Or because they have—according to some even crazier theories—technology that senses a distortion of reality in the vicinity of the text. How did I do?"

"Not bad." He looked impressed.

"See? I do listen. I don't know why, but I do." I granted him a smile that said this was all theoretical and we weren't really going to keep fighting over it for real. Debating things like this was one of the pleasures of our relationship when we weren't at each other's throats from too much cabin fever.

"But answer me this, Mark. How could someone put on a production of this play when not only is every printed copy seized by spooks who monitor every backwater of the internet for mentions of it, but *also:* anyone studying their lines or directing rehearsals, or even participating as a member of the crew or the venue or whatever ... would lose their mind? It doesn't sound like a very sustainable piece of work, right? You wouldn't be able to get everybody to hold it together long enough to put on a performance."

"You would think so."

"But?"

He shrugged. "The virus seems to have changed that. Maybe it's a coincidence, but for months now, people seem to have developed a limited tolerance for the material. I don't think you could call it immunity, but people have been staging it with some safety protocols—to protect them against the script, I mean, not the virus. Boston won't be the first. There was one in Austin. Another in San Diego, Salt Lake City. And those are just the ones that garnered some reviews online. Before SPECTRA took them down, of course."

"What kind of safety protocols?"

"Things like using different actresses to play Camilla and Cassilda between the first and second acts so the actresses from the first half are never exposed to the second half until the night of the performance. Rotating the crew as well. And only casting people who have already had Covid to work on act two."

"That's insane."

He gave me a wry smile that seemed to say, *the whole point of the play is insanity but haven't we talked at length about society's definition of sanity?*

He believed the play was a dose of pure reality. Too strong for most minds to bear and then go on playing the game of life as scripted by the status quo. It was a pretty radical idea for an insurance broker, but then I had my own theory about how the straighter he got with age, the more rebellious he needed to be in his side interests. Especially the ones he still clung to from his psychedelic twenties because they didn't present him with any problems he needed to act on. At least, most years they didn't. This year was different, apparently. I wondered if he thought even the year was symbolic—2020. A time for humanity to finally open its eyes and see things as they really are. With perfect clarity. But I held the idea back, not wanting to encourage him.

Instead, he offered something that sounded even crazier to me at the time. Now, not so much.

"You know why they call it coronavirus, right?"

"Yeah. It's those little spikes on the microbe that enable it to attach to your cells."

"Right. They—"

We finished the sentence in unison: "—resemble a crown."

We argued on and off about it for the next week. I knew the date and time of the event but not the place. He knew I didn't want him to go. It seemed insane enough to me that he was attracted to something with a reputation for driving people crazy, but when you added in the risk of getting sick, I just couldn't understand it. It was a strange compulsion for him, like an addiction to a drug he'd never tried. He had become obsessed and I knew there was nothing I could do to stop him.

Nevertheless, I stayed close to him on Thursday, waiting for his phone to chime with the update, the address. Not that we could get very far from each other anyway, living in the same house. It came through while we were eating dinner, his phone on the kitchen counter.

We both looked at it, though we couldn't read the screen from where we were sitting at the table, and he didn't make a move for it. I guess that would have been impolite—reading a text while eating dinner with your wife, even though ditching her for a night on the town and returning with a virus was another matter.

When our eyes met again, all he said was, "There are masks. You know that. They insist on it, they even hand them out."

"Why do they do that? Why do they provide them instead of having people bring their own like everywhere else?"

"I think it's so everyone in the theater matches the theme," he said. "I saw a photo from Utah. The masks all had the yellow sign."

"That question mark thingy you draw on everything?"

"I don't draw it on *everything*."

"Grocery lists, car windows, foggy mirrors …"

"I'll be safe. I promise."

"So you've made up your mind. You're going whether I like it or not."

"People are taking bigger chances than this every day."

I scoffed. "People are stupid. I thought we agreed on that."

Silence pooled around us like an incoming tide.

"Go ahead," I said. "Check it."

He got up and snatched his phone off the counter, glancing at the text before thumbing the button to black out the screen as he settled back into his seat.

"So where is it?"

"It wasn't the event update. Just spam."

I wasn't sure I believed him but I wanted to. And it was getting late. If they hadn't announced the location by now, maybe it wasn't happening after all. Mark looked disappointed. Maybe he was coming to terms with the fact it had been a hoax all along. Like those steel monoliths that started appearing and disappearing all over the world. A viral meme that required a metal shop and welding gear for the copy and paste. If that was possible, then how hard would it be to manufacture evidence of a viral theater production?

I hadn't showered or changed my clothes all day, too anxious about keeping an eye on him, but now I began to relax. He just looked so deflated.

"Maybe another performance will happen after all this is over," I offered, touching his hand beside the darkened phone on the table. "Then you'll be able to lose your mind without risking your body." It was a teasing joke, but when it didn't elicit a smile, I announced I was going to take a shower and left him to clean up the dishes from the meal I'd cooked.

They were still on the table when I stepped out of the bathroom in my robe twenty minutes later. I called his name—knowing I would get no response—as I marched to the front door. His keys were gone from the hook beside the alarm keypad.

My next stop was his office, dripping beads of water on the floor. I woke up his computer and pulled up his perpetually logged-on Facebook page. The message at dinner hadn't been spam. His disappointment had been an act worthy of an audition for the venue named in the latest message: *The Life House Theater Workshop. Password: Carcosa.*

The theater wasn't hard to find. A two-story brick building with a darkened marquee hanging over a side street a couple of blocks off Somerville Ave. just outside Porter Square. If you weren't looking for it, you would've thought it was shuttered. The only message on the marquee read *RENT A PRIVATE SCREENING FOR YOUR POD.*

I'd parked on the main strip and used the GPS on my phone to preview the rest of the route. A gentle rain was falling when I got out of the car. I was dressed for it, but even with the hood of my parka pulled up, I felt exposed on the empty street. Doubt bloomed as I approached the theater. Maybe I had the wrong address after all. I didn't see Mark's car anywhere on the street, despite ample parking spaces. If there really was a performance happening tonight, there were no signs of it. But as I stepped under the shelter of the marquee, one side of the double glass doors swung open, revealing a hollow-eyed young man in a dark gray hoodie.

"Can I help you, ma'am?" He looked at me expectantly over a black mask emblazoned with the yellow sign.

"Carcosa," I replied.

He tilted his head in the direction of a dimly lit lobby. I wondered if the light bulbs in the wall sconces had been dialed down on a dimmer switch to avoid drawing attention from the street. The place had a hushed atmosphere, but I detected the murmur of voices from

"Come," he said. "The play is already starting."

somewhere above. So far, crowds hadn't been an issue on my trip, but it seemed that one had assembled after all. "Come," he said. "The play is already starting." He gestured at a basket on a low pedestal, filled with masks in sealed plastic packages. I took one, tore it open, and fitted it over my nose and mouth, finishing up with a squirt of hand sanitizer from a pump bottle situated beside the basket.

"Fitting weather tonight," he commented.

"How so?"

"It's as if the Hyades are weeping."

I didn't know the reference, so I just nodded, hoping to maintain the impression that I was an insider, one of the invited.

"But don't worry, it's not raining upstairs."

This seemed even stranger, and I had to ask: "Is it an open-air performance?"

"Of course." Was he reappraising me? "But only in the second act."

He returned to his position at the door, watching the street for stragglers, and I climbed the stairs alone. The murmur of the crowd had ceased, and my thoughts turned to the attention I might draw upon entering a hushed theater. His words had made no sense and I had no idea what awaited me on the second floor. A rooftop stage beneath an awning? That wasn't consistent with a converted movie theater. I had no ticket and found no usher to greet me at the door.

For a moment, I hesitated and considered fleeing. I was doing exactly what I'd warned Mark against—entering a public space with a crowd—and no evidence he was actually here. It was something I'd had anxiety-ridden dreams about over the past eight months— finding myself among a crowd, and realizing with dawning dread that I'd forgotten a pandemic was raging. Yes, there was the reassurance of masks, but I knew they offered little protection in an enclosed space for any duration. That was why the movie theaters had closed. I knew this, but I was beyond reason. It was the betrayal that was driving me. The heat of knowing Mark had chosen this over our safety. Over our marriage, even. I needed to understand the obsession he'd risked it all for. I opened the theater door and slipped into the darkened room.

I could make no sense of my surroundings. At first, I blamed it on my eyes adjusting to the darkness. The dim space reminded me of a double-exposed photo, both a forest and a hall of gilded columns. I moved down the aisle, sensing the shadowy forms of the audience members around me. Or were they statues?

A second glance at a pastoral vista ahead and to my right resolved into a faded mural painted on peeling plaster beneath a scrollwork arch. But a third look found the same scene obscured by a rolling cloud bank, the lines between art and nature blurred. My mind scrambled to attribute these illusions to tricks of set design, theatrical lighting, and fog machines. Exotic perfume scented the air and a seismic bass tone droned in my bones, like the baritone chanting of a Himalayan choir. How had I not heard it outside the theater?

Above, the vaulted ceiling was pricked with violet stars burning in a mustard-gas sky.

A figure in the aisle ahead waved me onward with a handheld light, wreathed in fog. An actor or an usher? He was dressed in tattered robes that rippled like rills of oily smoke, moved by a current my slick skin failed to detect on the torpid air. His face was concealed behind the same featureless ceramic mask I'd seen in Jack's artwork for the event.

I followed the daunting figure, thinking that he would lead me to an empty seat. We approached the stage, where Cassilda sang a lament for lost Carcosa, the haunting melody turning like a wounded bird above the trembling vibration of the dark drone.

Glowing motes floated on the air, reminding me of dandelion spores, then of viral particles, and as the comparison arose in my mind, I realized that I had left those concerns behind me at the theater doors.

Was I even in a theater anymore? I seemed to follow the robed figure over black sands along the shore of a lake. Twin suns shone through the cloud bank, burning it off with rays of such a molten hue that I could not imagine it was cast by electric light.

I was alone. I was moving among a crowd. I was seated in a theater.

I was a sheep led by the shepherd god, Hastur. We were all sheep, in our masks. All afraid of the air. Afraid of sickness and death. Of each other. But the Yellow King had come to liberate us from our fear. To offer us the sacramental poison.

We were dancing at a masquerade. Each of us pretending to be an abiding form, when in truth, beneath our masks, we were decaying each day while our egos grasped at patterns to deny the terrible truth.

The lyrical speech of the play reached a hypnotic crescendo. Lines repeated throughout the second act struck me with the force of a Zen koan, and suddenly I was sitting in a shabby theater draped not with mist but veils of rotting silk. Three actors stood on a dusty black stage marked with masking tape, flanked by unfinished plywood sets. One read from a folded sheaf of paper. Had I stumbled into a rehearsal?

No. It was another layer of the illusion. Another metaphor encoded in the living art.

This life was a rehearsal. Earth was a waiting room.

Two women and a man stood on the stage, dressed in black jeans and T-shirts. The women wore no masks. The man's back was to the audience.

They were replaying a scene we had already witnessed, the refrain here at the end giving new meaning to the words. I'd never read the play. Mark could never find a copy. But I felt in that moment that I had heard these lines countless times. That they were engraved on my mind like a nursery rhyme. I mouthed them aloud as the actors spoke, and Mark, now seated beside me, took my hand in his.

"You, sir, should unmask."

"Indeed?"

"Indeed it's time. We have all laid aside disguise but you."

"I wear no mask."

Those four syllables echoed around the room. I spoke them, Mark spoke them, the people in the rows ahead of us and behind us, across the aisle, and in a balcony I hadn't noticed before all chanted them, a rhythm ricocheting around the theater. *No mask! No mask! No mask!* A vow, a revelation, a clarion call.

I tugged the cloth from my face, my fingers grazing the melted maw where my lips had been. Lips that had told countless human lies of safety and virtue and permanence. Mark's mask fell to his lap.

He'd released the ear strap one-handed, the other still entwined with mine. And together, we inhaled the cool, fragrant air, and the sublime madness of Carcosa.

The Enigma Signal

"**B**ut haven't you ever longed for the feeling that you're a part of something larger than yourself?"

Ricky wouldn't let it go. According to the latest Quinnipiac poll, more than half of the religious folks on Earth had questioned their faith at least once in the months since the satellite photos of Antarctica had hit the news, but Ricky "the Stick Man" wasn't one of them. I sighed, thinking of the five days at sea that lay ahead of us, of all the hours I still had to spend with this cat.

I relented. "Sure. And that's what I get out of music. What I get from jamming with a good band."

Ricky winced, like I'd just compared a Big Mac to filet mignon. But for me it was true and always had been. I'd never been a religious man, but I did get something spiritual from music, and that was enough for me. I didn't need the answers to Life, the Universe and Everything, just a sense of connection, a moment of elevation at the peak of a good solo. Getting a paycheck for *that* was all it took to satisfy my sense of wonder.

Ricky was a good drummer and a decent dude. I didn't understand why he needed more than that, why everything has to *mean* something for some people. Six days into the cruise I was trying to be tolerant, but even a big boat is still a boat. Not much personal space, and our trio was bunking in adjacent cabins. I wondered not for the first time why Ricky didn't nag Paul with his existential questions. Because Paul was a Jew? I never should have copped to being an atheist.

"That's not the same," Ricky went on, immune to my irritation. "Joining a band or the Army isn't what I mean about being part of something greater. I mean like ... when you look out from the deck of this ship at the majesty of nature, that pure white wilderness ... Or when you look up at the stars and the aurora ... Doesn't it make you feel small?"

"That it does."

"And do you ever get the feeling that that beauty isn't random? That there must be a creative force behind it?"

Kneeling over my guitar case on a bold-patterned carpet that reminded me of casino gigs in Vegas, I shook my head. I'd once had a music theory teacher who taught a whole lesson on the golden ratio and the Fibonacci sequence in Bach's counterpoint, the foundation of Western Harmony. The perfect proportions of a human face or a nautilus shell as reflected in art and nature. Bach's patron was the Church, and you don't even have to listen to the music to know their love for order and harmony. It's right there in the architecture. But one look at the cratered face of the moon will tell you that nature favors chaos and violence with brief intervals of peace and harmony that feel long to the flickering minds that inhabit them. We're just good enough at pattern recognition to fool ourselves into *believing* there's order in the chaos.

I said none of this to Ricky, just folded my guitar strap and laid it over the fret board of my 335 hollow-body, lowered the velvet-lined lid, and snapped the latches. Case closed.

But the drummer prattled on. "I hear spirituality in your playing, Marcus, I do. It's like you can't help it, it just comes out. I think under your hip modern skepticism, you're a deeply spiritual brother."

I winced.

"You say things with your axe that are spiritual, whether you know it or not. Like it's in your blood."

"What's that supposed to mean?"

"Well ... you weren't *born* atheist, were you?"

"How do *you* know? You think all black people are Christian or Muslim?"

"I didn't say that, man." He raised a placating hand. Like I was threatening him.

I picked up my guitar case and looked him in the eye. "Sammy Davis Jr. was old enough to be my grandfather, and he was a Jew *and* a Satanist."

That twisted his brow for a second, but he recovered. "Sammy was a Satanist for like fifteen minutes in the seventies for the pussy."

A beat passed between us and we laughed and were just musicians again. At least Ricky could still joke about the devil. I swirled the ice in my glass, tossed back the dregs of my Scotch, and winked at him. "If you'll excuse me, I'm gonna take in some of that majesty up on deck."

◆

I lit a smoke at the port rail, downwind of the artists in their orange parkas with their sketchpads and easels. Mostly sketchpads, because paint tended to freeze at those latitudes. The subject of their studies was still distant—a monolithic structure jutting from a calved glacier. Everyone who looked at it saw something different, and what that was kept changing. Photography and video didn't work on it—some kind of electromagnetic interference, they said. When the military had figured that out, they'd enlisted this group of artists to capture it. The cruise was funded by the U.S. government, with a pair of Canadian Coast Guard icebreakers enlisted to escort the cruise ship *Ortelius* through the Northwest Passage.

Most of the artists had been recruited from Hollywood art departments. A few of them worked in publishing, painting sci-fi and fantasy book covers. Apparently their usual work paid well, because the only way the government could entice them to freeze their tits off was to provide an open bar and entertainment, just like on a commercial cruise. That was how I fell into the gig, having worked the same route for Crystal Cruises out of Anchorage on two previous voyages. So far, this crowd was more interesting than the birdwatchers I'd played for on those runs. The tips were better, too. Probably because the drinks were on the house.

Looking over their shoulders on my cigarette breaks, I'd seen sketches of all kinds of improbable structures. Domed cathedrals with vented arches, stairs climbing to nowhere, faceted minarets, renderings in which construction and biology were fused in what looked like chains of architectural nucleotides. Crazy stuff.

As for me, when I looked at the horizon, I saw a black tree the size of a skyscraper, dripping coagulating ropes of oil like Spanish moss. An ecological disaster, always the same whenever I gazed north. I wondered if the seabirds migrating from the towering cliffs of Prince Leopold Island saw it that way, too. They foraged widely in this thawing region but gave the naked glacier a wide berth.

Down at the opposite end of the globe, the Antarctic city that had emerged from the melting ice on Google Earth last year was different. That structure had gradually revealed its contours to the satellite eye with no interference and no mutations. Before the UN resolution to block the satellite feed and ban journalists from the site, its public documentation had caused a tectonic shift in humanity's view of history. Granted, you'll always have your flat-earthers and dinosaur deniers. Psychological contortionists who will do anything to maintain a literal reading of Genesis. But now *thinking* people had to grapple with proof that mankind was not the first intelligent species to build a civilization on the planet.

You might have caught that clip of Neil deGrasse Tyson calling it the "second Copernican shift." Mankind—not just the Earth we inhabit—was no longer the center of the universe. Someone had come before us and they'd left their mark on an architecture undeniably designed to suit a different anatomy, sweeping all our creation stories off the table with a single image as iconic as the Blue Marble.

But at least you could study the properties of a lost city that didn't defy documentation, didn't defy the laws of space, time, and perception. At least reality was more or less *behaving* down there around the South Pole.

When the ice receded from this northern outpost, all bets were off.

Finishing my cigarette, I sensed an agitated uptick in the activity of the artists. The one closest to me at the end of the line was a portly white dude with long, snowy hair and a goatee that blended into the fur-lined hood of his parka. His eyes, just visible through polarized prescription lenses, darted back and forth between the approaching enigma and the sketchbook in his lap, a charcoal pencil racing furiously over the page. Before I could get a look at what he'd rendered, he flipped the page—so fast it snagged on the spiral—and started over on a clean sheet, leaning toward the railing with rapt attention.

He scribbled on the new page for less than a minute before flipping and starting over again. Wary of breaking his concentration, I edged closer for a look. In my peripheral vision, I detected similar urgency from his fellow artists down the line. If electronic drawing tablets had been reliable in these temperatures and conditions, the flurry of activity might have been less obvious, but given their tools, it was a riot of paper shuffling and scratching. Rough sketches tossed aside in rapid-fire iterations.

I flicked the butt overboard and walked behind the line of artists, glancing from the titanic structure on the horizon to their unfurling depictions of it. Out there, my black tree was morphing, the branches curling upward into a concave bowl, the hanging strands forming a net stretched between the boughs. And for the first time, I saw the same basic shape emerging on the sketchpads. Some of the artists stole glances at their neighbors' work, catching on that they were finally acting in concert, reaching a consensus.

A young woman wearing a Doctor Who scarf and fingerless gloves held up her drawing and said what I'd been thinking already: "It's a radio telescope."

The man beside her dashed out a triangular bracket pointing skyward at the center of his dish, blinked, and focused on her with the hazy demeanor of someone roused from a dream. "Or a parabolic antenna."

"What's the difference?" I asked, prompting both heads to turn. The man scanned my clothing quickly, trying to place my role on the ship—maybe to assess whether or not he was talking to a G-man. He shrugged. "Nothing, really. Just a matter of whether it's sending or receiving."

I nodded and strolled back to the stairs with no inkling at the time that I would be the one to tune in the first transmission later that night.

◆

Douglas Wynne

We were in the midst of the brooding noir groove of "Equinox" by Coltrane and I'd just stepped on my auto-wah pedal to add a brass tone to my solo when there was a loud burst of static from my amp. I thought maybe the pedal was on the fritz, but it cleared by the time Paul finished his descending piano lick and picked up the bass line again to support my solo. The audience didn't seem jarred by the noise like I was. They were deep into their drinks and conversations by that hour, well past midnight and nearing the end of our second set. They'd been more attentive earlier in the evening, coming off the exhilaration of a breakthrough day. But the booze had mellowed them in the trough of that adrenaline wave, and now only the dude with the white goatee—seated alone and doodling on a cocktail napkin with a felt pen—was still tapping his foot to our jam.

I remember watching him and thinking that my solo was starting out like a doodle on a napkin. Maybe that's what all improv is—a few lines out of context tentatively alighting on a suggestive shape, then maybe becoming something, taking on detail, themes, and emotion if it doesn't all just fall apart. I thought I knew where this solo was going. It was a familiar tune for our trio and I had a few licks I liked to touch on and weave together in this section. The auto-wah guitar is similar to a trumpet with a plunger mute; both sounds mimic human vocal tones. I used it a lot with the jazz trio, but that night, it sounded different. I was leaning in toward the speaker grille of my Fender Twin, eyes closed, fingers finding the winding path around the chord structures, like ivy climbing bricks, when I heard an overtone harmonizing with my guitar. I shot a look at Paul to see if he was playing it. Maybe he'd split the keyboard into two sounds: piano in the bass and some kind of synth tone in the treble register, but his right hand was just poised over the keys, giving me space.

The sound was both more vocal and less human than anything I could mimic, even with a stomp box, but I'll be damned if it wasn't coming from my amp.

In between phrases, I reached over and turned it up. The phantom melody continued on its own, like an echo or some kind of radio interference, like you sometimes pick up through a poorly shielded cable.

128

The past few nights of the cruise, I'd been surprised my amp worked at all so close to the enigma. We knew it interfered with digital equipment, cameras and phones, and our contract promised we'd get paid even if we couldn't play through the crackle, hiss, and hum. We were prepared for that, even though it would put an end to the tip jar real quick. This was the first malfunction we'd encountered, and at least it happened near the end of our set. We could wrap up early and I'd have time to troubleshoot my rig in the morning.

But as interference goes, it was just ... too musical. Too harmonized with the song to be accidental and too alien to be a stray song roaming the arctic airwaves.

I reached around behind my amp, finger lingering on the power switch.

Ricky gave me a raised eyebrow: *Wrap it up?* But I couldn't bring myself to switch it off. I took the guitar pick from where I'd tucked it between my lips and struck up a new riff, digging in and playing off of the weird melody, mimicking and poking at it, as if it were coming from another musician on the stage, one I could coax into a lively exchange.

At first, the strange sound wave seemed to respond to my melodic flirtations. But the more I played around it, the less like a conversation it felt, and soon I was watching my fingers move of their own accord, compelled to find new shapes to support the exotic melody, building a scaffolding of chords I'd never played before, climbing the fret board on the trail of an alien acrobat scaling rarefied sonic heights.

I was lost in the music, eyes closed, when Ricky stumbled on a beat trying to keep up with me and I looked up to see the room clearing out. I don't know if it was the atonal sounds coming from my amp or the lateness of the hour, but the crowd was milling out of the lounge through a wedge of light from an open door. Only the old dude with the goatee remained, seated at his table beside the stage, leaning into the music and scribbling with even more intensity than he'd shown on deck that afternoon in his effort to capture the enigma.

The melody spiraled upward. My fingers couldn't keep up and the trio crashed in a jumble of notes just as my amp popped and fizzled out, leaving me slicked with sweat, my left hand cramped into a claw.

Paul leaned back from his keyboard and tossed his hair away from his eyes. "Dude. What the hell was that?"

I squinted at the glowing red power indicator on my amp and struck my muted strings. Nothing. I shrugged. "Dead power tube?"

Paul shook his head. "No, man. What you were playing. What the fuck was that?"

Ricky, sticks crossed on his knee, watched with interest, waiting for my answer.

Truth was, I didn't know. I'd played like a man in a trance. A man possessed. Turning to my microphone, I meant to apologize to the stragglers for cutting our set short. But we were alone in the room. Even the old dude with the goatee had left. I found myself staring at the ice cubes melting in his abandoned whiskey glass, at a loss for words.

♦

I kept a spare set of tubes in my cabin. Swapping out the 6L6s in the morning brought the amp back to life. I'd slept fitfully, with a repeating phrase from the musical interference looping in my mind. I knew it was just a rhythmic pattern of static, but in that midrange of frequencies between one and six kilohertz, anything can start to sound like a voice. More of that pattern recognition. Except the words that had tumbled through my restless mind all night weren't in any language I knew. They sure weren't in English or French, those most likely to be heard on a transmission in this region.

"Tekeli-li. Tekeli-li." I said aloud to the empty cabin, pushing the last power tube into its socket with a bandana wrapped around the glass cylinder.

I'd skipped breakfast and made my own coffee. My stomach was growling when I switched the amp on and plugged my guitar in to the familiar crackle and hum that told me the signal was restored before I played a single note. There was no interference that I could hear at this volume level, which was just a fraction of how loud I played in the club. The bedside clock read 9:16. Early enough for my neighbors to still be asleep. I tuned up and fiddled with the cable, the same one I'd played through last night. Jiggling it in the jack didn't cause the rig to pick up any noise, either.

I let my fingers roam, searching for the exotic chord shapes I'd discovered the previous night and coming up empty. Both the interference and the inspiration had passed.

There was a knock at the door.

Housekeeping didn't do much to staff rooms, just replaced our towels and linens every few days, so I figured it had to be one of my bandmates. I opened the door in my boxers and Miles Davis T-shirt and found myself peering up at the big old dude I'd seen sketching in the club, his polarized lenses clearing as if he'd just been out in the Arctic sun and they were still adjusting to the dim corridors below decks. His goatee, white as ermine, concealed the contours of a smile, but his brow looked wrinkled more by uncertainty than age.

He offered his hand. "Joe Schumer. May I come in?"

"Marcus," I said. I gave his hand a quick shake and stepped aside, waving him into my messy lair.

He entered, with a spiral notebook tucked under his arm, and cast around for a place to sit. I moved a pile of clothes and sheet music from the lone chair onto the unmade bed while he zeroed in on my amp and pointed an ink-stained finger at it. "You get it working again?"

"Yeah. Dead tube. I saw you in the club last night."

He nodded. "That was a hell of a jam." The words sounded less like a compliment than an allusion to some illicit act.

"Yeah," I said again. Then, thinking he might take me for an idiot if I didn't start speaking in more than single syllables, I said, "I don't know what came over me. My amp ..."

"Picked up some interference, right?"

"Right. I tried to roll with it and riff on it. Jazz is about responding to the moment, you know? Whatever comes up. But it took me to some strange territory."

"We're *all* in strange territory on this ship, amigo."

"I saw you drawing while we played."

He nodded. It was his turn to weigh his words. "You know what synesthesia is?"

"Sure. Seeing sound, smelling colors, getting your sensory wires crossed."

"Something like that. I've always thought of it as more of a gift than a disability."

"You have it?"

He leaned back in the stuffed chair and drummed his fingers on his notebook cover. His Hawaiian shirt (octopus-themed) was neatly pressed, and I wondered who he worked for off the boat. He looked pretty L.A. to me, but for all I knew, he could be on the SPECTRA payroll. The once-secret agency had become more visible following the Antarctic discovery and that business up in Boston in 2019, and word on the street was that they employed all kinds of specialists. I knew an audio engineer who claimed to have done some classified work for them for a big wedge of cheddar.

"My type is *chromesthesia*. That's a fancy word for seeing sounds as colors. Mostly they're clouds of color. *Your* voice is robin's egg blue to me. And when I first heard your lead guitar tone last night, it was amethyst purple—bright in the middle with a darker glow around the edges."

"That's interesting. Most cats talk about musical timbre as bright or dark, but it's not that specific."

Joe flipped his notebook open and picked through the pages. He continued his train of thought as if I hadn't spoken. "But after the interference joined the mix, and you started playing along with it, your color changed and took on distinct shapes. I keep a variety of ink pens handy and I did my best to capture what I could by the tea light on my table." He passed the notebook over to my perch on the corner of the bed, where I sat with my guitar in my lap.

The subject of the sketch was so intensely represented in the foreground—leaping off the page in bold strokes fringed with ink spatter from the pressure he'd put on the nib—that it took me a second to see my own silhouette in the background. He'd captured in minimal lines my posture while leaning over the neck when I'm really going for it. The focal point of the drawing—the *creature,* for lack of a better word—spilled out of my amp in a riot of iridescent fluid bubbling with lidless eyes and lipless teeth.

I searched the artist's face for a sign that this was some kind of punch line but found no humor there. Reconsidering his long white

132

hair and Hawaiian shirt, I wondered how much acid he was enhancing his art with. "You saw this," I said.

He nodded. "I nursed one drink all night, if that's what you're wondering. Haven't touched drugs in decades."

"I guess you don't need them. You get enough enhancement from the synesthesia."

"Well. It's never been like this. Colors and shapes are normal, but this full-blown phantasmagoria. It was more like dreaming awake."

"So you tracked me down to see if ... what? If I saw it, too?"

"Well, did you?"

"Nah. Not this. I saw shapes, like I usually do when I'm playing. Musical shapes in my mind. But they were different. Weird."

Joe looked from the guitar in my lap to the glowing power light on the amp, a bright red ember glowing in the dim room. I shifted uncomfortably. "You want me to play. So you can see it again?"

He swallowed, like a man afraid to ask for something he's not sure he wants, then closed the notebook. "It was flowing across the floor when your amp died. Had almost reached my table. I couldn't look away. Then it just ... disintegrated, faded out, like your chords."

I didn't know what to say to that.

Now he met my gaze. "There was a theme you kept returning to. Mimicking that staticky voice. Do you remember it?"

I stepped on the auto-wah pedal and rolled the volume knob up on my guitar. It took a second of fiddling, but I found the notes. I played the phrase three times while he stared at the silver cloth speaker grille, his eyes widening until I stopped. "You see anything?"

"Bubbles. Play it again."

I did. And this time, when I stopped, the phrase continued cycling in the speaker. I checked the pedal board but the light on my delay box was dark. So where was the echo coming from? It morphed as it looped, twisting into something distinctly more vocal: *Tekeli-li ... Tekeli-li ... Tekeli-li ... TEKELI-LI ... TEKELI-LI ... TEKELI-LI.*

Joe jumped backward, almost spilling the chair over. His notebook hit the floor, falling open to a random page: a sketch of the black dish on the horizon. Looking at the speaker, I could see it too, now—what he was retreating from: a black wave of rolling eyes reconfiguring itself

133

with motions that looked divorced from the regular flow of time, like a stop motion video. I jumped, the guitar tumbling out of my lap like I'd found a scorpion crawling out of one of the f-holes. The inky pool spread around the amp. I knew shutting it off would probably make it disappear, but I couldn't reach the power switch on the back panel without stepping in the stuff, and the wall outlet where I might pull the plug was even farther away. There were mouths forming in the oil among the bubbling eyes. Teeth growing. Tongues lolling.

Joe was already in the corridor. I scrambled after him, shutting the door behind me as the living liquid overtook his sketchbook.

He clapped a big hand on my bony shoulder and we stared at the gap under the cabin door. I could still hear the chatter, as clear as it had been before I'd shut the door, only now it was reaching my ears in surround sound. I turned on my heel, following the sound to its source—an industrial gray intercom speaker mounted in a high corner at the end of the corridor. The grille dripped with more of the viscous, bubbling goo that had poured from my amp, drooling it onto the floor where it pooled and leapt with excited sentience. I grabbed Joe's hairy wrist and pulled him away from it, down a stretch of worn carpet toward the stairs.

He had a glazed look in his eyes, like a man in shock. I grabbed a fistful of his Hawaiian shirt, tugging him away from the discordant sound and its physical manifestation. "Joe! Look at me. What is it? Do you know?"

His thousand-yard stare passed right through me without focus, and I gave him a slap on the cheek. "Look at me, man. What the hell is that stuff?"

He blinked and I could see the rational part of his mind lumbering into gear, grinding against the paralysis of fear and astonishment. "The dish on the horizon," he said. "The enigma. It's transmitting a signal. And you picked it up."

"No shit."

"But it's a living signal. And when it made contact, when you tried to communicate back to it …"

"What? What happened?" I pulled him along, up the stairs.

"I think you woke it up, made it triangulate on us and manifest."

"I don't get it. Come on, man. Keep moving."

"When it first came through, it was subtle. Mostly made of sound." He spoke between labored breaths. Fleeing my cabin and running for the stairs was probably the most exercise he'd had all year. "Only I could see it. Because of my condition."

"Keep climbing, Joe."

A burst of semiautomatic gunfire ripped the air somewhere up on deck. We flinched and ducked in the stairwell.

"That must be why they chose me for the boat. Early detection. Fuck. I should've gone to one of the agents, not to you." He looked terrified. Not at the gunfire or whatever it was aimed at, but at what he'd done. He'd prompted me to provoke the thing.

At the first landing, I pushed him through a swinging door into an empty dining room. Tables lay overturned around a deserted breakfast buffet. Icy wind howled through a shattered window spanning the length of a wall. Faint shouts and screams reached us from the deck, almost drowned out by the alien chatter filling the room. Strings of inky iridescence dripped from the in-ceiling speakers. They pooled on the floor, merciless eyes in a rolling boil, percolating mouths chanting their ceaseless mantra with escalating urgency: *TEKELI-LI! TEKELI-LI! TEKELI-LI!*

I stepped through the broken glass and out onto the lower deck, buffeted by the stinging wind. The dining room overlooked the port side of the *Ortelius*. I could see the enigma, stark against the pale horizon, unfolding like a black flower against the icescape. A woman in an orange parka nearly knocked me over careening blindly up the deck in a panic, a scream trailing like a bright yellow ribbon from the fur lining of her hood. The gunfire was louder outside but no less difficult to pinpoint with the wind howling in my ears. Looking up, I saw runnels of red and black liquid washing over the side of the upper deck, staining the churning foam of the ship's wake some fifty feet below.

Joe and I had switched roles, him shoving me along behind the woman who'd just body-checked me. She clambered up a flight of stairs, her boots slipping on the ice-glazed treads. As best I could tell, she was climbing *toward* the gunfire and chaos, toward the source of that wash of fluids that spoke of violence. And Joe wanted me to follow? It seemed insane until I looked aft and saw what she was fleeing. An exterior intercom speaker mounted in an eave of the upper deck drooled another monstrous form into being. Watching it lurch toward me, I froze, paralyzed by fear.

Joe shoved my shoulders with such force that I had no choice but to move or land on my face. My feet found the metal stairs and climbed. I wasn't dressed for the exposure and couldn't tell if my extremities were numbing from fear or cold. I grabbed the handrail to pull myself up and my skin bonded with the cold steel, leaving behind a layer when I ripped it free. I wiped my bloody hand on my shirt and focused on my feet. One shoe in front of the other, one stair at a time with Joe's firm hand on my back until we spilled out onto the upper deck.

One look and I knew it was over. The *Ortelius* would never complete the Northwest Passage, never reach the Atlantic or dock in Boston. I'd played my last set, cashed my last check, smoked my last cigarette. I thought of Cecilia, the girl I always imagined settling down with someday. The knowledge that that future had been canceled spread like hoarfrost in my chest. What was happening here would spread.

The speakers the crew used to pump music onto the pool deck in warmer climes were giving birth to the vast limbs of a massive creature, joined at a nexus in the bottom of the drained pool. I caught flashes of human faces and limbs in that roiling stew, white-eyed and terrified, twisted in a symphony of agony and awe as they were devoured or assimilated, and in a flash I comprehended the ecosystem laid out before me. Those who struggled were consumed for raw energy, while those who surrendered merged with the monster, their eyes and mouths bulging and stretching like ink smeared under an invisible thumb, taking on the curvature and coloring of those features I'd first seen depicted in Joe's sketch.

Men and women in white parkas and black Kevlar encircled the pool, firing rifles into the mess. Bullets plunked in the soup with no effect, except when they struck the heads of the victims swimming in the sludge. My stomach lurched when I realized those were their *targets*. Whether to prevent growth or end suffering, I couldn't say.

One agent had taken to firing at the big speakers, peppering the gray metal grilles with ragged holes. But the only result I could see was that the iridescent black tide poured faster from them. Whatever was manifesting here may have started with a sound only Joe could see, but we were beyond that now. The birth canals were open like sewage pipes, and there was no shutting them down.

Sensing that Joe was no longer at my side, I tore my eyes from the pool and scanned the deck for his print shirt. I spotted him at the railing, where passengers were jumping overboard into the icy water. Was our Canadian Coast Guard escort down there, or had they been overtaken, too? Were the jumpers choosing quick hypothermia over the gruesome transmutation unfolding in the pool? If they were, it was the right choice, and I embraced it as soon as I recognized it.

Joe sat on the railing like a man taking a load off on a park bench. He flicked me a resigned salute and tumbled backward, taking my stomach with him. Part of me still wanted to believe there was a Canadian Coast Guard life raft down there to catch him.

Walking to the railing through the tide of blood and oil, I thought I heard my name, and cast a final glance back at the pool. It was Ricky the Stick Man, I'd swear to it. Ricky shedding his flesh like snakeskin, melting and merging, his throat piping that ragged mantra, the incantation I'd invited into the world. And in that moment before the laser-sighted rifles found him, I knew he'd achieved it. Apotheosis. A shade of ecstasy in his wild, rolling eyes. He'd become part of something larger than himself.

... horned and radiant, its flesh rendered translucent ...

Contact

Ritter knew it was a bad idea to walk in the daylight. Except on rare occasions when they were intentionally trying to draw fire and lure the enemy out of hiding, they almost always traveled under cover of night. But today there had been no reasoning with Staff Sgt. Payne. He'd been insistent they needed to meet with the tribal elders to discuss reparations for the tobacco field that had caught fire the previous month when phosphorus munitions rained fire down the valley during an attack on an ISIS-occupied ridge. The meeting had been a success by the ambiguous standards Ritter had become accustomed to in Achin district, which was to say that his gut told him most of the Pashtun red-beards he'd had tea with this afternoon were unlikely to actively help the insurgents blow up their squad on the trek back to the outpost. Of course, that didn't mean they wouldn't get hit. They were overdue.

"Scarlett Johansson ... or Daisy Ridley?" Huff asked, taking a breath between the two names. Slogging up the trail in full kit was sucking hard in the August heat. They relied on small talk to take their minds off it. Conversations that required little attention while scanning the terrain for hints of anything suspicious. As Alpha Team leader, Sgt. Ritter had almost ten years on PFC Huffaker, but when it came to Marvel movies, they were all boys again.

"Who's Daisy Ridley?" Ritter asked. They ascended the trail in a long line with a wide spread, to keep from offering clustered targets to snipers on the rocky hilltop. He and Huff were essentially alone.

"Rey. You know, from Star Wars."

139

"The new one?"

"Right. Chick with the metal staff."

"My kid likes the emo Vader guy from that."

"He's a whiny bitch. So? Scarlett or Daisy?"

"Scarlett."

"Really? My money's on Daisy."

"We're talking actors not characters, right? Your Daisy can't use Jedi mind tricks."

"Right. No lightsabers, no gunplay. Just hand to hand."

"Exactly. Scarlett has how many action movies under her belt by now? She was already badass in *Iron Man*. Then you've got the two Avengers ... Age of Ultron. By now she's had a lot of fight training, and that body is tight as shit."

"That's the suit, dude. And a lot of the melee is stunt doubles."

"How are you supposed to know how much of it is stunt doubles?"

"You can't. But dig it: Daisy channels some real anger. And she's hungrier. You can just see it in her eyes, she might sound posh with that British accent, but in a fight? She'd go dirty. Scarlett's had the good life for too long. Daisy's probably a year out from living on ramen and kneecapping other bitches for auditions. She would fuck ScarJo up."

"I don't know, man. If it ends up on the ground, Scarlett has the grappling chops to—"

Matt heard the familiar snap of a round breaking the sound barrier, followed by a sensation like a bee buzzing past his head. Huffaker's brains sloshed out of a hole at the back of his helmet right above the pouch where he stored a strobe for air-support recognition as a counterweight to the NVG mount on the front. His body wobbled for a second before crumpling in a heap, leaking blood over the rocky ground.

Matt knelt and raised his M4, returning suppressive fire without the benefit of a clear target, just buying time to get his bearings. Even while they'd been talking like bros around a barbecue, he'd been aware of the options for cover presented by the terrain. An ingrained survival habit. He knew there was a drop-off to a rock shelf beside the trail just to the left of the scraggly tree at his eleven o'clock. He unloaded another burst and then ran for it, leaping over the edge and bracing himself for the landing. The dead leaves at the bottom weren't as deep as he'd expected, which was good. Better to be too tall than too short when you wanted to fire over a ledge.

He could hear Brozek, the comms officer, shouting over the incoming PKM and AK fire. "Contact! Troops in contact! Taking fire from the southeast. Man down."

They were pinned down and spread out, with no chance of the medic reaching Huffaker, but who was Ritter kidding? Huffaker was dead.

He couldn't see any of his other team members when he popped up to return fire, but one of the Automatic Riflemen had found a perch for his SAW. The belt-fed machine gun drowned out all other sounds, vomiting two hundred rounds per minute, every fifth round a tracer—a pyrotechnic bullet that left a trail, enabling the gunner to adjust the trajectory based on the visual feedback. The ghostly streaks floated on the hazy air, and Ritter trained his fire on the place where they converged until the glass of a rifle scope flared from a stand of holly trees prompting him to duck for cover again.

Fragments of rock peppered his helmet as bullets stitched across the ledge. He crouched and ran, scanning for a new spot to fire from when his gaze fell on a pipe like an old car muffler poking out of the ground among the rocks and deadfall. The sight stopped him in his tracks, his mind lurching from battle mode to registering the significance—the flared cap on top to keep rainwater out and the grid of holes dotting the rusty tube.

An air vent. Like the ones found around the Tora Bora cave complex.

Fixated on this evidence of a hidden tunnel system, a few seconds of silence elapsed before he noticed the pause in the exchange of fire. Seizing on the opportunity to be heard, he drew a breath to shout out the discovery to Brozek, but before he could form the words, a rocket-propelled grenade whizzed into the trench, and exploded at the base of a tree, hurling dirt, splinters, and shrapnel in all directions.

Ritter covered his face with his elbow at the last millisecond and was pitched forward off his feet into the rock ledge.

The impact almost knocked him out, dimming his vision for a second. His head cleared just in time for him to find himself sliding down a mini-avalanche into a fissure in the rocky ground where there had been none before the RPG went off. Blood gushed into his left eye and a stinging pain shot through his right thigh where a fragment of shrapnel had ripped a gash through fabric and flesh. But there was no time to take stock of injuries. Everything was being sucked down a dirt slide in the eerily muted world beyond the ringing in his ears.

Then he slipped through the crack, falling in a shower of debris toward the bowels of Hades.

♦

Ritter regained consciousness on a cold stone floor in total darkness. His injuries lit up in a slow sequence like a string of Christmas lights with bad connections. He felt around his helmet, and finding the tactical light still attached, clicked it on. A pool of light spread around him on the dusty cave floor, throwing stark shadows away from the debris that had accompanied him, but there was no sign of his rifle among the litter. He looked up at the ceiling and switched the light off to search the heights for a glimmer of daylight. Nothing. Whatever hole he'd fallen through was plugged up again with dirt and rock.

He coughed out dust and switched the light back on.

The air vent. The image returned to him; the last thing he'd seen before the explosion. A telltale sign of an occupied cave system. Sweeping his beam around the undefined chamber, he picked out calcium deposits, bat guano, and against the gray wall a young man in ragged clothes with dust-powdered hair pointing what looked like his own M4 at him.

The man squinted when the light found his eyes and Ritter clambered to his feet. The two stood in silence, facing each other. Was this the one that killed Huff? The memory of the private's brains spilling out the back of his helmet flashed through Ritter's mind on a wave of rage. But it couldn't be the same man. Not unless he'd been blacked out for longer than he thought. That fire had come from the crown of the hill. And this guy—this *kid*—looked nervous. Not likely a battle-hardened ISIS fighter with precision aim.

If the insurgents from the firefight had found him, he'd have woken in restraints (if at all), stripped of his gear. That the one who'd found him was apparently armed only with his own rifle told a different story, but he didn't know it was.

He raised a placating hand and patted the air. "Easy," he said, his voice echoing in the damp space over the continued ringing in his ears. "Just take it easy. *Salam Aleikum.* Uh … *Sta noom sa de?*"

"Nawab. My name is Nawab."

"You speak English?"

The man nodded but didn't lower the rifle.

"Good, because I'm running out of Pashto. Nawab, my name is Matt, and I think we should discuss our situation. Cool?"

Nawab shot a glance at the darkness beyond Ritter's right shoulder, then locked eyes with him again. The kid was drenched in sweat despite the cool environs of the cave. Ritter resisted the temptation to check behind him. He just hoped his hearing was adequate to detect a threat from behind while recovering from the blast that had almost deafened him.

"What are you looking at, Nawab?"

"Nothing."

"Are you black flag or white?" ISIS or Taliban.

Nawab shook his head.

Ritter tried a different tack. "Who are you with? Are you alone?"

Nawab shifted his posture around the gun, aiming it more deliberately at Matt's chest, telegraphing that he meant business, that surrendering his name was not the same as surrendering.

"You ever fire one of those before?"

The insurgent nodded. "You are the reason they are here. You Americans leave your shitty footprints all over the world, and then fanatics decide they have to burn everything down to get rid of your stink."

Matt smiled. "Fanatics, huh? That mean you're not one of them? Your English is too good for a goat herder."

"I was a student. In Jalalabad. Now I'm driving white devils out of my homeland."

"Care to show me the exit then? Because if you were going to shoot me, I think you would have by now. You're not a killer, Nawab. I can tell."

"You don't know that."

"I do. I'm not a killer, either. I'm a soldier. And it sounds like you're a scholar. But even for a soldier, there's a difference between shooting a man in the heat of a firefight, and shooting one point-blank when it's just the two of you."

Matt's helmet flashlight was the only illumination in the room, and he tried not to blind the man with it as they spoke. He considered detaching it and throwing it at Nawab, using the darkness for cover to flee or draw his folding knife, but he knew he couldn't move fast enough once the rifle started going off.

Nawab's face contorted. "You lie. You guys kill civilians. For sport, even. You want to know why Daesh is tolerated here? Why the tribesmen protect them after all of the evil they do? It's because you guys are worse."

Matt laughed. He couldn't help it, even with his own rifle pointed at him. "You hear about that village where they made the tribal elders sit on explosives and painted the sky with them? Don't give me bullshit about how we're worse."

"Shut up! Americans pose for photos with the bodies."

"Don't believe everything you've heard on *Voice of the Caliphate*." But he knew it was true. There had been incidents. Civilian mass murders. Fingers cut off as trophies. Guys who'd enlisted because they were sociopaths, getting bored with clearing IED's in low-action areas with no engagement and deciding to go on the hunt.

"Get over there," Nawab said. "*Move.*" He gestured with the barrel of the assault rifle, waving it off-center of Ritter's chest, indicating the direction he wanted him to move in.

It was the moment Ritter had been waiting for. He'd closed the distance between them quietly while they talked, shining his light in the other man's face each time he took a step. Now he was close enough to seize the opportunity. He slammed the rifle barrel with the heel of his hand, shoving it away as he closed the remaining distance. Nawab squeezed the trigger, whether out of reflex or intent Ritter didn't know, but the result was the same: white fire barked from the muzzle, riddling the cave wall with bullets, the shots obscenely loud in the tight space. Ritter punched Nawab in the face and slammed his

144

lanky body into the rock wall, still holding onto the weapon with his left hand.

The rifle let loose another volley of bullets, this time across the ceiling, sending limestone chips raining down around them, dust swirling in the fan of light from the helmet. Now they were on the ground, grappling and Ritter was struck with the absurd thought: *Which of us is Daisy and which is Scarlett?* But as soon as it arose, the joke was blasted away by the image of Huff's body collapsing like a puppet with its strings cut. The memory should have added fire to the fight, but instead, it punched him in the gut, and he was reminded of how weak his body still was underneath the surge of adrenaline. His wounds and the time he'd spent knocked out were still impediments in a hand-to-hand fight. And if he didn't get the *upper* hand soon, his enemy would at the very least crack his skull with the butt of the rifle and he'd wake up even more compromised, if at all.

On their knees, struggling for control of the gun, Nawab used the weapon as a lever to force him into a corner. The young man was stronger than he looked, not a stranger to hard work before he'd gone off to university. He was thin, but sinewy, like so many of the Taliban who'd lived their lives laboring in the thin mountain air and didn't break a sweat lugging a 50-caliber up a ravine.

What was Nawab pushing him toward? A fissure in the rock floor? Did the former student have fewer scruples about tossing him over the edge of an abyss than he did about shooting him in cold blood? But in the darkness, Ritter's other senses were heightened, and he felt no atmospheric indications that a chasm loomed nearby. What he did sense, was something shuffling in the darkness. Some living thing, leathery and bristling, possibly waking from slumber and coiling to strike.

Nawab's twisted hand was still wrapped around the grip of the rifle, his finger in the trigger guard even as Ritter wrenched the gun at an angle intended to dislocate it. Now, sensing danger behind him, he clasped Nawab's hand and squeezed it, depleting the last of the thirty-round clip he'd been firing from at the start of the ambush on the hillside. When it clicked empty, he let go of the weapon and drove an elbow up under Nawab's nose, knocking him backward, off balance. Ritter drew a spring-assisted folding knife from his belt, flicked it open, and slashed at the bare arms the man had raised in defense.

Nawab tripped and landed on the seat of his pants, dropping the spent rifle as he fell. Ritter snatched it up by the strap and finally turned to look over his shoulder sweeping the unmapped space with his light.

Blue fire crackled in shadows. But as his beam tracked toward the source, the white light was sucked out of his headlamp. It shot like a meteor into the amorphous darkness, which swallowed it like a physical thing.

As the ball of light was extinguished, the shape of a creature emerged from the darkness, traced in lines of violet light. The anatomy was difficult to reconcile: a bipedal body easily twice the height of a man, the head set with luminous electric blue eyes beneath spiral horns. The entire form appeared to be cloaked in translucent wings of laser light, shifting and wavering like water. It was visible only for a moment, the light growing like an indrawn breath fed by what it had stolen from Ritter's headlamp, then vanishing again, leaving the two men in pitch blackness that smelled of ozone.

"What the hell was that?"

Nawab was curled up in a ball against the wall, knees to chest, praying in Arabic, blowing into his hands, and passing them over his body. Ritter couldn't see these gestures in the darkness, but he'd encountered them before among superstitious locals. *Ruqyah,* they called the practice. A type of spiritual cleansing to ward off demonic spirits and the evil eye.

Unarmed except for his knife, Ritter felt intolerably vulnerable. How long before the sound of the gunfire summoned other insurgents to the chamber?

He removed the flashlight from his helmet, slapped it against his glove, and triple-clicked the switch. Still dead. Deciding to delay replacing the battery until he was more confident of his situation, he took a chem light from his vest, cracked it, and tossed it at the ground, lighting the empty corner of the cave, where just a moment ago something impossible had bloomed in and out of existence.

The desiccated bodies of what looked to be a goat and some other small animals were revealed in the eerie green glow, but there was no sign of the beast he'd seen. Could the light show have been a symptom of a concussion? No. The dead goat on the ground couldn't have been mistaken for the horned humanoid form he'd seen towering above him.

He took his NVGs from his fanny pack and snapped them onto the mount on his helmet, pulling them into position and viewing the cave in their noisy green light. The shadow spaces the chem light couldn't reach were now delineated, the glow stick providing enough ambient illumination to augment the power of the goggles. The cave was larger than he'd imagined, pockmarked with bullet holes, but even the newly revealed areas were empty of living creatures.

So where did it go? The other man had seen it too, or he wouldn't be carrying on like that, rocking and praying.

Ritter bent over Nawab and shook him by the shoulder. "What was it?"

Staring at the dead animal bodies in the jaundiced light, Nawab spoke without making eye contact.

"The Daesh … they thought it was a djinn. But the local tribes tell stories about these caves."

"What stories?"

"They would mean nothing to you."

"Try me."

"The followers of a heretic, a false prophet named Alhazred, once kept a hermitage here. They studied his book, the *Kitab Al Azif.* A book of conjuring."

"You're talking about black magic? You're saying that was a demon?"

Nawab touched a silver charm on his chest. Ritter couldn't be sure, but it looked like the hand of Fatima. "Have you ever considered there might be things in this world your technology and weapons have no power over?"

Reminded of his tech, and no longer fighting for his life, Ritter clicked the comm button on his belt and spoke into his headset mic. "This is Sgt. Ritter, anybody copy? This is Sgt. Ritter. Do you copy?"

Not so much as static in reply.

"My tech is no match for solid rock, I can tell you that much. As for my weapon ..." He took a magazine from his tactical vest and reloaded the rifle. "Last I checked, it can kill anything that can kill me. Anything *real*, that is. Keep that in mind, friend. And keep your hands off."

"I don't know what I was thinking." Nawab dabbed his bloody nose with his scarf and Ritter saw runnels of blood streaming down his forearm where the knife had grazed him. "I should have let you kill me."

Ritter coughed out a dry laugh. "I haven't yet *tried* to kill you, pal."

"It would be best if you did. What you saw wasn't a djinn or a demon. It is something far worse: a god."

"I thought you only believed in one god."

"Alhazred believed in many. This one is the messenger god, the All-Seeing Eye, the Haunter of the Dark."

"Messenger god? What's the message?"

"The end of the world. The coming of chaos."

Ritter shook his head. "Whatever that was, it was made of light. It had to be a projection of some kind. A trick."

"Smokeless fire. What the legends say the djinn were made from. Maybe those legends started here in these caves, when the ancients saw what lives in this place. Maybe the acolytes of Alhazred came here to worship because they knew what it really was."

Ritter rose from where he'd knelt to sort out his gear in the aftermath of the struggle. Equipped with night vision and a reloaded weapon, he began to hope he might see his men again.

"On your feet. Show me the way out of here."

"There is no way out of here."

"Bullshit. You came from somewhere. Did they send you to find me?"

Nawab shook his head, staring at the animal carcasses.

"Answer me! You fuckers killed one of my men. I have every reason to kill you right here."

The threat met with silence. Nawab shuffled to his knees. He pulled his bloodstained shirt open to expose his chest, his hands, clutching the fabric on either side with raised middle fingers, a grim smile on his face.

"*Fuck,*" Ritter sighed. "You really want me to."

Nawab let go of his shirt and slumped against the wall. He dabbed at his bleeding nose with his scarf. "There's no way out," he repeated.

"You came from *somewhere*. You didn't fall through the same hole I did."

Nawab crawled to the glow stick and picked it up. He waved it over the rock wall where bullets had chipped away at geometric sigils and thorny words painted in a forgotten alphabet. "You Americans have no sense of awe. No curiosity about what you see with your own eyes."

"Mysteries can wait. My men come first, and I need to get back to them. But what I *am* curious about is what you're doing down here alone. You could have killed me while I was knocked out but you didn't. They sent you down here unarmed. Are you supposed to be the next sacrificial goat?"

Nawab ran his fingers over the painted wall, his back to Ritter. "I never wanted to be a part of this. I was at school when they came to my village and nailed a shabnoma to my mother's door. A threat. They were recruiting anyone with connections to the government. Forcing us to swear allegiance to their new state. Most of them aren't even Afghan. They come over the border from Pakistan and work their claws into the cracks in the tribal leadership. They thought I was with the government because I went to the university, but I wanted nothing to do with politics. When my sister called, I knew they would slaughter my family if I wasn't there to join when they returned."

"So you joined."

"I had no choice. They knew I studied history and languages. They wanted me to explain what it was, the beast in the cave. When I translated these inscriptions and told them it was one of Alhazred's gods, they called me an infidel. I knew they would."

"But they didn't kill you?"

"They needed me. The caves in this region are unmapped, unknown to your people and the Afghan Security Forces. They have great strategic value. The Daesh didn't want to abandon them if the beast could be killed. I let them believe I could learn its weaknesses if they gave me more time to study. It kept me out of the firefights. But then men began to disappear."

"And that's when you suggested sacrificing animals."

Nawab nodded.

"Let me guess. They ran out of goats and you ran out of time. You were down here waiting for death in the dark when I came crashing through the roof."

"There is no escape."

"Because the only way out is through the insurgents."

"You are one man with a gun. There are twelve in the upper chambers."

"Those carcasses don't look chewed on."

"Nyarlathotep does not feed on flesh and blood, it consumes energy, life force, consciousness. It drives you mad, feeds on your madness until you die of insanity."

"Nya-what?"

"It has many names."

As if summoned, the horned form reemerged from the rock wall, hovering and shifting through myriad forms—man, beast, angel, devil, nebula, glyph.

♦

Wings of light enveloped the two men, and the walls of the cave fractured in prismatic shards. Ritter felt a sickening lurch as his mind was wrenched from his body and shot down rails of light faster than a 50-caliber round.

When the world resolved around him again, he was perched on a precipice in the open air, overlooking a barren plain that climbed rocky steps to an onyx city of crenelated turrets and domed towers. The titanic scale of the castle city gave him vertigo, and he looked away, grounding his gaze on his dusty combat boots. His body had traveled with him, or at least he inhabited the illusion of it as he would in a dream. Was he dreaming? There was no such place as this in Afghanistan.

Beside him Nawab looked equally dumbstruck, eyes transfixed on the city, mouth agape. Hovering in mid-air beyond the cliff's edge was the entity from the cave—horned and radiant, its flesh rendered translucent by the glow of its incandescent bones, like violet filaments at the heart of a bulb. It was held aloft by webs of laser lace, beating like the wings of a hummingbird, intricate patterns blurred by speed.

"*Kadath.*" Nawab spoke the word in an awestruck sigh.

"Is this heaven?" Ritter asked his companion. "Are we dead?"

The entity answered with a voice like wind howling through glass pipes. Ritter heard it more with his mind than his ears. "You are on the borderland of the city of the gods, outside the bounds of time and space. Your body still breathes in the sacred cave."

"What are you?"

"I am the messenger and the message, the living matrix of all that is and is to come. I consume life so that I may assimilate its permutations. I offer apotheosis, infinite and eternal knowledge of the trials and triumphs of your seed."

"I don't understand," Ritter said. "Take us back."

"Do not refuse what you cannot comprehend. I offer a gift, but only one of you may claim it. Witness."

The creature waved its hand—if it could be said to possess one—sending a wave of distortion rippling through the air. Nawab absorbed it with a shudder and a subtle transformation. His body was the same, but his face, took on a resemblance to Ritter's ten-year-old son as if the man were an older brother.

"Gavin?"

"Daddy!" Nawab spoke in the child's voice, and despite the chill it sent across Ritter's flesh, his heart leaped at the sound and a lump swelled in his throat. It was a sound he had only heard through the metallic filter of computer speakers and phone lines since shipping out. "I *miss* you, Daddy."

Ritter swallowed. He couldn't bring himself to reply. It was a trick. A lie.

"I was lonely when you left us, but then I made friends with Rainbow Dave. You remember him, right?" Dave was a YouTube star with a multicolored mohawk and a charismatic way of rambling incessantly about video games. Gavin was addicted to the guy's channel, Scream Time.

I must be dead or dying. Or captured and drugged. Whatever this is, it's harvesting my memories to fuck with me.

"Mama's worried about you, but you wanna know something funny? It's that I get blown up. In Boston. You went all the way to Afghanistan to fight the terrorists and I get blown up in America. But it's okay, Daddy. Because sometimes you have to blow up to level up. Do you know that, Daddy? What level are you on in the game? It looks pretty high."

"Stop...."

"Are you ready for the boss battle?"

"Stop it. Stop talking. You're not my son. You're not my son!"

The air rippled between the two men, and the resemblance to Gavin drained from Nawab's face. As soon as it passed, Matt felt a presence seize hold of his own nerves like an electrical current. It contorted muscles he didn't know he had, animating his face and modulating his vocal cords. He spoke without knowing what the words would be until they left his mouth, the desperate pleadings of a young woman.

"They're coming back, brother. You left us to join them for nothing. When they return they will string me up and rape me and slit my throat like a cow. Mother will go to her grave knowing you are one of them. They are coming, Nawab. They are com—"

Nawab slapped Ritter across the face, knocking the possessing spirit out of his body and leaving him reeling at the cliff's edge. The anguish on the other man's face confirmed that a shard of the woman's soul, complete with her memories, expressions, and voice had inhabited him.

He addressed the entity hanging in the sky. "His sister and my son. Do they know they were here?"

"Their waking minds are unaware. These were fragments of their souls that know the future. Time and space have no dominion over me."

"Are we really here?" Nawab asked, touching the healed skin of his forearm where the wound from Ritter's knife had been.

"Your bodies slumber in the cave. You can not remain long away from them. Now you must make a choice: which of you will join me and which will return? Come. Follow and see the way."

The entity led them up a winding stair carved in the cliff face, crowned with a stone arch. A brass instrument fitted with an array of

152

lenses and dials stood perched atop a swivel mount beyond the arch. It was flanked by a pair of steel monoliths, each taller than a man, their mirrored surfaces facing each other across the path.

Nyarlathotep floated down to ground level and engaged the instrument, tuning the dials, and aiming it at a precise location on the ashen plain at the foot of the onyx fortress. "Come," he said to Ritter. "Gaze upon what stalks toward your loved ones even now."

Ritter approached, not as a soldier but as a husband and father. He had left all other duties behind in this time outside of time.

The instrument reminded him of a tower viewer on a pier. The kind of device that takes quarters in return for a closer look at a city skyline. He squinted into the eyepiece without touching it, for fear of jostling the delicate optics.

What he'd taken for a cloud shadow moving over the cracked ground now came into focus—visually, if not psychologically. For there was no sense to be found in the creature's strange anatomy. It appeared to be a mass of trembling glass shards and black feathers, though it was impossible to say where feathers ended and glass began, the two shifting in and out of each other in constant flux. The head was comprised of a pyramid of stone or bone set with what he believed was a great eye, until it opened to reveal a downturned grimace of red gums and sharp teeth. Clouds of brown dust kicked up in its wake. He could only stand to look at it for a few seconds.

"Its name is Choronzon, ruler of the tenth aethyr beyond the abyss. Among the Other Gods, it is Lord of Chaos. It has been granted dominion over your homeland and crosses the boundless waste to infect the mind of mankind."

"My homeland?"

"Your son has already seen it in a dream. He is a chosen witness."

"Why?"

"You know enough to make your choice. Should you accept my gifts, you shall know all. Now step aside."

Nyarlathotep readjusted the instrument and beckoned Nawab to gaze through it at a different location, higher on the stepped plain. Ritter could only discern a cloud of oily black smoke in the targeted spot. Nawab's breath hitched in his chest.

"Do you recognize it?" Nyarlathotep asked.

Nawab's voice quavered. "Only from nursery tales. The bloody kind."

"The Black Goat of a Thousand Young. It feeds them on the curdled milk of man's fear and despair. She approaches your village in the guise of the Daesh."

"They said my village would be spared."

Nyarlathotep raised his arms, palms upturned, the sleeves of his diaphanous robe shimmering with iridescence, and the twin monoliths glowed white against the perpetual dusk. Inside each slab, a tableau was revealed. In one, Gavin sat on his bed, his back to the wall, an iPad in his blanket draped lap, the screen lighting his face from below in the darkness. In the other, a young woman seen from behind knelt in the dirt as if about to pray, dusty strands of dark hair spilling from her headscarf and floating on the wind. Both figures appeared frozen in time, trapped in amber or glimpsed through a torporous underwater light, thick with motes.

Nawab approached the slab that held his sister's image, moving like a sleepwalker, extending his hand to touch the translucent surface.

The messenger god turned his hand, fingers twisted in a sorcerous contortion, and the figures inside the monoliths rotated like mannequins on a revolving stage.

The side of Gavin's face that had been concealed by shadow came into view like the surface of a planet rotating toward the sun, but the light couldn't shine on what wasn't there. The boy's skull was fractured—a ragged cavity caked with clotted blood and brain matter framed with singed hair. His exposed teeth leered in a horrid grin, as if what he saw on the screen in his lap amused the slaughtered side of him. A plastic lizard with glowing green eyes sat perched on his blood-stained shoulder.

Ritter turned away, a bolt shot through his heart, and his gaze fell upon the woman, also rotating into view, and the ragged gash across her throat from which a frozen fountain of blood gushed to the dusty ground.

Three simultaneous sounds shattered the spell: the dark god's metallic laughter, the piercing whine of an F-15 Strike Eagle, and the ringing of a dagger drawn from a silver sheath.

"I am the Voice of Kadath, and I bring these tidings from days yet to come." He pointed a black-taloned finger at the fighter jet screaming across the sky. "The airstrike summoned by Sgt. Ritter's compatriots lies mere minutes in the future. It will collapse the mouth of the cave system and your bodies will never be found. The fates of your families, however, lie farther off. I grant one of you the chance to be a messenger to your kin, to travel in the aethyr and warn them. The other ..." He raised the dagger and a corona of golden light flared from its razored edge. "Will die in sacrifice to provide the force required for the transformation."

These terms declared, the god tossed the weapon at the ground between the two men, where it spun like the wheel of fate.

Nawab was scarcely more than a boy, scrawny and untrained. Ritter could see the naked fear in his eyes, could almost taste it on the dry air. He had no desire to kill the man and no doubt that he could. The dagger was the only weapon present—not even a single flash grenade had made the journey to this place with him. If Nawab made a move for it, things would happen fast. His mind protested the reality of their predicament. How could death in a dream realm harm their cave-bound bodies? But as with the insanity of the war itself, he had to take the situation on its own terms or not at all.

"He's lying," Ritter said. "The demon is lying. It's what they do, right? In every culture. Demons lie."

Nawab had dropped his center of gravity, stalking around the dagger with his fingers spread, knees bent, waiting for the moment to strike out and seize it, his eyes locked on Ritter's. Maybe he'd been an athlete of some kind. Maybe the outcome wasn't as certain as Ritter assumed.

"He is no demon," Nawab said. "His cruelest weapon is the truth." On the last word, Nawab tried a feint, moving right before diving left. Ritter saw it coming and acted faster kicking the dagger aside to ricochet off one of the monoliths. But Nawab was light on his feet and quick to reach the new location. He seized the weapon by the hilt and pivoted to face Ritter just as the larger man crashed into him.

Ritter half expected the collision to send the pair of them crashing through the monolith like a plate-glass window, but the impact was hard. They struck the steel slab with bone-crushing force and rebounded, landing on the ground where they scrambled for control of the blade. Ritter's mind was racing. How could this be a dream? Every detail was vivid, the pain absolutely physical. Even the sound of the fighter jet had reached his ears with the exact delay of the differential between the speeds of light and sound. Was it really heading for the mountain they were buried under in the waking world?

His men didn't know about the cave system. The insurgents must have censored all hints of it from their radio communications, suspecting the U.S. intercepts that had netted so many other key pieces of intel. No wonder they'd been able to supply seemingly endless munitions in the battle for the valley. They'd had it stockpiled in the tunnels. All of this flashed through his mind as he wrestled Nawab for the dagger, the mental struggle more agonizing than the physical. If he believed what was at stake, he would act decisively when the moment came. But If the threats they'd glimpsed were real, was there a way to warn everyone and change the trajectory of the future?

And did the master of this game know him well enough to understand that a struggle was necessary to force his hand when he would balk at taking a life in cold blood? What if the chance to save his son was bait to bloody his hands in an effort to claim his soul? Nawab said it wasn't a demon, but Ritter knew of only one true god. He might be known by many names, and men might even kill one another over which they called him by, but Nyartlathotep was not among them.

The dagger trembled in the air between their faces.

"Your sister," Ritter said through clenched teeth. "Tell me her name."

"Why?"

"So I can warn her ... before I warn my son. Neither of us is getting out of this."

Nawab let out a growl with his last reserves of strength. Then he surrendered, his muscles gone slack, his eyes wide. With his last breath, he said her name. "Farishtah."

Ritter plunged the dagger into his throat. The whine of a laser-guided bomb crested to an earth-shattering explosion and his dream body was tugged through the onyx arch into the cold and glittering sky over unknown Kadath.

♦

Later, Farishtah would decide she must have dozed off from fatigue while taking a break from laboring in the summer heat. Surely the message had come to her in a dream. This explanation satisfied her intellect, though it didn't for a moment cause her to consider dismissing the content. Angels had been known to speak through dreams.

She was alone in the one-room school where she'd once taught the children of Pikha before the militants ransacked it, sifting through the rubble to salvage whatever pencils and books she could reclaim. She was surprised to find her portable transistor radio in the drawer of her broken desk where she'd left it, and even more surprised to find that it still pulled in songs from the Pashto station broadcasting out of Jalalabad with no more static than before.

She fed the wire for the earpiece under her scarf and sang along under her breath as she worked. Music was forbidden. Drivers had been shot on the road for playing car radios, and it occurred to her as she worked that this was one of the few secret pleasures a woman could indulge with a slight advantage. Her hair and scarf concealed the earpiece and wire, allowing her to listen furtively. With her other ear free to hear anyone approaching the building, she felt secure. It had been months since ISIS had visited Pikha, but it was impossible to know who in the village was keeping a list of sinners for them.

She prayed every day for her brother Nawab, who had been forced to join their ranks or face public execution for the crime of secular studies. That boy had no business carrying a gun in the snowy mountains. Their mother feared he was dead already at the hands of the Americans. Farishta feared she was right but had vowed not to give up hope without evidence.

She was musing on these thoughts, seated on the floor with a damp rag and basket of writing instruments, when a voice spoke her name in her ear. She'd taught the children a little English—one of the most practical skills for trading and begging with the occupying troops.

157

Telling the Americans where an IED had been planted could earn a child an MRE. Her own English was limited, but the voice that spoke to her now was unmistakably American, crackling through the earpiece, icy and thin.

"Farishta ... Listen carefully ... Farishta ... Nawab sent me."

Were the Americans targeting her radio directly somehow? There was no telling what their technology could do, but surely an intrusion on public airwaves to deliver a message to a single woman would make no strategic sense. And this was when she began to feel that she must be dreaming. Mishearing a word as her own name on the static laced broadcast wasn't hard to do—everyone was biased to hear their own name in similar sound patterns. But to hear her brother's name as well? That was too unlikely to be a trick of her mind. Perhaps because she had only just been thinking of him?

"Farishta ... Listen to me ... Write this down."

Her fingers trembled as she took a clean pencil from the basket and opened a torn but mostly intact math book to the blank back cover. The signal was partially scrambled by strange modulations, less clear than the broadcast it had interrupted.

"Nawab sent me. Your family is not safe. Daesh will return soon. Go to the American checkpoint at the bridge. Tell them ... have information about a cave system ISIS is using in near Khas Kunar. They will he- ... your family ... set you up in Kabul ... exchange for this information. This is very important...." The signal faltered. When it returned, the American's voice sounded even thinner, more air than tone. "I'm running out of time, Farishta. I'm going to give you a security code and coordinates that will lead to the recovery of a soldier's body. Write this down...."

Tracking the Black Book

When it came to grimoires, Eric reminded Peter of a jeweler digging through a bag of dirty rocks that had cost him dearly, examining each under his monocle, breath held in anticipation of an elusive refraction of the light combined with just the right weight in his hand. But some stones were simply out of reach, even with their authenticity untested, and Eric could usually let these go. Until he found the *Necronomicon*. That was different, and for the first time in their long friendship, Eric asked Peter for money.

The year was 2003 and the seller, a Mr. Qassim, claimed to have been a clerk at the Iraq National Library and Archives in Baghdad. In a series of emails, Qassim relayed the story of how he had discovered the book in a moldering stack while conspiring to sell rare manuscripts on the antiquities black market ahead of the American invasion. The UN was still wringing its hands over sanctions and inspections amid rumors of war, but in those days one didn't need magic to divine the future, and Qassim had fled with his plunder to Cairo where he put out feelers on the internet. Two weeks later, Eric broached the subject with his old conjuring partner.

"I know you wouldn't ask if you didn't have good reason to take it seriously, but we both know forgeries are a cottage industry. And five grand is ... significant." Peter bit his thumbnail and stared at the laptop Eric had placed on the coffee table in front of him.

"This is different," Eric said. "You don't know what it took for me to even find this."

"And that might be coloring your judgment a little."

Eric raised an eyebrow, "When has it ever?"

"You've had your guy translate parts of it?"

"I wouldn't be asking you if I hadn't."

"So, apart from the seller's story, what do you make of the contents?"

"The syntax of the conjurations is dead-on. Those scans you're looking at? There are a lot of them. I've barely slept this week going through them with a fine-tooth comb."

"Are there any diagrams? Glyphs?"

"Yeah. Click on that. I've never seen anything like them. In fact, I'm starting to worry about some of them blooming in my dreams the next time I do sleep."

Peter sat back, dragged his thumb and forefinger across his closed eyelids to the bridge of his nose and said, "Okay, how sick are we? I have the kid's college fund to think about and I'm considering spending five K on a book that at worst is a forgery and at best will give us nightmares."

"C'mon, Pete, you know nightmares aren't the worst it can do," Eric said with a tone that suggested he wanted Peter to challenge the idea.

Peter sighed. They had spent more hours on the nature of the fabled *Necronomicon* over the span of their friendship than on any other topic. Considering how elusive it was, there was an absurd proliferation of rumor in occult circles about the hazards of even possessing the book. The original Arabic text was nothing but a wisp of smoke drifting through the footnotes of history. And yet, whenever the title was mentioned to a practitioner, it provoked dire warnings that the book was cursed.

Peter slouched into the couch and shot a glance at his watch. Lily was at the supermarket with Robbie, but they would be home soon. "Are you referring to the curse, or to actually using it to conjure?"

"The curse is probably bullshit. I mean nobody can ever back that up, since nobody credible has ever seen an original."

"My thoughts exactly."

"I'd be more concerned about what we might encounter if we use it."

"Okay. Now we come to it. Just what do you have in mind, anyway? Because what we're looking at here is basically an artifact that belongs in a museum. It's worth a hell of a lot more than the asking price, if it's legit—and why *is* that, anyway? But all that aside, you're thinking of vibrating the incantations and spilling candle wax on it, aren't you? You want to work some mojo with it, I can see it in your impish grin, you crazy little fuck. So tell me, to what end?"

Eric leaned forward, hands clasped between his knees. "To find out first hand if it works. Same as ever."

"But this is on a different scale. If it does work, what then?"

Eric stared at a blank spot on the wall for a moment, then met Peter's eyes and said, "Then we'll know. Unequivocally. We will have answered the central question of our friendship: *Is this shit for real?*"

"I wonder at what cost," Peter replied.

"We're not dabblers, Pete. We've been doing this a long time. We'll be okay."

Peter took a swig of iced tea from a can and shuffled the sheaf of email printouts against the coffee table. Eric was looking at him for a verdict.

"Why so cheap, if it's real? Not like Lily won't kill me if she finds out, but considering what it appears to be …"

"He's scared. I think it's that simple. Let me show you his last email."

Eric riffled through the papers, and withdrew a page that was warped from frequent sweaty handling.

Dear Mr. Marley,

I must have your decision presently. This object has become a burden to me and I need to be rid of it. Perhaps I risk frightening you away, but it seems that someone of your proclivities may be assured of the authenticity by what I will tell you.

Yesterday I carried the book with me when I went to meet with a scholar at the Boulak museum. On the way there, I was attacked by dogs. And in my hotel room at night, insects have gathered around the box I keep it in, beetles and even a scorpion. The book seems to hum in their language, and they want to be near it. There have also been accidents when I walk the streets, and I fear that soon Allah will cease to protect me.

Our haggling is over. You may have it for the $5000 U.S. dollars. And do not think that I will give you a cursed book for free. I will burn it first. You must tell me within 24 hours if we have a deal, or it will burn. You can wire the money Western Union. Forgive my rude haste.

Sincerely,
Mr. Qassim

Peter set the page down and shook his head.

"I think he'll do it," Eric said. "I think he'll burn it."

For a moment neither of them spoke. A gentle breeze lifted the yellow curtains in the living room of Peter's house on Hubble Street, and the scent of lavender drifted in from Lily's flower box. Before the curtains settled again, sparkling silver light could be seen playing on the surface of the Merrimack River through the trees. It was a beautiful day after all of the spring rain they had endured, such an incongruous day to be discussing what might stir in the shadows at the bottom of the well of eternity.

Peter laid his fingertips on the printout as if it were a Bible he was about to take an oath on, and said, "Even considering Qassim's experiences, you don't think it's cursed?"

"He's a devout Muslim. It's spooking him out."

"Okay. I have some stocks Lily doesn't know much about. They've done all right and it's an account she won't be looking at. If we find a way to make money on this with … I dunno, a limited-edition English translation or something, then maybe we'll tell her the whole story. Maybe. For now, this looks like a once-in-a-lifetime chance. I'm in. We need to be careful, though."

"We will be. We'll take every precaution."

"All right." Peter sighed. "So now that you've finally found it, how do you feel?"

"Nervous as hell."

"Good."

On Monday morning Peter cashed out the stocks, and Eric had completed the wire transfer by noon. "Would have been a lot easier if the Mad Arab took Paypal," Peter joked. At home that night he checked his email before going to read bedtime stories to Robbie, and found a FedEx tracking number in his inbox.

> Ship date: June 9, 2003
> Estimated delivery: June 11, 2003
> Destination: Haverhill, MA
> Status: Package data transmitted to FedEx
> DETAIL
> Activity: Package data transmitted
> Location: Heliopolis, EG

The package was estimated to arrive on Wednesday, just two days hence. That seemed fast, but it was airplanes pretty much all the way. He closed the laptop lid and announced that it was story time.

Sophie, their aging German shepherd, woke him in the night to go out. While he awaited her return, he ambled over to the little rolltop desk where he paid the bills, blinking sleep from his eyes. He flipped the laptop open and hit refresh on the web page he'd left up. The status was now *In transit*. He didn't know whether to feel relieved or threatened.

In the morning, while trying to feed Robbie some oatmeal without getting it on his shirt, he reached for the laptop again. Setting it down inside the Flying Oatmeal Zone was not a chance he would ordinarily take, and of course he could check the tracking from his office computer as soon as he got there, but he didn't want to wait that long. The status now said *Redirected*. Strange. He had tracked his share of packages, but didn't recall ever seeing that particular status.

"What's so urgent?" Lily asked from the hallway where she stood wrapped in a towel, brushing tangles out of her hair, fresh from the shower.

"Nothing. Just checking on some stocks."

In the car, he turned on the radio. With the war in its opening phase he seldom strayed from NPR these days. As he backed the Camry out of the driveway, a segment about some baseball player testing positive for performance-enhancing drugs was wrapping up. This was followed by a summary of top stories delivered by a female reporter with a British accent. One item caught his attention.

"A Federal Express cargo plane made an emergency landing in Cyprus today. A spokesman for the corporation praised the pilot's skill under duress, but declined to identify the source of the problem with the Boeing 727. No one aboard was injured."

A horn blared and Peter slammed on his brakes. A car flashed by in his mirrors as coffee sloshed out of the hole in his travel cup. *Jesus.* He'd almost backed right into it. He shut off the radio with an irritated stab at the button, and eased the car out onto the road.

He was distracted all day, thinking of insects crawling out of the walls in a Cairo hotel room, of dogs chasing Mr. Qassim down trash strewn alleys, of a pilot diving his plane to avoid a flock of leather-winged, potbellied predators pouring forth from a fissure in the clouds like maggots erupting from the torn flesh of a gas-bloated corpse on the shore of some nameless ocean.

Stop it. He had to stop this train of thought. It was just an old book; the downed plane, just a coincidence. The dread tome had slept on the dusty shelf of a library in Baghdad for how many years?

And then something stirred, and war came to Baghdad. And what will come to you when you have the cursed thing?

Just stop it.

The tracking results didn't change all day. He drove home in a heavy rain, then surfaced from his fugue by force of will at the diner table.

Before going to bed, he lifted the laptop lid one last time. The machine whirred to life, clicking and breathing. The tracking page was already up; it was always up now, wherever he had a computer. He clicked and waited.

The page now showed an arrival scan for Paris. They were a mightily efficient carrier, he had to admit that, even with a worm of dread coiling in his stomach. Redirected. He went to bed, but sleep was slow to claim him.

Morning brought heavier rain. Pools had formed in the backyard where some of Robbie's toys now floated, and a dirty towel had taken up residence on the sliding-door handle in the kitchen, for wiping the mud off Sophie.

In the car he almost put on a CD to keep from brooding, but habit won out, and he left the news on. And then it came, as he knew it would, a little story, glossed over in a few seconds. A dreadful story. Charles DeGaulle airport in Paris was mired in delays after a partial runway collapse due to a ruptured water main.

Rain lashed the windshield in white sheets that his wipers couldn't clear on their fastest setting. He turned off the radio and craned his neck toward the glass, as if that would help him to better see the road ahead.

♦

He called Eric on his lunch break.

"Have you been following the tracking number?" He asked without a hello.

Eric laughed, "Of course. You too, huh? I still can't believe it's actually going to be in our hands tomorrow."

"I'm starting to worry about that."

"Relax."

"Eric, listen to me. I think Qassim was right. I think the book is cursed."

"You're kidding."

"I'm not kidding. You don't follow the news. I do. There have been accidents that I would bet anything are related to the package as it moves."

"I don't see how you could be sure of that."

"It's not hard to see a pattern when you compare the tracking data to the stories. Trust me."

"Pete, trust *me*. You're having prom night jitters, that's all. You're out of practice, and now we've found the real thing. You're nervous; it's understandable."

"You're not hearing me!" Peter barked and immediately sensed the conversational mute button that had been engaged among his coworkers in the cubicles surrounding his own. He continued in a hushed tone, "There will be no experiments with this thing. It's not safe. We made a mistake Eric, but now it's coming. It's coming to my house where my child is. We need to divert the package. We have to do a Return to Sender or something."

"How much coffee have you had this morning?"

"I'm not paranoid."

"Yeah. That's what you said after nine-eleven when you were on the computer all the time. And there's no getting your money back from this guy. You know that, right?"

"I don't care about the money."

"Has anyone been hurt or killed by any of these accidents you're talking about?"

"I ... I don't know. I don't think so."

"Then chill out. Right now the book is loose, it isn't bound by any of the defensive wards I'm going to put on it as soon as it gets here. Just let me take care of it. It'll be okay."

"You sure?"

"Yes."

"I have to get back to work."

♦

Wednesday morning arrived without a dawn, just a lightening of the gray water-world outside. Lily had the little TV on in the kitchen when Peter came in. Looking up from the toast she was cutting into strips she said, "They're predicting flooding. If it's anything like last time, we're screwed. Would you check the basement before you go to work? Get the pump set up if you have time?"

"Sure." He kissed her temple, and poured a coffee.

He was less than halfway down the basement steps when he realized he would be calling in to work. It was an idea he had entertained anyway so that he could be home when the package arrived. Now he had a legitimate excuse. The basement was already flooded with what looked liked six inches of water. As he stood there surveying it, the lights dimmed for a second, then returned to full brightness. He trotted up the stairs, plucked his cell phone from the charger, and called his boss.

After setting up the pump and digging out flashlights, candles and batteries, he sat down at the computer. In theory he could work a little from home as long as the power held out, but the first thing he did was log onto the tracking page.

The *Necronomicon* had reached the shores of America. There was an arrival scan in Boston and a departure scan immediately following. He was once again grimly impressed with the company's ability to keep things moving. Their fucking *tenacity*. He was definitely getting his seventy-five bucks worth of International Priority. Still, maybe now that it was on the ground, the weather would keep it away for one more day. It certainly couldn't be delivered if the local roads were closed.

He turned the TV on and caught a news brief in progress. A reporter holding an umbrella was standing in front of an animal shelter in Lawrence according to the text bar. She said that four dogs were dead and several others were in veterinary care after a fight erupted in an outdoor kennel that morning. They cut to a clip of a woman at a reception desk responding to an interview question. The text identified her as Denise Norton, Manager. "I've never seen anything like it, and I've worked here for twelve years," she said, still visibly shaken. "They were out in the run to do their business this morning and they just turned on each other. I didn't see it myself, I was signing for a package at the time. But the handler who was with them said it came out of nowhere. They just went berserk. He's in the hospital over to Beverly now."

I was signing for a package at the time. Peter turned off the TV and looked at docile old Sophie curled up on the couch. He didn't need anyone to tell him which carrier was delivering the package Denise Norton had signed for. He was pretty sure there was another box on the same truck with his name on it.

The doorbell rang and set his heart hammering at double its resting rate in less than a second. Sophie barked her territorial alarm, but Peter found it hard to get up. The chime came again, and it was the sight of Robbie toddling toward the door that got him moving. He scooped Robbie up and deposited him in the pack-and-play in the corner of the room.

He peered through the curtain, looking for a white truck with the familiar logo, but couldn't see it. His hands felt wet as he gripped the knob, took a breath, and swung the door open with the hurried determination of a man jumping into a cold pool before he has time to think about it.

Eric stood on the porch in a charcoal-gray hoodie with a shoulder bag slung across his body. He smiled his wolfish, bearded grin and said, "Took you long enough. It's raining, if you haven't noticed."

"What are you doing here?"

"Saw your car and figured you took the day off."

"Yeah, the basement's flooding."

"The whole road will probably go under in the next couple of hours, depending on the tide and the moon and all that shit."

"Come on in. What's in the bag, dare I ask?"

"You know, equipment."

Peter lifted Robbie under the arms and set him down on the carpet. The boy beamed up and said, "*Ehwik!*"

"Hey, little man." Eric tousled Robbie's shaggy hair. His smile faded when he looked at Peter and said, "We should have sent it to my place. I don't know what I was thinking. I guess I thought you'd feel better about getting it directly, since you ... fronted the funds. Lily home?"

"Yeah, she's in the bathroom doing the laundry."

"Well, I thought I should be here when it arrives, since you're kind of, you know, worried about it. But in this weather it might not get here at all today." Eric sounded disappointed.

"Yeah. We'll see. You want some coffee?"

"Love a cup."

In the kitchen Peter took a Bic lighter from the junk drawer and tucked it into the front pocket of his jeans before returning to the living room. He set the mugs down and asked Eric what he meant by 'equipment,' nodding at the black bag.

"A banishing dagger. I wasn't sure if you still had one. And a lead box that I hope is big enough."

"A *lead box?*"

"I made it at friend's metal shop a few years ago when I was experimenting with the Lesser Key spirits. Remember King Solomon was said to have kept them imprisoned in a brass vessel with a lead seal? I thought, why just a seal? Why not make the whole damned thing out of lead?"

"Too bad you didn't have the book shipped in it. Then we might know if it helps or not."

Eric chuckled. "This bitch is heavy. Would have cost a fortune to send it back and forth, and we'd have the FBI up our asses right now for trying to move a box that can't be x-rayed in and out of the Middle East."

Peter watched Robbie playing with his trucks on the floor under the coffee table and considered these precautions. It was tempting to think that Eric had it all worked out. It was a temptation he didn't trust.

Peter checked the basement again. The water level had climbed higher in spite of his electric pump, and the bottom step was now submerged. He wondered if it could possibly reach the electrical outlets if it kept up. Maybe he should get the hip waders on and slosh through it to the breaker box, turn everything off down there. The thought was interrupted by an explosive outburst of barking from Sophie, a rapid, followed by the clacking of her claws across the floor above. Peter bounded up the stairs, taking them in twos before the doorbell even rang. When he got to the living room and saw Eric stepping away from the curtained window, reaching for the doorknob, Peter yelled, "*Wait!*"

Eric turned to look at him.

... a flame bloomed and wavered in the wind ...

"The dog," Peter said, "Get her out of here while I sign for it. Put her in the mudroom."

"She always barks at strangers. She's fine," Eric said, squeezing the knob in his hand.

Peter scooped Robbie up and set him in the playpen, all the while keeping his eyes locked on Eric's. "Do it," he said, "It's not a suggestion, Eric, I'm telling you, get her out of here. Now."

"All right," Eric said with a raised eyebrow. He gently plucked a handful of fur at the scruff of the dog's neck and nudged her side with his knee, "Come on, girl, come." She went with him, but maintained a low growl and a sidelong stare at the door.

Peter waited until they were out of the room, and then opened the door on a scruffy young man dressed in a navy blue shirt and matching shorts with a white box in one hand, and an electronic signature pad in the other. The guy looked okay, not like someone who had seen nameless horrors. So that was good.

Standing in the shelter of his covered porch, Peter scribbled something that didn't render anything like his name in the little gray LCD bar, then felt the box thrust into his sternum. He watched the driver sprint through the pelting rain and wondered if his was the first electronic signature in history to bind a covenant with chthonic forces.

Moving fast, he found the cardboard tab and ripped the box open along the seam, thrust his hand inside and withdrew the bubble-wrapped book. He unwound the plastic shroud and let it blow away on the wind. Now he held the book in his hands: sand-blasted leather bulging with vellum leaves tied by a rough hemp cord. There was no title on the cover, which seemed to thrum with magnetic resonance in the bones of his hands, only an elaborate glyph rendered in cracked and tarnished gold leaf. He opened it. On the first page was the same sigil in sepia ink. On the second page dense and beautiful Arabic script began to flow.

Peter took the lighter from his jeans pocket and flicked it. The wheel was slow and stubborn after lying inert for so long in the kitchen drawer. He tried again. On the third strike a flame bloomed and wavered in the wind. Cupping the flame in his hand for shelter,

171

he held it to the edge of a stiff vellum sheet that protruded a little farther out from the edge than its brethren. The page caught, drawing up the flame and curling inward. He bent over the book, like a pilgrim doing prostrations, acutely aware of Eric's imminent return. He blew on the orange line of consumption to help it along. When it reached the writing the ink appeared to be far more flammable than the paper. It sucked up the scintillating terminus from the vanishing edge of the page and drew it along into a living blue flame that traveled to infuse every detail of the flowing script, as if the ancient ink were made of some black fuel.

Peter watched with dread as the edge of the page ceased to burn and the line of flame jumped from page to page across the entire book until cold blue light spilled from the spaces between the leaves.

"What did you do?" Eric's voice came from over his shoulder, calm and close.

"I tried to burn it," Peter said looking up at him.

"It looks hungry for the fire." Eric said.

"What's happening to it?"

"I think setting the words alight might have the same effect as chanting them. Jesus, maybe that's how it survived the inquisition. *A black book that can't be burned.*" Eric whispered the words with awe.

A wild fit of snarling and barking that didn't sound at all like Sophie echoed through the house as they watched the book not burn but illuminate, neither of them moving, neither knowing what to do, when a shadow moved into the doorway behind them eclipsing the warm yellow light from the house. It was a strange double-headed figure, but Peter quickly fit it into its place in the mundane world: Lily holding Robbie.

When she spoke, she sounded frightened, a tone that didn't suit her at all. She didn't ask what they were doing kneeling huddled over something on the porch in a storm, or why Sophie was locked in the mudroom, she just said, "Peter, there's something in the basement, like a ... I don't know, a big animal or something."

"Don't go down there," Peter and Eric said in near unison.

"Like hell I would. What is it? Is that what Sophie's going psycho about? You know about it, don't you?"

"No," Peter said, standing up beside Eric, trying to hide the book from view with his body. "We'll check it out. Listen, Lil, we might have to go to your parents' house if this flooding keeps up. You should pack some things, maybe get Robbie in the car before the roads go under, okay?"

She nodded agreement but kept her eyes fixed on his lower body as if she were looking through him at whatever they were hiding. When she raised her eyes to meet his, she said, "What did you two do? Did you make this weather? I know you're into some weird shit together, I hear things when you've had a few drinks between you."

Peter smiled weakly and said, "We had nothing to do with the storm. That's crazy."

The dog's maniac barking filled the space that hung between them. Then a sound of thrashing water erupted from below, followed by the crash of a shelving rack being knocked over. Lily stared at her husband.

"We'll check it out," Peter said. "Pack some things."

She shook her head in disgust and turned without another word. When she was gone, Peter closed the book, surprised to find it cool to the touch. Shutting the cover reduced the strange fire to a dim blue glow along the edges.

At the top of the basement stairs, Eric lifted the flap of his shoulder bag and withdrew a ceremonial dagger with double crescent moons on the hand-guard. The light in the stairwell flickered as they descended. Little waves of dark water splashed over the bottom steps, sent forth by whatever was stirring down there. Eric went first with the point of the dagger held out before him. Peter followed, holding the book in both hands, feeling it vibrate the bones in his fingers.

Peter said, "We didn't even call anything up. How did something come through?"

Eric cocked his head to be heard over his shoulder and said, "You should have waited for me. When you put fire to the words ... it's the same as if you chanted them, somehow."

On high shelves that spanned the room, family-sized boxes of crackers, jumbo bags of cheese curls and cases of soda flashed their garish colors as the light swelled and faded. The boxes and cans on the shelves that lined the bottom of the stairwell were now wet with filmy floodwater where the creature had splashed them. The air was infused with a fetid stench that thickened the mucous membranes in Peter's throat, leaving him with a sense of physical violation.

He scanned the sloshing surface of the dark water but could find no physical thing to account for its disturbance. What if it was lurking around the corner behind the stairs? The thought chilled him and he glanced down at his shoes expecting some blasphemous sinewy anatomy to seize his ankle through the gap between the planks.

Something stirred in the water, sending out a wake, and Peter had the distinct impression that this sort of cleaving of the water's surface could not be caused from below.

"Is it *invisible?*" he asked.

"Yes," Eric whispered. "Look at the droplets falling. They're not dripping from the ceiling."

The roiling wake sped toward the stairs. Peter retreated two steps and almost tripped. Eric raised the dagger, slashing the air in geometric forms and bellowing the solar invocation he had prepared against whatever native of the darkness this was.

"*A ka dua tuf ur biu! Bi a'a chefu! Dudu nur af an nuteru!*" His voice crackled into a high, panic fraught register at the end of the phrase.

The thing responded with a sound that arose first from the depths of Peter's own mind, unfurling into physical manifestation until the pressure of the sound pressed his skull from both within and without. It would have been impossible to know if the sound was in the air at all if not for the visible vibration of the water and the resonant buzz among the cans on the shelves. He wondered if those cans of beans and soup would explode like grenades as the syllables hummed and snapped like whipping power lines, droned and gurgled like the rotting plumbing in some hive of hell, punctuated by the clacking of mandibles and the slimy sibilance of an alien tongue. Amid the wreckage of primordial language he could hear the foreshadows of words forming in his brain stem, "YOG! FTHNAGGA! CTHUN … ZAZAZ CTHUN!"

Peter's knees gave out. He collapsed in a tangle on the stairs, one foot caught between the planks. Eric stabbed the dagger thrice at a space in front of him where a shimmering haze like a heat mirage, stirred the air. With each thrust of the blade, he roared a syllable, "Yah! Ra! Shammash!"

There was an almost ultrasonic squeal in return, rising and merging into quivering harmonic union with a high howl of pain from the dog upstairs as it passed out of human range. Peter put the *Necronomicon* down on a step to try to free his foot from the stairs. The blue light playing along the brittle page edges appeared to be burning out. He dislodged his foot, almost losing his balance in the act, and shouted at Eric over the din of psychic interference ricocheting around in his skull, "*THE BOX! GIVE ME THE BOX!*"

Eric shrugged his shoulder to free the strap of his bag, catching it when it slid down his arm and handing it back to Peter without ever taking his eyes from the boiling air in front of him. Peter opened the bag's flap and removed the lead box. Eric drew the dagger and the flat palm of his other hand up beside his ears, then shot both hands forward with a roar, "*HEKAS, HEKAS, ESTE BEBELOI!*"

The cacophony that rebounded upon them from this attack sounded more like fury than pain. Peter was lashed across the face with stinging droplets of water. He couldn't see the limb that had just whipped past him, but he could see Eric's shirt wrinkling and twisting where something was wrapping around his back and constricting.

Eric screamed and dropped the dagger. It tumbled through the stairs and plunked into the water. Eyes watering, jaw agape in horror and pain, he strained to turn his face away from something neither of them could see.

From the top of the stairs there came a rapping on the door and a cry of distress, "Daddy, Daddy!"

Peter scrambled upward, knocking items off the stairwell shelves with his elbow. "Get away, Robbie," he yelled in his sternest voice. "Go find Mommy. *Go.*"

He grabbed at the railing and spilled a little row of baby powder bottles from the nearest shelf. Watching them tumble around his feet, he remembered something he had once read about shamans blowing corn flour into the faces of demons to see them. Without thinking he seized a canister, cranked off the cap and tossed the white powder over Eric's shoulder at the invisible predator.

In the days and years that followed Peter would experiment with all varieties of sleeping aids and anti-anxiety drugs to erase the image that formed in that white cloud from his dreams. Partly arachnid—perhaps from a dimension in which great spiders made their nests in ocean caverns, catching some mutant species of shark in their nets—it also resembled an octopus in the way that pulses of light flowed along its oddly jointed limbs toward a nexus where concentric rings of teeth chattered with mechanical speed. And the elephantine eye, roaming and blinking through a putrid membrane … there was no correlation to the geometry of Earth in the corona of that eye.

Eric was being pulled toward the chattering teeth by the tentacles that embraced him, but it was the eye he was screaming at.

The cloud of powder only hung in the air with enough density to reveal the thing for a moment and then it was gone again. Eric vanished with it, entwined in the writhing anatomy, shrieking to burst blood vessels all the way down.

Peter did the only thing left to him in this uncharted nightmare. He opened the lead box, shoved the book inside and shut the lid. The roaring cyclone of alien language in his mind was muted instantly as a presence was sucked from the air with the force of a vacuum. There was a pattering of droplets striking the dingy water, then silence.

The river washed over the streets of Haverhill. National Guard trucks arrived to set up detours, and the local police went door to door to help people evacuate. Peter, still in shock, stood on his doorstep watching the flashing blue strobes of the police van, oblivious to the rain on his face. He felt a crazy urge to tell them that his friend had just died in his basement but there was no body because it had been devoured whole by an invisible monster. He would be required to see a psychiatrist, and maybe lose Robbie. So he said nothing. Lily threw hastily gathered essentials into the car and they pulled onto the road mere minutes before it became impassable. They drove to her parents' house, Sophie licking Robbie's face in the back of the car, Peter shooting agitated glances at the rear-view mirror.

Lily didn't ask Peter what had happened to Eric. She wasn't a closed minded or incurious person, and while Peter knew she didn't particularly like Eric, she had always been kind to him. There had been a time when she would have been all questions, would have made him pull the car over until he explained what had happened. But now they had a child, and she didn't want to know.

They spent a week with the in-laws. When the roads reopened, Peter took a few days off from work, rented a dumpster, and got busy fixing the damage to the basement. Then he did the thing he'd been putting off; he reported Eric as a missing person. The river was dredged, divers went down, and in the end Eric Marley was presumed dead, washed down the Merrimack and into the Atlantic past Plum Island.

The book, secured in its lead encasement, went into a safe-deposit box at the bank. Peter didn't want it in the house. When he had stopped by Eric's apartment before calling the cops, he let himself in with a key that was still on his ring from times when he'd watered the plants. Walking through Eric's rooms had broken the chains on the gates of grief, and he was thankful for the privacy to let it out, sitting on the couch they had so often shared, weeping.

When the wave passed, he put Eric's laptop in a shoulder bag and left with it. The scans would save him from ever needing to open that box again. He didn't know what the auction would do to his eBay feedback rating, but there would be a heavy shipping fee and no returns.

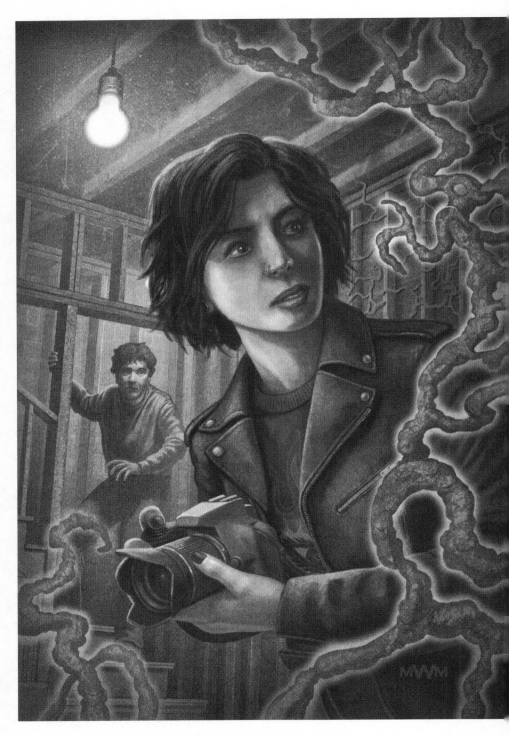

... awash with shapes that resembled fractal branches or tentacles ...

Time Out of Mind

Becca was close to making a sale, telling a Cambridge geneticist and his wife about the infrared technique she'd used in the photo series, when she spotted the fidgety guy across the gallery. Nothing about him fit the scene. Dressed in work boots and a Carhartt jacket and jeans, he stood out among the sport-coat and little-black-dress art crowd, but it was the way he moved that caught her eye first. Agitated, bouncing from one foot to the other like he needed to pee, and moving from one photo to another like he was searching for something.

"I love the juxtaposition of the ethereal aspect over the urban blight," the geneticist's wife was saying. Becca hadn't caught her name but knew she was on her second glass of wine and already had a wall picked out for the photo.

"Thank you," Becca said. "Would you excuse me for just a moment? I'll be right back."

The couple made polite noises and Becca maneuvered through the crowd. The exhibit had drawn a better turnout than she'd hoped for, a credit to the gallery owner's instincts for a punchy press release. Becca had initially pushed back against Sarah's insistence that they remind the public the photos were taken during the 2019 Starry Wisdom terror attack on Boston and that Becca had briefly been a person of interest in the investigation.

That brief moment of infamy when her pursuit of urban exploration and art photography had placed her between an apocalyptic cult and a government counterterrorism agency was a chapter of her life she was trying to leave behind. The photo exhibit, for all of the financial hopes she had pinned on it, was, more importantly, a way for her to finally confront her memories of that time and hopefully attain some semblance of closure. Sarah Junger was shrewd enough to remind Becca of that motive, and in reminding the public of her brief moment in the news they'd already managed to sell some of the smaller prints at prices she couldn't quite comprehend. She was almost starting to relax and enjoy herself when the ginger-haired guy in the canvas jacket got her hair up. Whatever his deal was, he wasn't an art-photography aficionado.

Making her way through the elbows and past the hors d'oeuvres table, she wondered if she should be wary of confronting the agitated man. But despite his stocky build and the intensity he radiated, his working-class dress somehow made him less intimidating than the rest of this crowd. Becca felt out of place trading her usual cargo pants and heavy-metal T-shirt for black slacks and a blouse but quite comfortable cutting a beeline toward potential danger.

"Hello," she said to his back when she reached him. "May I help you? I'm the artist."

He raised a finger and tapped the air in front of the photo. "I saw this," he said. "I saw something just like this. I forgot all about it, but it's coming back to me now."

His eyes were fixed on the centerpiece of the exhibit: a 36-inch print of a crumbling brick wall in an abandoned textile mill on the north bank of the Charles River. The image showcased a signature element of the series, an anomaly in the infrared spectrum she'd captured that year and never again. The brick wall was awash with shapes that resembled fractal branches or tentacles, rendered in ghostly silver light. The brochure for the exhibit explained that this was not something she'd achieve with a double exposure or Photoshop process. It was in the images themselves, captured by the modified sensor of her DSLR.

A physicist she'd consulted with at MIT at Sarah's insistence in the run-up to the show theorized that the shapes could have been artifacts of a solar storm around the time of the celestial event the Starry Wisdom church called the Red Equinox. Becca knew the real cause of the phenomenon and it was much stranger than that, though she'd sworn to never reveal it publicly when SPECTRA had conscripted her into their investigation after confiscating her cameras and computers. Though her relationship with the agency had got off to a rocky start when they raided her apartment and abducted her with a helicopter, she'd worked a variety of assignments for them in the years following what they called the First Incursion Event. Some of the rank-and-file officers from those days now held senior positions and even considered her a hero, but that didn't make it any easier to get permission for the exhibit. The solar-storm cover story had greased the wheels.

Now here was this man off the street, possibly Exhibit A of their fears: *what if the images trigger somebody?*

He turned to face her, the scent of marijuana wafting from his clothes and hair, his eyes bloodshot. Maybe she was overestimating the significance of the encounter. Had she really just walked away from a sale to babysit a wandering stoner? Where was Sarah when she needed her? She scanned the crowd for the woman's platinum-blonde hair and spotted it at the center of a small ring of patrons.

Too far away to easily get her attention, and probably best not to do further financial damage.

"You took this picture?" The man looked her over for the first time, his eyes narrowing with suspicion.

Becca nodded. "How did you hear about the show?"

"I seen a postcard for it on a corkboard at Harvard Square. Stopped me in my tracks. I couldn't stop lookin' at it, so I put it in my pocket, took it home. Couldn't stop thinkin' about it. Took it to work with me ... to the pub. Asked some people if they ever seen anything like it. Nobody did."

"But you have?"

"Yeah." He scratched his scruffy chin. "It's like ... imagine if a big thing happened to you in your life. A big, crazy thing. Like you were standing in line at the bank when it got robbed. Or you had a one-night stand with a movie star. Or got abducted by aliens or some shit. And then you forgot all about it. But years later, somebody shows you a picture from that day, and you're like: how'd I forget that? How the fuck did I forget the wildest thing that ever happened to me? That would be pretty crazy, right?"

Becca swallowed and found her throat was dry. "It would be."

"That's how this feels. Wicked fucked up."

And maybe he *was* high, but he sure didn't act like it. He was too animated, too agitated, his eyes darting around the room as he spoke, checking the exits and the crowd whenever they weren't being tugged like ball bearings toward the magnet of the giant photo print.

"You can see a lot more detail at full size. Makes my head ache. Is that the price tag?"

"Yeah. Crazy, huh?"

"I've been staring at this picture for the past week trying to remember. Counting the days to the exhibit so I could ask you about it. But I can't imagine anyone paying money to see that fuckin' thing on their wall every day. It's a monster, right? Or a swarm of them, getting ready to break through a brick wall and eat people. Ain't that right? You seen it, too. In 2019?"

"You sure know how to cut to the chase. What's your name?"

"Dan Mulvaney."

"I'm Becca."

"I know. Like I said, I've been staring at your postcard for a week."

"Are you high right now, Dan?"

"Why, you want some? You got a nose ring with your fancy clothes, so I know you party. Or are you implying that I'm of unsound mind?"

"No, I'm just trying to figure out where your head is at because you're attracting some attention here. You seem a little nervous. Maybe we could talk another time when I'm not in the middle of a show. I'd be interested to hear more about your exper—"

"I'm not high. I'm just trying to take the edge off. You gonna pretend you don't know what I'm talking about?"

"There's no need to raise your voice. I want to help. Are you looking for someone? You keep looking at the exit like you're expecting someone."

"They'll be here. They've been following me since I started remembering."

"Who?"

"The hounds. I call 'em that because they catch your scent and don't let up. Just wait til they get a whiff of you. You remember all of it, don't you? Don't lie. I see it in your eyes. You remember every goddamn thing."

His voice modulated on the last two words. It sounded like someone had switched on an electronic effect, making the words ring with metallic resonance. Becca instinctively took a step back, the old instincts kicking in. She angled her body away from the man and caught sight of movement in the corner of her eye. During the events of the Red Equinox, she'd encountered cultists with strange powers. The modulation in the man's voice prepared her for the possibility that he was more than human, but what she saw out of the corner of her eye was far stranger than the sound he'd made.

The east wall of the gallery was a plate-glass window overlooking foot traffic on Newbury Street where a pale shade of February dusk was settling on the city. The street lamps had yet to come on, and it wasn't dark enough yet for the full-spectrum track lights of the gallery to be reflected back at her from the windows, but something at the street level—the high-tech headlights of a passing car?—sent a cascade of bright angles rippling across the glass, like laser beams refracted through ice.

Only, that wasn't quite right. The shards of light moved in a way that was more animal than mechanical, reminding her of a porcupine's quills, if a porcupine were the size of a compact car. There for a fleeting second and then gone, it sent a tingle down her spine and she turned away from the sight as she had the sound of the man's voice, nearly knocking over a waiter carrying a tray of bacon-wrapped scallops in the process.

The young man flashed her an annoyed look, then realizing she was the star of the show, fixed his face and carried on.

"Did you see them?" Mulvaney asked. "You did, just now, didn't you? Out there on the street." But before she could answer he was looking away again, scanning the room for exits. "They found me again. I gotta bounce."

"Who found you?"

"I told you. The hounds. They've been running me down ever since I saw your postcard. This is *your* fault. You must know something about them. I mean, you *did* take all these pictures. I don't see *them* in your pictures but I see the ones who sent them. Pieces, anyway. Azathoth … Yog Sothoth …"

Becca's nostrils flared at the sounds. She could feel her fight-or-flight reactions ramping up.

"Yeah, I know their names. Some of their spells, too. Wish I didn't, but I do. It comes to me in my sleep. I keep a notebook next to the bed."

She could see Sarah now, moving toward her through the crowd. A moment ago she'd wanted the gallery owner to take notice of this man who was quickly becoming a disruption. But that was before he'd begun talking. A whole five minutes ago, when she'd thought the great horrors of her life were firmly ensconced in the past. Now here they were, bubbling over again. Just when she'd got her act together and summoned the courage to move forward and maybe even allow herself to reap some rewards from the darkness and pain that had fueled her art. But who was she kidding? Of course she couldn't have that without summoning the darkness again.

"Is everything all right, Becca?" Sarah was appraising Dan Mulvaney, ruling out profit and calculating threat level in the space of the half-second it took her to scan him top to bottom.

"Sarah, this is my uncle Dan. I didn't think he'd make it to the show. I'm afraid he's not feeling well." As an aside, "He's not so good with crowds. Is there a quieter exit he could use? A door that doesn't let out onto Newbury Street?"

Sarah nodded at a hallway beyond the restrooms. "All the way down the end, past my office on the left. Make sure the door latches behind him. And don't dally. I'm going to go see if I can save one of your sales before this place starts clearing out. Remember, dear—they're not just buying art. They're buying a moment they had with the artist."

"I know. I'm sorry. I'll only be another minute."

It was dark outside when Becca shouldered open the steel door that let out onto a cramped alley surrounded by the mostly windowless backs of brick buildings. The thin sport coat she wore over her black blouse did almost nothing to keep out the chill of air so dry it almost smelled of snow.

"Why did you say I'm your uncle?"

"To get you out the back door before that thing finds you."

"You *did* see it!"

"I saw something. I don't know what. Where do you live?"

"Forest Hills."

"Can you get home on your own?"

"What do I look like, a child?"

"No. You look like someone afraid for his life. I know people who might be able to help, but ..."

"But what?"

"It's complicated. You might only want to call them as a last resort. How much do you remember about wha—"

A high-pitched whine sped toward Becca's ears like a bullet. It rose in volume and fell in pitch so fast that before she could turn her head toward the source the alley was alive with vibrations. It came on like an earthquake. Trash cans danced across the buzzing asphalt. A fire escape shook so violently she thought it would come free of its moorings and crush her. An icy web of white light spread over the air, shifting, folding, and gnashing like the jaws of a great beast.

A shard of light passed through her arm, chilling her marrow. Then the frenetic geometry converged on Mulvaney. He ducked and rolled away from it, then launched himself off the ground, palm out, striking Becca squarely on the chest and sending her careening backward through the open door. She landed on the carpet, and before she could regain her feet, he'd slammed the heavy door shut. Something thudded against it hard enough that she expected the steel plate to dent. She rose and pressed her hands to the latch bar, expecting resistance, but the door swung freely open when she pushed, and she fell through the opening into an empty alley just as a gust of air was sucked out of the space, leaving a silent vacuum in its wake. There was no trace of Dan Mulvaney or whatever had hunted him.

Becca worked her jaw until her ears popped. An empty bottle from one of the overturned trash cans rolled marimba chimes across the pavement, and the first flakes of a flurry settled in her hair.

"*Becca!*" Sarah called from the far end of the hall where art connoisseurs still chattered and sipped cabernet as if the fabric of the cosmos hadn't recently been rent in their vicinity. "Come *on,* dear. We just sold your centerpiece!"

The rest of the night was a whirlwind. The first big sale caught fire around the room and many polite handshakes and evasive anecdotes about her inspiration later, Becca was astonished to find all but two of the photos tagged as sold, the buyers milling out onto the street in search of nightcaps and desert. Tomorrow the pieces would be packed up and shipped to houses and apartments she could only dream of living in, but tonight she was assured the fattest check she'd ever seen for her art. She'd done well enough as a research photographer scouting locations for private clients over the years, and her government work, weird as it was, had provided a significant if sporadic supplement. But this was the first time she'd sold work that was close to her heart. The experience left her reeling. Exhausted and elevated all at once by both the social buzz and the brush with danger that had interceded on her opening night.

It was hard to focus on whatever Sarah was rambling on about as the crowd thinned out. Becca was relieved that her patron and champion was visibly happy with how the night had panned out, but her thoughts were with the mysterious Dan Mulvaney.

"Congratulations, dear. Stop by tomorrow and we'll settle up. And give my regards to your uncle." Sarah winked, signaling she was in on the joke and knew what the cat had dragged in was likely a lover. An amusing incident in hindsight, but only from the higher ground of a successful show.

"Thanks," Becca said. "I'll do that. Do you mind if I leave through the back door?"

"Don't want to be waylaid by lingering admirers? Suit yourself."

Becca had avoided the wine throughout the night, and her mind felt sharper as soon as she stepped outside of the overheated gallery. She tucked her scarf into her wool overcoat and looked around at the grimy alley, the overturned trash cans. *Something* had knocked them over. But the only tracks in the thin scrim of snow were the tiny prints of a rat.

Something glistened on the concrete curb, an almost phosphorescent shade of blue. She stooped and examined it: wet liquid, like paint.

Nothing obvious in the spilled trash barrels accounted for the substance, and she abstained from touching it. Instead, she took her phone from her pocket and snapped a few shots, wishing as she did so that she'd brought her infrared camera.

She took two shots with flash and two without. Then she pulled up her quick contacts and tapped *Brooks*. He picked up on the third ring.

"Hey, Becca. Listen, I'm sorry I didn't make it to your show."

Before he could deliver his prepared excuse, she cut him off. "You're forgiven. That's not why I'm calling."

"Really?"

"Yeah. I would have said it mattered if it did."

"Okay...."

"I don't mean ... I just mean that it's probably better you didn't come."

"I get it. Things have been weird since ... I shouldn't have told you how I felt. I'm sorry—"

"No. Jason. I just mean I would have been even more nervous if you were there. That's all. Can we please have that conversation another time? It's not why I called. Something weird happened tonight. Like *weird* weird."

"Go on."

"Can you find out if a Dan Mulvaney was one of the people exposed and processed by SPECTRA in the 2019 incursion?"

The house, a slate-blue cape on Wenham Street in Forest Hills, wasn't hard to find. SPECTRA was still keeping tabs on all of the witnesses from 2019, no matter where they lived now, but Dan Mulvaney had stayed at the same address. A dyed-in-the-wool Bostonian, he'd worked for the MBTA before going into construction. He lived alone in the house he grew up in. His mother had moved to a hospice facility right after Christmas. Becca knew she shouldn't be surprised by how much info Brooks was able to pull up with a few clicks, but it did make her wonder how much they still knew about her own life.

The morning after the exhibit, she took the Orange Line to the last stop and walked the three blocks to the Mulvaney house, a route she'd mapped in advance on her phone. At a glance, the house looked well maintained, the white porch railings repainted not too many seasons ago, but mounting the stairs she saw that the Christmas wreath—still tacked to the front door in February—was dry and brown and had shed most of its needles on the deck boards beside a half-empty bag of ice melt. What windows she could see from this angle were blinded by curtains and other fabrics, giving the house a dark, un-lived-in appearance. There was no car in the driveway, but a single-car garage stood at the end of a cracked concrete slab. From the telephone wires, a flock of starlings regarded her silently. Boston winters had grown warmer in recent years, and it seemed like the birds never entirely left. Becca plucked dog hair from the sleeve of her wool coat and rang the doorbell.

The curtain in the nearest window shifted. A moment later she heard the sound of a deadbolt turning. Dan Mulvaney squinted at her through the narrow gap as if she were the Queen of England. He was unshaven, dressed in gray sweatpants and a Celtics T-shirt. In the daylight, she could see gray in the ginger stubble that dusted his jawline. He was older than she'd first estimated, or maybe just more haggard and hollowed-out after a rough night. But he didn't smell like alcohol or pot, so at least there was that.

She almost retreated, wondering what the hell she was thinking, visiting a man she'd met the night before when he crashed her show, raving about being hunted. She should've explained more of this to Brooks and brought him along for backup, but she hadn't wanted to say too much the phone for fear that the agency might swoop down on this troubled soul before she had time to learn what was happening to him and what it had to do with her.

"Becca. What are you doin' here? How did you know where I live?" He looked up and down the street as if he either shared her fears about SPECTRA or was still keeping an eye out for whatever had pursued him in the alley behind Newbury Street.

"You told me your name and that you lived in Forest Hills. I'm just glad to see you're okay. You disappeared so fast last night, I thought …"

"You thought what? That they ate me?"

"It sounds crazy when you say it, but I've seen some weird shit in my time."

"You wanna come in?" His voice rang as he reached the end of the sentence, as if metallic bangles buzzed in sympathetic vibration, throwing off harmonic sparks.

"Your voice …" Becca said.

"It's doing it again, huh?" he whispered, touching his throat.

"What is it?"

He opened the door wider and stepped aside. The interior was dark, cave-like. "I don't know, but you should come in. It doesn't happen as much if I stay in this room."

Becca reluctantly stepped over the threshold and looked around. The room was draped in heavy fabrics. Bed comforters of various patterns and colors, some of them stained and torn. They were tacked to the ceiling and walls and bundled in the corners. There were no chairs, but a couch lined one wall, and something that might have been an upright piano was draped with more blankets. A sleeping bag, rolled up lengthwise, was spread along the bottom of the longest wall, reminding her of sandbags arranged against a flood. She'd thought the room resembled a cave, but now that she stood in the center of it Becca felt more like she'd set foot in some kind of white-trash harem tent.

The man was clearly troubled, but she lacked concrete details about his mental well-being and personal history. Her mind went to the slim folding knife she kept clipped in a pocket of her pants and the pepper spray in her camera bag. But the greater reassurance was his demeanor. She didn't know what Dan Mulvaney looked like on a good day, but today he looked too scared and depleted for violence. The high-voltage agitation he'd radiated at their first encounter was burned off.

"Have a seat. I'd offer you some coffee, but there's too many angles in the kitchen and I'm already feeling weird from opening the door. I need to stay in here for a while. Does my voice still sound weird?"

"No, not like it did on the porch."

"Good. You could make some coffee yourself if you want to."

"No, thanks. I'm good. Do you live here alone?"

"Yeah. I grew up in this house. I got a brother in Delaware. Nieces and a nephew. But I moved back in here with my mom after Ricky moved for his job. My dad died a decade ago. Leukemia. Now my mom's in hospice with Alzheimer's and heart disease."

"I'm sorry to hear that. My parents are gone, too. So, what's the deal with all the blankets?"

"I have to cover up all of the hard surfaces. The angles. That's how they get through—they use angles. Curves throw them off. It took me a while to figure that out. Like, I can mostly walk in the woods and not see them. Not too many straight lines in nature. But that place last night was too much. All the glass and frames. City architecture. I knew it was a risk but I didn't know how else to find you after I saw your postcard."

Becca looked around at the fabrics with a new appreciation of how thorough he'd been at making sure every corner was rounded. "Your voice doesn't change in here?"

Dan shook his head. "I don't know how it's related, but I'm pretty sure they use sound as a way to get physical. Like, they can be right next to you, but you can't tell. They could be drooling on your neck and you wouldn't even know it if they stay on their own side of reality. Because they have no substance. But if there's angles and the right kind of echoes, it makes them tangible. You know what I mean?"

"I think so. I probably wouldn't if I hadn't had a similar experience."

"The stuff in your pictures."

Becca nodded. "It makes sense that sound would play a role. That's how it started in 2019. How much do you remember of what happened back then?"

"Not much. I was an engineer on the T back then. I don't drive trains anymore. Had to get out of the tunnels. There's a whole piece of my memory from that time, the time of the terror attacks, that's blacked out. Like those CIA pages they take a sharpie to. They told me I was exposed to something like a nerve agent. Affected my memory. But I don't know if I believe that. They gave me some treatment for it and I never had any side effects till now. Is that what this is with my voice? A side effect from back then?"

"That's what I'd like to find out. You remember the cult that was in the news back then?"

"Sure. Church of Starry Wisdom."

"They developed an acoustic weapon. The man who made it, his name was Darius Marlowe, and he was a student at MIT. He called it the *Voice Box of the Gods*. It was like a larynx made from bovine cells and electronics. It was designed to produce sounds the human voice is no longer capable of but that supposedly were used by ancient people to chant magic spells. I know how that sounds, but I've seen it firsthand." She shrugged. "Maybe there's a scientific basis to what people used to call magic. I don't know anything about your own beliefs ... but the practical effect of Marlowe's machine was to tear a hole in reality and let predatory entities into our world from the other side. He thought they were gods. I still don't know what they were, but anyone who heard the sound would find themselves among them. See them and be seen *by* them. The Voice summoned them. And if you heard it, you were their prey. Marlow set it off on a subway train, the Red Line. Soon there were incursions from the other side all over the city, but given your line of work, I'd guess you were exposed in that first event. Do the words 'Red Equinox' mean anything to you?"

"I don't know. It almost rings a bell."

"It's the name of an astrological event that was important to the Starry Wisdom cult. They timed the attacks to coincide with it because the membrane between our world and the other was especially thin at that time. The two worlds were aligned. They said the stars were right."

"You know a lot about it. Were you exposed too?"

"The things from the other side had been gaining substance for a while when they started showing up in my infrared photos of abandoned buildings where the cult had been active."

"So you work for the government? You don't strike me as the type."

"Not back when this all started. I was an art student and an Urbex photographer."

"What's that?"

"Urban explorers. People whose hobby is exploring abandoned urban spaces. That's how I got tangled up in all this. Well, sort of. My family also has some entanglements with the occult, truth be told."

"And I thought *my* life was weird." Mulvaney laughed. Becca was glad to hear that he could. He seemed relieved to at least be in the company of another crazy person.

"The thing is, Dan ... I thought all this was over. When the government got involved in shutting down the church and stopping the incursion, I did end up working with them. I even deliberately exposed myself to the sounds so I could see what I was fighting. The whole story is too long to tell, but we finished it. And we helped people like you to forget it ever happened. I'll be honest: I found your house by getting in touch with a friend at the agency that handled the crisis. They're called SPECTRA. What they told you was treatment for a nerve agent was actually a drug called Nepenthe. It was designed to heal the part of your brain that was exposed in the attack, the part that was activated and could see the monsters. It worked so well it made people forget everything they'd seen from that other world. But now you're starting to remember. And you're apparently being pursued by something from the other side. I feel responsible because my photo might have triggered this. And if it's happening to you, it could be happening to other people who were exposed back then."

"You're telling me an awful lot. You planning to wipe my memory again?"

Becca chuckled nervously. "That's not my area. But you may need their help. Or maybe my friend who I trust can help you. But it's only fair you should know what you're dealing with if we do have to bring in SPECTRA. They tend to put national security ahead of individuals. I learned that the hard way."

"You shouldn't feel responsible for what's happening to me. It started before I saw your postcard. It started back in November. Before my mom went into hospice when I signed up for a drug trial to make a few extra bucks for Christmas."

"Wait, *what?* What was the name of the drug?"

"Liaotrevex. The money was good—the study was funded by a Chinese pharma company. They said it had to do with long-term memory recovery. I qualified because my own memory was full of holes, and I wanted to support the research because my mom's memory was failing. But once I started getting flooded with images from 2019, it was like I got stuck there. It was terrifying."

Becca took a pen and notebook from her camera bag and jotted down the name of the drug and the company that had funded the study. "Did you meet any of the other subjects? Do you know if anyone else had a similar experience? Horrific memories they'd forgotten from that year?"

"No. All of my appointments were alone. No one else in the waiting room. They set it up that way so the data doesn't get contaminated because memory is such a subjective thing. Like dreams. At first, that's what I thought they were—dreams I was remembering. But it kept getting more and more vivid until I knew they were memories. I started remembering normal things from that time, too. Things that got blurred, I guess, by that ... what did you call it?"

"Nepenthe."

"Yeah. Son of a bitch. And all this time I thought I was exposed to a chemical weapon in the tunnels. Guess I should be relieved, but this is worse. I think I'd prefer nerve damage to getting hunted by these ... *things.*"

"Did you talk to the researchers about what you were seeing? Not just the memories but the hounds?"

"No, the hounds started showing up after I completed the trials. They're not really dogs. At least I don't think so. There's just something about them that reminds me of dogs. Something about how they move. Like dogs made out of glass shards, but then sometimes they seem more humanlike. I can never get a good look at them. And the way they track you, it's like how bloodhounds run down fugitives. That's what I am now—a fugitive in my own life. The more my voice changes, the closer they get. When I started taking the drugs at Harvard, it was different. Almost nice, remembering."

"How so?"

Dan had taken a small glass pipe and a bag of weed out of a Tupperware container while he talked. Becca wondered if he'd chosen the container for its rounded curves. Now he packed the bowl, struck a lighter, and took a toke. From his perch on the piano bench, he offered her the pipe. She shook her head and waited for him to exhale a long, fragrant plume.

"Hope you don't mind. I've been under a lot of stress, as I'm sure you can imagine."

"Of course. You were talking about remembering?"

"It's hard to explain. I was kind of excited at the beginning about what things I might recall from childhood. I had a pretty happy childhood, but like anybody you forget most of it. Lot of things fall away as you grow up. Fall out of your life. Sports. Music. Even church. I used to be an altar boy, but now I'm not even a believer. Used to sing in the church choir when I was a kid.

"Anyways, like I said, I didn't really get farther back than 2019 with the memories, but I did start thinking more about the pieces of me that got lost along the way. Turning my mind to the past. I don't know how it happens but you end up in your 40s and realize there's nothing left but work in your life. So I started thinking about the piano again and singing, which I hadn't done in twenty years. But also, like I started seeing signs everywhere pointing me back to it. Like the universe telling you to do something, what you're *meant* to do. You know?"

"Is that your piano?" Becca gestured at the blanket-draped shape against the far wall.

"My mom's piano. She taught me when I was a kid. I wasn't never very good, but back in November, I started hearing songs on the radio that I used to play and sing. Songs that didn't used to get much airplay, all of a sudden they were back. I listen to a lot of talk radio, some classic rock. But I'd get in my truck, turn on the engine, and the station would be changed from where I left it. Next thing you know, I'm listening to some hymn we used to sing at Sunday services or some Irish folk song my mom taught me. Then the birds came, the starlings."

"I saw some on the wires when I came up your driveway just now. I thought it was a little odd. Birds in February."

Mulvaney pointed at a dim square of light shining through one of the blankets that covered a window. "You can see the telephone wires from the piano bench through that window. They line up like a musical staff. So after I started poking around on the keyboard again, the birds would come and line up a melody for me to play. It felt like a little game I was playing with God. Almost brought my faith back because they sounded like real melodies, and it happened so regular it was hard to call it a coincidence. I realized I was starting to write music. Or the birds were writing music *through* me. Or something was writing music through the birds and me. It was eerie—the experience *and* the music. But it was really music, not random notes. I even figured out how to tell by a bird's posture if it wanted me to play a flat or a sharp. Pretty fuckin' schizo, right?"

Becca gave him a sad smile. "I've been accused of the same, so I don't judge."

Mulvaney nodded, took another toke on his pipe, then set the spent thing down on the shrouded piano. "By then I was having dreams, too. Dreaming words and colors, mostly, with the new music playing in the background. It was always playing in my head by then. When I was awake, when I was asleep, when I was at work. It was around middle of January I started dreaming these … *lyrics*. Not words but syllables. I started keeping a notepad by the bed and writing them down."

Becca rubbed her forearms. She felt chilly in spite of the ridiculously well-insulated surroundings. She, too, had gone through a phase of singing in her sleep when the Great Old One, Cthulhu, had reached out to her dreaming mind from the ocean floor.

"That's when my voice started to change. When I would sing those weird syllables, harmonize them with the piano tones. The birds got agitated as fuck when I got going. My mom's knick-knacks would buzz on the shelves. That's also when the hounds started showing up, attracted to the sounds. But it wasn't like you whistle and a dog comes. I had the feeling more like the sound caused cracks in the air that they could smell me through, like what you said happened from that boom box of the gods."

"It sounds a lot like that," Becca said.

"I got freaked and stopped playing the piano. I'd made some recordings of the songs I used to play when I was a kid, but I didn't record the starling songs. I was afraid to. The last song I recorded, when I listened back to it, there were places where my voice sounded like it had metal in it, and like a flute in the background. That's when

I covered up the piano and quit. It was starting to have an effect on the house."

"What kind of effect?"

"In the basement. I'll show you," he said getting up from the piano bench. "But we have to be quick or they'll come. There's no blankets on the walls down there."

The basement smelled like sawdust and gasoline. Smells that reminded Becca of her father. But there was something else underneath, a scent both florid and musky. It made her close her mouth and slow her breathing for fear of lining her throat with something alien and infectious.

The bulb at the foot of the stairs was too weak to throw more than a dim circle on the floor. Mulvaney plugged in a utility lamp on a tripod and the room came alive with a blast of pure white light that drove all but the deepest shadows from the pockmarked concrete walls.

The space was mostly empty except for a neat workbench, an antiquated water heater, and a washer and dryer in the corner.

"I stopped doing laundry down here," Mulvaney said. "I do it in the tub now when I have to. Dry it on a clothesline."

"What *is* that?" Becca could barely focus on his talk about laundry. She guessed he'd covered the bathroom with a similar array of blankets. He would have had to. Everyone needs to use a bathroom. And if angles and hard surfaces enabled the phenomenon ... the thought of bathroom mirrors and tiles gave her a shiver. But the details of his daily routine were irrelevant. The idea that anyone could sleep in a house infested with this iridescent blue ichor undulating on the walls like a quivering jellyfish was nauseating.

"I was hoping *you* would know. It started like mold or fungus. Dusty, like spores. But the more it grew, the more liquid it got. Reminds you of an internal organ, don't it? Like it's breathing real slow ... the patch of it on *that* wall connected to the patch on *this* wall. Like it's one living organism taking over the whole foundation of the house."

Becca realized her head was nodding agreement but she couldn't manage to get words out, subconsciously holding her breath against the fetid stench.

She took her camera from the canvas bag at her hip. "How long did it take to spread this far?"

"Couple of months. It was slow for a long time, then one night it just exploded."

"Exponential growth. Like a virus."

"I think it was my voice that sped it up." His words were husky, and she realized he feared powering the phenomena with full-throated speech.

Becca approached the wall where the stuff was most active, the hot light of the work lamp blasting at her back. She shot a series of photos from various distances, then angled the lamp away and took another set in partial shadow. "How do you mean? That your voice sped it up."

"I told you about how I was learning those melodies from the birds and the syllables from my dreams. I had those songs running loops in my head all day when I was away from the piano. I was probably always humming and singing under my breath by then. Doing the dishes, shoveling snow, folding the laundry. I probably wasn't even aware of what my mouth was doing most of the time. But this is where I was the first time I noticed my voice changing. At first, I thought the mold was active down here because of the damp and it being underground, but now I think maybe it was the sound of my voice echoing around this concrete box that got it started."

Becca snapped another photo and listened to the click of the shutter reverberating around the room, sharp and wet. "What if it isn't about angles versus curves?" she said. "Not exactly, anyway. Maybe it's about the acoustics. Curved spaces have less sound reflection. The waves die out sooner. Your living room is practically soundproofed with that treatment you gave it. Maybe that's why you're safe there."

"Guess that makes some sense," he said, still keeping his voice low. "What do you think your pictures will show?"

"I don't know. That's why I'm taking them. You saw how the infrared sensor in the camera revealed things that weren't visible to the naked eye in the days leading up to the Red Equinox. What we can see with our eyes here is bad enough, but if it's even farther along in the range we can't see, we need to know that as soon as possible."

197

Mulvaney pressed the heel of his hand into his eye socket and swayed on his feet.

"What is it, Dan? What's happening? Are you okay?"

He let out a low moan. "You don't hear that?"

"Hear what?" To Becca, the room was silent except for the sound of the blue ichor dripping from a pipe it had overrun.

"*Shush,*" Mulvaney begged. "Your voice is echoing around my head like broken glass. *Jeeesus.*" He drew out the word, and as it trailed off Becca detected a halo of harmonics ringing out around it.

The throbbing membrane on the wall reacted to the sound, leaping up in jagged spikes. Becca recoiled, grabbing at Mulvaney's forearm and pulling him away from the volatile substance. A jutting crystalline spear reached the limit of its range mere inches from Becca's thigh, splashing droplets of the iridescent liquid on her pants. It burned through the fabric like acid, sizzling on her skin. She gritted her teeth against the pain, determined not to add any more sound to the cacophony ricocheting around Mulvaney's head.

Is he causing this? Is his extra-perception amplifying even my speech? Using it as kindling for the fire?

She persisted in tugging him toward the stairs, trying not to think about the wisps of purple smoke rising from her leg, and resisting the urge to press her palm to the wound, which would only drive the poison deeper into her. Mulvaney snapped out of his fugue and followed. By now the substance was erupting from the wall like lava and pooling across the floor. They mounted the stairs seconds before it reached them, clambered up into the hall and through the curtain of blankets to the relative safety of the insulated living room.

Mulvaney fell onto the couch, hands clapped over his ears, eyes shut, swaying in place, waiting for the torment to subside.

Even away from the manifestation and the reflective environment in which it thrived Becca was afraid to speak. She took up her notebook and pen, jotted an urgent message, and shook him by the shoulder to get his attention. *We need to get out of here. I think we triggered it, accelerated its development. Do you have a car?*

He read the note and nodded, took the pen from her, and wrote: *In the garage. Where do we go?*

Becca: *Someplace safer than here. I'll drive. Trust me. Get the keys and a towel.*

♦

"Jason, it's me. I need a safe place to take this guy. There's another incursion happening and he's ground zero for it. It's sonic."

"Whoa. Slow down. What do you mean it's sonic?"

"The way they're coming through. It's related to his voice, like before. But it's also different. I took photos but I haven't been able to look at them yet. The address you gave me ... Something's taken hold in his basement. I don't know if you should send a team in to contain it. I just want to get him somewhere safe and I don't know what SPECTRA would do to him. He trusts me."

"Okay. I hear you. If whatever's going on at his house isn't going to eat the neighborhood, we can maybe keep it to ourselves a little longer. Good thing you called my burner phone. Where are you?"

"I'm driving. He's in the back seat with a towel wrapped around his head. His voice has been prying open a crack and letting something through, giving it substance. But even *my* voice was starting to contribute to it. Maybe because I used to have the same ability he has now? I'm scared, Jason. I'm afraid it's coming back."

"I'm gonna text you a map link. Go to that address. I'll meet you there after I swing by Mulvaney's house and make sure it's secure. Just wait for me in the parking lot. What are you driving?"

"A red SUV. Where are you sending us? Is it a SPECTRA facility?"

"Not exactly. It's a university lab. Northeastern. We funded it and use it sometimes, but it's off the grid. I'll meet you there. Keep the radio off in that car."

"No shit."

♦

The place looked like a warehouse, a brick block with no windows at the end of a mostly deserted parking lot. It was raining when Becca parked the SUV. She didn't see Brooks' car, so she kept the engine running for warmth and waited. In the backseat, Mulvaney leaned forward and straightened the towel wrapped around his head. It looked like a turban, held on with a winding of duct tape. It covered his eyes as well as his ears, mostly because it had slipped down during the drive. He didn't seem to mind. She imagined it was somewhat snug and reassuring in there. More so than her experience with the black nylon bag agents had yanked over her head back when SPECTRA landed a helicopter on her roof in 2019.

This was all feeling too familiar. They had sacrificed too much along the way for this to be happening again. She had sacrificed loved ones and pieces of her sanity to rid the world of these monsters and, though he didn't talk about it, she knew Brooks had too.

As if summoned by the thought of him, his car pulled into the lot, circled around, and parked beside her. Becca reached between the seats and adjusted the towel on Mulvaney's head, tugging it up to reveal his eyes. She couldn't help thinking he resembled a farm animal wondering if it was being led to slaughter. She pushed the thought away, tried to telegraph a reassuring look, then unbuckled her seatbelt and stepped out to meet Brooks between the two vehicles.

Brooks bent over and squinted through the rain-glazed window, gave Mulvaney a two-fingered wave.

"How exactly did he find you?"

"He showed up at my gallery show. Saw a postcard that triggered his memories of '19. Whatever's happening to him it's accelerating. I don't know if that's from proximity to me or something else. He's dangerous." She looked at the long monolithic building as she spoke, moisture beading in her hair. "What is this place? Why no windows? He had them all covered up with blankets at his house. Did you go there?"

"I did. Didn't go down to the basement, but at a glance the place looks stable for now. You have the photos you took there?"

"On my camera card. We can view them on my laptop. It's in the car."

Brooks nodded. He looked like he wasn't sleeping well, but then again, he'd always looked like that as far back as she could remember. At least whenever circumstances brought the two of them together. They had tried to hang out a few times outside the context of an operation, but they'd both found it weird to be in each other's company without the adrenaline, the cosmic upheaval, the taste of the promise of death. Last time, they drank a little too much to compensate, and there'd been a moment ... not a kiss exactly, but a proximity that could have become one. It was complicated between them. She used to wonder if there was a Stockholm syndrome component to the attraction, but he had become an ally very soon after they'd met as adversaries. On the other hand, his ex-wife was her ex-therapist, so ... Complicated.

She knew a small but excited part of her was weirdly grateful for this new calamity because it gave them something to focus on that made more sense than their relationship. How crazy was that?

"It's a test lab for wave emitting electronics. Antennas, drones ... We tested the dragonfly here. Reason I picked it for your current predicament? There's an anechoic chamber. You know what that is?"

Becca nodded with dawning comprehension and the hint of a smile. "Great minds think alike. I was trying to remember what you call those places. A room designed to snuff out all sound, right?"

"That's right, a perfectly silent space. I figure that's what he was trying to approximate without realizing it in his living room."

"He didn't understand the acoustic aspect of it," Becca said. "He thought it was all about angles. He thought if he could surround himself with curved surfaces, he could keep the beasts at bay. He'd worked out that much from experience. Do you really think it will be safe? What if we're wrong?"

"We may be. If we're wrong, we throw a blanket over him and try to get him out fast. A theory is all I have right now, but it might buy us some time to figure out our next move."

"You haven't told anyone at the agency?"

"Not yet. But one thing I've learned: never assume they don't already know."

"That's comforting."

"Just being honest. Anyway ... are you going to introduce us?"

"Yeah. I bet you two would hit it off if you could actually have a conversation. He's a Masshole, too."

Brooks laughed. "I believe the term you're looking for is townie, darlin'."

201

"Sure." She opened the back door of the car. "Dan, this is my friend Jason Brooks. You can trust him."

They were fine until Mulvaney set eyes on the room. Every square foot of the place—the walls, the ceiling, even the floor—was crowded with spiky cones. It was an orgy of angles, an endless grid of gray stalagmites and stalactites. He shuffled back through the door frame, nearly knocking Brooks over, digging in his heels like a condemned man facing the execution chamber.

A porous metal plank extended from the entrance to the center of the room. Becca walked across it and waved for Mulvaney to follow. It was unsettling how her footsteps made no sound. The air had a dead quality. It seemed strange that it could even carry the light waves from the LED pin spots mounted high up in what would have been the corners. But in this chamber, everything was a corner, and nothing was. At least she felt safe enough to speak without the fear that her own voice would rebound and resonate in the peculiar way that fed raw material to whatever metamorphosis the man was undergoing.

"I know it looks like your worst nightmare, Dan. So many angles. But there are so many, they cancel each other out. Don't try to talk, but I bet you could do it safely in here."

Mulvaney stared around in wonder, then took a few tentative steps across the plank.

"It's a short-term fix," Brooks said, "until we figure something else out. It isn't booked for any tests this weekend, so I would say you could even sleep here. But you probably don't want to. The absence of reflected sound messes with you after a while. You lose your sense of balance, inner-ear equilibrium ... all that stuff depends on audio feedback we get from our environment. Stuff we're not even aware of most of the time, but once you take it away, it's not long before you start going crazy. You should be okay for a while, though. Just warning you what to expect. You'll become hyper-aware of the sound of your own heartbeat, your breathing, your eardrums moving when you rub your fingers together. Like I said, short-term solution. But you can take the towel off."

Mulvaney unwound the towel and handed it to Becca. His ginger hair was a sweaty bird's nest and his freckles stood out starkly against his pallid skin. He looked disoriented, like a trauma victim, in shock. Brooks held up a small device between thumb and forefinger. A copper-colored earbud.

"I'd like you to put this in your ear, Dan, so that we can talk to you. It receives on a frequency that the room will allow because the transmitter is inside here with you. If you have any problems, just pull it out and I'll turn it off. Okay?"

Mulvaney nodded, still afraid to speak. Brooks closed the spike-studded door and turned to Becca. "You're right. He has that same look in his eyes as most of the poor bastards we treated in 'nineteen."

"He says he's remembering more of it every day. Whatever they gave him in that sleep study, it seems to have undone the effects of the Nepenthe."

Brooks led her to what looked like the control room of a recording studio, only without the big glass window. Instead, there was an array of widescreen monitors. On one of them, she could see various angles of the anechoic chamber. Mulvaney was seated on the metal plank with his arms wrapped around his knees, staring up at the spiked walls, the copper earbud catching the light when he turned his head. Brooks took a seat in a swivel chair and pressed a comm button. "Can you hear me?"

He released the button and Mulvaney's voice came through the speakers, thin but otherwise natural: "Loud and clear."

Brooks pulled up a computer program on an adjacent monitor and selected a few options. "Talk to me a little more, Dan. I'm putting some processing on your mic. Just a precaution in case your voice morphs again. I don't think you'll be able to have an effect coming out of our speakers in here, but I'm gonna scramble you a little just in case. You can say anything while I set it up. Pledge of Allegiance, the alphabet, song lyrics ... I just need to get some levels and make sure we can still understand you."

There was a pause long enough to make Becca wonder if he'd heard Brooks' last transmission, but then Mulvaney's voice rang through the speakers, singing in a tone so pure and sweet, it caught her off guard.

O Danny Boy, the pipes, the pipes are calling
From glen to glen and down the mountainside.
The summer's gone and all the roses falling.
'Tis you, 'tis you must go and I must bide.

Brooks clicked and scrolled. With each parameter he adjusted, the voice in the speakers grew more alien. At first, Becca was afraid that these enhancements represented the manifestation of the strange and dangerous harmonics, but it soon became apparent as the voice shifted down an octave and assumed the robotic character of an auto-tuned pop singer, that it was Brooks' doing. He was preventing the voice from triggering the trans-dimensional vibrations that might otherwise emerge from it in an acoustic space. The effect was no less disturbing in light of this knowledge.

"Well, that's not freaky at all." She rubbed down the gooseflesh on her arms and removed her laptop from the bag at her feet.

Brooks swiveled his chair toward her. "I don't care how freaky it sounds as long as tentacles don't start pouring out of the speakers."

"Point taken. What now? You said he won't be able to stand it in there for very long."

"No, he won't. I heard the longest anybody could tolerate it was about fifty-five minutes. We're on a ticking clock. Last night when you brought this guy to my attention, I did a records search. Found contact info for the doctor who ran the memory drug study at Harvard. I've been in touch. Got him on standby. He wanted to come here and meet with us, but I argued against it."

"Why?"

"I'm just trying not to introduce too many variables."

"Like dude freaking out if he sees the guy who did this to him?"

"It's a consideration. And Dr. Huang doesn't have clearance to watch weird shit go down, if it does. I don't need him becoming one more person who needs a fresh dose of Nepenthe when I have to account for my actions later."

"I get it. So you're gonna call him?"

"Yeah." Brooks nodded at the laptop she'd set up on a stretch of table clear of other tech. "What do you have?"

Becca clicked and frowned at the screen. "These are the infrared shots I took of the substance on his basement walls. None of this was visible to the naked eye." She turned the computer toward him.

"Jesus. They hurt to look at."

She nodded. "But he's right: they do kinda look like dogs."

"Dogs made of broken glass, maybe." Brooks turned to a third monitor and typed in a phone number from a spiral notepad. A moment later the system brought up the slightly laggy video feed of a young Asian American man in a V-neck sweater and tortoiseshell glasses. He looked more like a tech CEO than a pharmacologist. The expensive furnishings in the background suggested he was at home.

"Hello, Agent Brooks."

"Thank you for taking my call, Dr. Huang."

"Always happy to assist the government and help a patient." Though his tone suggested otherwise. Becca figured he was cooperating out of curiosity for any details he could glean about adverse side effects. Or maybe he was suspending judgment about whether or not said side effects *were* adverse if they were interesting enough to suggest new avenues of research.

"How is Mr. Mulvaney? You mentioned hallucinations."

"Possibly, yes. Have you heard from any other subjects about that kind of thing?"

Dr. Huang bobbed his head side to side. "I'm not at liberty to discuss the data. I mean, the NDA is pretty extensive. You flashed a SPECTRA badge on our first call, but you'll have to forgive me for taking my employer's corporate espionage concerns into account."

Brooks sat up straight and leaned into the camera. Becca could hear his Boston accent coming to the fore, the way it did whenever he switched modes from *appeasing eggheads* to *not fucking around.* "I have a man in a foam room right now, possibly going schizoid because of an experimental drug you gave him and you want to talk about NDAs? Are you kidding me with this shit? Because if you're still eager to join this party in person, I can assure you the armed escort and helicopter ride will erase any doubts you might have about who I work for."

"Is that an invitation, Agent Brooks? I have to admit it's tempting."

"More of a warning, really. Once you're in with us, it's hard to get out. As my associate Ms. Philips can attest."

Over Brooks' shoulder, Becca fluttered her fingers in a little wave. "Hi, Dr. Huang. He speaks the truth. You don't want the debriefing. It either puts you on the payroll—talk about NDAs!—or on the receiving end of those experimental drugs."

Dr. Huang shifted in his chair. "The answer is no. I've received no reports of hallucinations related to the study. Just some bad dreams."

"Any recurring themes in those nightmares?" Becca asked. "Any shared images reported by different subjects?"

Even on a screen, she could tell from the look on his face that she'd hit pay dirt. "You want to know if other test subjects have dreamt the same content Mr. Mulvaney is seeing in waking hallucinations. That is very interesting. I might even confirm it, if you go first. What is he seeing?"

Brooks gave Becca permission with a look.

"He imagines that something is pursuing him. He catches glimpses of it in his peripheral vision, so the details are scant. But it seems to have canine characteristics, only sharply angular, even crystalline."

Dr. Huang took a sip of water.

"Ring any bells?" Brooks asked.

"I would very much like to interview Mr. Mulvaney. His experience suggests that he's tapped into what we call *genetic memory*, accessing an archetype that has presented itself throughout history to people in visionary states. This one was first documented by shamans on the plateau of Leng."

"What did your other test subjects dream? Don't evade the question with jargon," Brooks said.

"Some of the reported dreams have been consistent with this archetype, yes. But when I recorded them I believed I might be making inferences prejudiced by my own knowledge of the subject. What you've described is interesting because it's more specific. That is to say, I've had reports from people who feared they were being pursued by dogs in their dreams, but that's not unusual. Dogs are part of life. They can symbolize different things to different people. This, however ... is closer to the mark."

"What mark? You clearly recognize this. Just tell us what it is." Brooks was losing his patience. Becca knew she should intervene to keep their delicate relationship with the doctor from breaking, but before she could speak, movement on the video feed from the anechoic chamber drew her attention. Mulvaney was snapping his fingers, listening to how quickly the sound was snuffed out, like a match lit in a vacuum. He didn't look well. But then Huang's voice drew her back.

"The active ingredient in our memory-enhancement drug is a fungal compound with mild psychedelic properties. Too mild in the amounts we're testing to produce full-blown hallucinations. But this compound has a well-documented history in Chinese alchemy as well as a fantastical reputation for inducing psychic time travel."

"Time travel," Brooks shook his head. Becca marveled that he still defaulted to a low threshold on his personal bullshit detector after all they'd seen and lived through together.

"I know how that sounds," Huang said. "But I've never interpreted the myths surrounding the drug in terms of actual physical time travel. I always believed it made more sense that this was a primitive and poetic way of describing vivid memory regression. My hypothesis was that if we could induce vivid memories with finely calibrated low dosages, we would have a basis for treating brain injuries and Alzheimer's."

"And what about your colleagues?" Becca asked. "Did they share your opinion that the descriptions of time travel in the literature were just poetry?"

"We would never get our work published if we entertained notions of psychic time travel."

"That's not an answer," Brooks said.

"I parted ways with my original partner in the work when I found out he was interested in past-life regression. Some subjects in early trials before we adjusted the dosages regressed so rapidly through childhood memories that they began to tap into memories that appeared to be from earlier eras. The memories of people who lived before they were born. In most cases, we had no way of verifying these reports, and I was afraid they would taint our data." A Siamese cat hopped onto

Huang's desk and arched its back. He petted it while he talked. "I argued with my colleague that these cases could likely be explained by genetic memory, subjects accessing traumatic experiences of their ancestors buried deep in their DNA. Such a mechanism could even have evolutionary value in that it might prevent later generations from dying of the same causes. The universal primal fear of poisonous snakes and spiders is often cited as a potential example of this sort of thing. But it wasn't our focus, and I didn't want to get sidetracked by something that would bring the stigma of New Age quackery. Chinese medicine has enough superstition attached to it without bringing in reincarnation." The doctor sighed. "Klinger would have loved to hear about Mr. Mulvaney's experience. It's straight out of the magic scrolls of Zhang Daoling."

"Dr. Huang," Brooks said, "I have a man in a box for his own protection right now, but there's a clock ticking on that. I need you to get to the point."

"Understood. But remember: you asked for it. The lore surrounding the drug claims it makes one vulnerable to attack by predators that track time travelers. They're called the Hounds of Tindalos, named after the their city of origin. Some say it's situated on another world, or nested in another dimension. They're supposed to leave a residue behind in the form of blue slime with strange chemical properties." Huang must have seen something pass between Becca and Brooks at the mention of the substance because he stopped his explanation abruptly and asked, "You've *seen* it?"

"No comment," Brooks said.

Huang set his cat on the floor and slumped in his chair, covering his mouth with his hand and shaking his head. "This is all too much. And why Mulvaney? He didn't regress as far as some of the others. What would make *him* a target of ... This is crazy talk. Did Klinger put you up to this? Is he there? Is this some kind of prank?"

"I'm afraid not," Brooks said. "Are you familiar with a drug called Nepenthe?"

"No. What is it?"

"We administered it to victims of the Starry Wisdom terror attacks. Our working theory is that it may have effected long-term brain changes that caused Mulvaney to process your drug differently because both are memory agents."

"It's clear you are in a moment of crisis with Mr. Mulvaney. What other symptoms or side effects is he presenting besides 'hallucinations' that leave a trail of blue slime?" Dr. Huang hooked air quotes around the word.

"I never said there was—"

Becca cut Brooks off. "His voice is changing. I think this all got started because of him singing. It was like the universe was conspiring to get him to start singing, and once he did his voice started changing. I've seen enough to be convinced that the creatures pursuing him are using resonant sounds to manifest. I don't care if you think they're a myth. What do they want?"

"What does anything want? To eat and propagate. But these things are supposed to be literal hellhounds. If they feast on a man, his soul is devoured. Cast outside of time and space."

"You believe in a soul?" Brooks sounded honestly curious.

"I don't believe in any of this. I'm just quoting the lore. But just between us, the past life regression data convinced me that consciousness likely survives death."

"We have him in an anechoic chamber right now," Becca said. "He was acting as an amplifier. Not just his own voice but mine and any other vocal sound in his vicinity was feeding the process."

"I might be able to help you if I could analyze the structure of this Nepenthe drug, but for now I can only speculate about how it might be interacting with the Liaotrevex," Dr. Huang said.

Brooks shifted restlessly in his seat. "I'd need authorization to send it over and right now I'm not sure—"

The sound of a crash crackled through the monitor speakers. Dr. Huang started and nearly spilled out of his chair, his cat yowling and leaping over the furniture. Within seconds the room was crowded with Kevlar-clad men brandishing rifles. Huang was on his knees, his hands raised, his head still level with the webcam. "What is this?" he asked the camera. "I thought you said you weren't bringing me in?"

Brooks killed the feed and jumped up from his own chair, which spun in circles behind him as he rushed to the entrance hall of the lab.

"You should get out of here," he said to Becca. "I'll take the fall for this. Go to the basement and hide out in a utility closet until we're gone."

"Like they don't know I'm part of this. I'm staying." She leaned over the control desk and clicked through a series of camera views until she found the security feed from the parking lot. Two black SUVs blocked the front entrance to the lab. A third was parked in the back, where a pair of armed men watched the exit. In the chamber, Mulvaney lay on his back, staring at the ceiling. Locked in the soundproofed room, he didn't flinch when door at the end of the hall flew open.

It occurred to Becca that the agents making their entrance likely had a key to the lab, the same as Brooks did. They didn't need to kick the door in, but they'd still burst in with enough force to make their intentions clear. No matter that she and Brooks worked for SPECTRA; this was a raid, the same as at Dr. Huang's house.

Within seconds the entry hall was filled with agents, their guns trained on Becca and Brooks. The pair stood beside the door to the anechoic chamber with their hands raised. Becca recognized the man in the lead. Nico Merrit, chief of the Boston field office.

"Why is it always you two I find in the kitchen when the pots are boiling over and the smoke alarms are going off? Where is he, Brooks?"

Brooks nodded toward the door of the chamber. "He's a safe in there. Sound can't travel in that room, and sound appears to be the source of the danger. Again."

Even in the dimly lit corridor, Becca could see a jumpy nerve twitching at the corner of Merrit's eye. "So it's back? It's happening again?"

"Maybe not the same thing," Becca said. "He may be a solitary case."

Merrit ordered three agents to secure the rooms at the rear of the lab and motioned for a fourth to train his rifle on the door to the chamber. To Brooks, he said, "You're going to open that door and tell Mulvaney he's coming with us. Tell him he's safe with us but we're bringing him in in a hood and cuffs for his own safety."

"I just met the guy. He trusts Becca more."

"Then you do it, Philips. Open the door."

"I don't think that's a good idea. He's so resonant that exposure to any vocal sounds at all could feed the fire. Right now he's like a live wire that's been insulated, but if you transport him ... a hood won't be enough. We were lucky to get him here before it went full bloom."

Merrit worked his tense jaw. "Look, we don't know everything, and neither do you, and that's the point. But we've intercepted enough of your comms to have an idea, and the feeling at Government Center is that his mutation is likely exponential. Likely to reach a critical mass where your soundproofing won't matter anymore. When that happens, he needs to be in a more secure environment. This is an extraction. I packed light, and we need to hustle. Open the door."

Becca stepped forward and turned the latch. The tight-fitting door gave a hushed sigh as it swung inward on blackness.

"Dan? Are you okay?" she called into the dead air.

After a beat, the answer came: "I don't know." Three words. Dry and quiet at first, as if he were standing just inside the doorway. But the tail end of the third word climbed through a howling spectrum of harmonic resonance.

The sound pierced Becca's skull like an iron bolt and sent her stumbling backward, pressing her palms to her ears. The agent with the gun switched on a laser sight, a green beam trembling in the darkness. Brooks stuck his fingers in his ears and squinted through the pain. Only Merrit was unmoved. It took Becca a moment to realize he'd put on a pair of ear protectors.

Mulvaney crashed into the hallway like a man on fire frantic for a body of water to jump into. He flailed at the air, wracked with panic and pain. Behind him, something moved on the borderline of manifestation. It reminded Becca of giant insect wings formed of violet light. Then of the blades of enormous scissors made of cloudy quartz. Her final impression was of a great beast, hunched like a Scottish deerhound, dripping viscous rays of light—expanding, contracting, and flickering as if reflected by a series of moving mirrors in a carnival funhouse. Its eye fixed on her for a fleeting instant and she felt all of her will to resist its ravenous appetite draining from her body. Then its cold gaze darted toward Mulvaney again. The paralysis left her as quickly as it had come on, and the beast lunged at its prey.

She knew in that instant that the hounds had made a choice. They would sacrifice their living doorway into this world rather than go hungry. She didn't know for how long Dan Mulvaney's mind and body would sustain them, if it would be enough for the journey back to wherever they'd come from, but they sensed the opportunity to feed slipping away and seized the moment.

She would have to seize it, too. The fear in Mulvaney's eyes was as hot as their hunger was cold. He knew there was no escape this time. He was trapped.

In the days and years that followed, Becca would doubt what she'd seen in those eyes—the depth of Mulvaney's understanding, the presence of pleading. But she didn't doubt it now. She reached into Brooks' jacket and pulled his gun from the holster.

He tried to stop her, but the suddenness of the move caught him off guard and slowed his reaction. By the time his hand came up to grab her wrist she'd already tossed the weapon to Mulvaney, who caught it like a football, pulling it in to his belly. The hound was almost upon him when he raised the gun to his head.

"No!" Brooks yelled.

The agent with the rifle was now training his laser on the beast, but it was just one more thread of light in a shifting web. Merrit was lunging forward, raising a black hood in both hands, preparing to pull it down over Mulvaney's head, as if that would somehow stop the manifestation in its tracks. But it was too late for that.

Time seemed to slow. Becca felt a wave of déja vu pass through her mind, telling her that she'd lived this exact scene before, and would live it again. Somewhere in the cosmos, a shard of her mind would always be living this moment in a Möbius loop because time was holographic, every piece contained the whole in simultaneous synchronicity.

She felt alive in a way she hadn't since the tide of chaos had receded from her life, and it was horrible because she was failing even as her adrenaline surged. Mulvaney was going to die, and the only thing she'd managed to save was his soul, and she didn't even know if she believed there was such a thing. All she knew beyond the shadow of a doubt was that there were more horrors in the universe than any religion could ever catalog, and sometimes the only way to banish them was to blow out a mind like a candle.

Mulvaney pulled the trigger, and just like in the alley behind the gallery, there was a backward sigh, the sound of all the energy being sucked out of a pocket of air, and he was gone. Only, this time, he left a body behind.

Brooks parked the car and waited for the song to finish before shutting off the engine. Becca, in the passenger seat beside him, clicked the Stop button on her phone and tucked it into the inside pocket of her coat. Her chest hitched with a deep, sharp breath, but she kept the tears in check.

"He sure could sing," Brooks said.

"Yeah."

"You want me to come in with you?"

Becca shook her head and sniffed. "I'll be fine."

She could tell he wanted to reach over and comfort her in some way, that he was considering brushing her hair away from her temple with a gentle finger, but he hesitated and she withdrew before he could. It would have broken the dam, and she needed to hold it together a little longer. Maybe she shouldn't have played the recording before going in, but she'd wanted him to hear it. It felt important somehow. There wouldn't be much of a memorial for Daniel Mulvaney. He'd lived a mostly solitary life after 2019. This moment of reflection might be the extent of it.

"Be right back." Becca slipped out of the car, shut the door, and walked up the brick path between the dwarf pines flanking the entrance of the Gentle Shepherd Hospice Center.

She'd called ahead and spoken to a counselor, introducing herself as a friend of the family and explaining that Dan had died suddenly and unexpectedly in a tragic accident. SPECTRA had kept the incident out of the press except for the sort of boilerplate obituary used for suicides. It hadn't been difficult to arrange a visit with his mother,

Judith, but the counselor had advised Becca that it was unlikely to be rewarding for either party.

"Honestly, you'll be as familiar to her as any stranger off the street. I know it can be hard to hear this when you feel a need to inform a loved one of a loss, but you should be aware going in that it will mostly be for your own benefit to tell her. Most days, she doesn't remember her son. Maybe that will be a mercy in this case. I'm sorry for your loss, Ms. Philips, but I have to ask that you'll be respectful of Judith's condition and refrain from causing her any distress if the news is confusing to her."

The counselor Becca had spoken with on the phone wasn't available when she signed in at the front desk. A receptionist summoned a nurse to guide her through the facility to Mrs. Mulvaney's bedroom. The place had a homey vibe once you got past the green glass and veined marble of the reception area. Polished wood staircases and Victorian wallpaper gave the impression that it might once have been a boarding house or a funeral home.

Becca was relieved to find Mrs. Mulvaney sitting upright in her elevated hospital bed, unencumbered by medical equipment, gazing out the window at the bare trees of Jamaica Hills and the hazy gray Boston skyline in the distance. She was dressed for the visit, which caused Becca a brief pang of guilt.

"Judith?" the nurse said, "Your visitor is here. Do you remember Becca?"

"I can't say I do, dear." Judith smiled. "I used to pretend, but they tell me it's better to be honest about it. I'm sorry. Are you my daughter-in-law?"

"No, ma'am. Your married son is in Delaware. I'm a friend of Danny, your other son."

"Oh? Is he here?"

"No. He couldn't be with me today. But I know he misses you. He sent me to play a song for you. A recording of him singing and playing the piano. He told me you taught him to play. Would you like to hear it? I have it on my phone here. I'll set it on your bedside table."

"Those do everything now, don't they?"

"They are pretty handy." Becca set the phone down on a lace doily with the speakers aimed at the bed, her finger poised over the play icon. "Danny told me this is a song you used to sing to him when he was a baby. He took up the piano again around the holidays, and recorded himself singing and playing your old upright around Christmas time. He was planning to bring the recording to you because there isn't a piano here, but he ... he couldn't make it. So I came instead." Her voice was cracking, the old woman looking at her with a spark of sympathetic curiosity in her eyes, sensing the emotion in Becca's words, if not the reason for it. Becca tapped the screen and turned to face the window.

The blue ichor had been gone from the basement when she and Brooks returned to the house. Becca didn't know if that meant it had grown sentient enough to leave of its own accord, but she wanted to believe it had retreated back into the ether from which it had arisen when Mulvaney died. There was so much they didn't know and might never understand, but that much felt right to her. Time would tell, she thought grimly as the final verse came around in the train driver's smoky tenor. *Time will tell.*

Had he known, even as he recorded this song, how things would end?

> *O Danny Boy, the stream flows cool and slowly;*
> *And pipes still call and echo 'cross the glen.*
> *Your broken mother sighs and feels so lowly,*
> *For you have not returned to smile again.*
> *So if you've died and crossed the stream before us,*
> *We pray that angels met you on the shore;*
> *And you'll look down, and gently you'll implore us*
> *To live so we may see your smiling face once more*

Judith stared at the ceiling, her deep rutted cheeks glistening with tears. Becca approached the bed and patted her frail hand. "It's okay," she said. "It's okay."

"I remember now. I remember Danny. But I know I'll forget again."

"It's okay. You'll be together again soon," Becca said. "And then you'll remember everything."

The White Door

What would you say if I told you there is but one book in all the world that reveals a true account of the realms beyond death? You've heard the claim before, of course, from men of cloth and cap who would tell you the title for free and how to read it for a fee. But what if I told you there has never been more than a single copy of this book, and that it roams the libraries of the world at will? What if I told you that of all the books in the world, there is but one that reads the reader?

I first heard of *The White Door* when I was a student at Phillips Exeter Academy in New Hampshire. Even then, in my adolescence, I was predisposed to doubt the popular claims of the world's religions. Were they true, then surely their adherents would be endowed with powers and proofs beyond refute. Unlike men of science, the religious have failed to produce the miracles that would validate their claims. And yet, precisely because of this lack of empirical proof for a world beyond ours, I have searched for it since boyhood with a hunger all the more ravenous for the scarcity of crumbs from the philosophical table.

That embarrassing hunger, which I'd long kept secret from family and friends, came to the fore when at Exeter I found a small band of like-minded seekers in Professor Nourse's Parapsychology Club. I still considered myself a skeptic in those days, albeit one yearning for conversion, and I would often critique the tepid proofs of my fellow students when they offered anecdotal evidence to support their favorite claims. In retrospect, I suppose I was challenging myself, deriding my own obsessions aloud in order to test their veracity. Professor Nourse indulged my windy critiques, but he also maintained the core practice of the academy, adhering to the Harkness round-table method of discussion even in our student club, sketching a web of lines around a template of the table to keep track of who in our group had spoken and who deserved a turn. Only when Nourse himself brought forth an outlandish claim would I absorb it without debate.

Please don't think I took my teacher's claims on faith—I did not. But unlike my fellow students, the man had been a sifter of shadows for long decades before I was born and could be counted upon to present only the most veritable pieces of lore to our assembly.

I received the data on *The White Door* from him in scattered fragments over several semesters, and each made an indelible impression on my mind.

"There's a legend about a book that haunts the libraries of the world," he told us after school one afternoon in his classroom. I remember focusing my gaze on the chalk dust swirling in a shaft of autumnal light bisecting the wood floor as I listened.

"When it isn't roaming, it supposedly resides at Miskatonic University, where its leaves were bound by the school's most renowned librarian, Henry Armitage."

This met with grunts and murmurs. We were all familiar with Armitage and the collection he'd once curated. And for that reason, the conversation took a series of sharp turns touching on the more notorious tomes rumored to be kept under lock and key at the university.

Some months later, over dinner at the professor's cramped apartment where the club had gathered to ride out a nor'easter, I resurrected the subject.

"What more can you tell us about the roaming book?"

Nourse grinned. "Well, the call number, for one thing. It's 133.9 ARM."

I can still hear the crystal claws of ice flakes tapping against the glass in the brief silence that followed.

"One thirty-three for Paranormal and Occult Studies," Brett Wheaton said, showing off.

"And nine for The Afterlife," I finished for him. We didn't have the entire Dewey Decimal system memorized, but most of us were well versed in the section that catalogued our obsessions.

"Correct." Nourse said. "And ARM to indicate the editor, although as the story goes, Armitage did no editing whatsoever. He merely took a folio of loose incantations recorded in a single hand and had them bound to preserve them for the stacks."

Patrick Ellis interjected: "You've seen this book?"

"On the occasions when I've visited the university, it was … unavailable."

I noticed that he didn't exactly answer the question, didn't say that he hadn't ever seen the book, only that he hadn't seen it at Miskatonic. "Unavailable, but surely not listed as checked out," I said. "They would never allow an edition of *one* to leave the building."

He nodded. "However, I was able to study Armitage's firsthand account of the book's production. Very interesting, that. He never describes the contents explicitly, but he does express consternation over the fact that what he knew to be a book of incantations became something else once it was bound. He had quite a row with the binder."

In the spring of my junior year the professor hired three of our group to help with landscaping at his mother's house in Stratham. I recall sitting on the back deck at the end of a full day's work, drinking fresh-squeezed lemonade, the condensation on my glass turning the dirt on my fingers to tears of thin mud, when I revived the topic again.

"Professor, assuming that Armitage's account is true, what do you suppose caused the change in the contents of *The White Door?* Did he ever consider the possibility that the binder didn't bind the wrong pages?"

Nourse swirled melting ice cubes around a vortex in his half-empty glass. "Being a very rational sort of man, Armitage dances around the conclusion, but the pages he brought to the binder were hand-written on parchment, and the leather-bound book that came back was filled with pages of the same parchment, written in the same hand. He even recognized particular stains, having examined the leaves carefully before submitting them. Only the contents differed. He could not account for it. When he calmed down, he realized that the number of pages also matched. He never states what he read in the bound book, only that he asked a colleague to also read it so they could compare their impressions. He doesn't name the other man, yet makes it clear that to him it was a *third* text; one he found far more terrifying than what Armitage had led him to expect. The two men had read two different books within the same boards."

I chuckled at this, but the laugh sounded false to my own ears. "How is that possible?"

In his dirty jeans and white T-shirt, Nourse looked more like a gravedigger than a professor. He fixed his gaze on his earth-clotted shoes and shook his head. It was the first time I'd seen him at a loss for words.

◆

I embarked upon my own search the following week, starting with the libraries of southern New Hampshire before venturing further afield on weekends to Massachusetts and Maine. At school I began working detours through the library into my schedule, often arriving late for my classes when the errand sent me too far off course.

But the book never appeared on the shelves.

Summer vacation expanded my reach. When my classmates returned in September, bronzed from New England's beaches and lakes, I would be as pale as the day we'd left. In my senior year, I finally made the pilgrimage to Miskatonic University to examine Armitage's original documents. But there were no great revelations waiting in the source material. I had learned more from the kindred spirits I occasionally encountered in the stacks caressing rows of call-number stickers, the cellophane sleeves crackling beneath their desperate, sweaty fingers. Always the same numbers—a litany of cabalistic equation: 131, 133 ... 133.9 ... hungry eyes searching for leather under the laminate.

Most were older and had been searching far longer than I. They had the look of addicts in their gaunt faces. But were they all addicted to something they had never sampled? For a long time I was too timid to ask. And the more of them I crossed paths with, the more convinced I became that if the book even existed, it had long since been stolen by the last seeker who'd found it.

In time my curiosity overcame my temerity and I began prying the competition in the musty aisles, collecting theories about *The White Door*.

Most agreed it was an account of the afterlife and that each reader saw in its pages a different realm: the one to which he or she would be transported at the moment of death. This was the core mythology, but descriptions of the book's physical details differed widely, the legends of its legacy even more so. Some said the leather was black, others red or white. Most agreed that the spine had raised bands and that a geometric symbol from the text was stamped in gold leaf on the cover, but no two descriptions of the symbol aligned. One popular theory held that the binding-together of the spells had activated them.

In Rhode Island I met a lawyer from Cleveland who claimed the book was illustrated with woodblock prints that came to life like opium dreams. In London, where I studied abroad for a year after graduation, a homeless schizophrenic who claimed he'd once been a prosperous antiquarian book dealer told me he'd spent his life's savings traveling the world in search of our mutual obsession and had found it twice. On the first occasion, he had attempted to leave the library with it only to find a different book in his hands when he reached the sidewalk: a cheap fiction by a best-selling horror writer. When his second chance arrived years later, he read the book from cover to cover on the spot.

He wouldn't tell me what he saw in its pages, only that it was devastating. Now he needed to peer inside the book a third time in the desperate hope that his destiny had changed, that this time he might glimpse a fate he could bear for the remainder of his days.

Others told tales of heavenly dimensions, unfathomable ecstasies.

The lawyer's enthusiasm had been contagious, while the vagabond infected me with dread. I liked the lawyer more, but both men had reaffirmed what I already knew: to pursue the quest I would need capital and the freedom to travel.

After college I went into finance. I traveled the world and amassed a small fortune, but no amount of worldly success could diminish my obsession. To the contrary, the more resources I acquired, the more driven I was in my quest. The fuel with which I fed the fire was of no consequence to me. If subprime mortgages offered the biggest profit, the quickest return, and the earliest retirement, then what did I care if working people saw their homes devalued as neighboring properties went into foreclosure? I was on the trail of something sublime; something most people didn't even know existed. I rode the bubble until it popped, and when entire neighborhoods fell, overtaken by a tide of graffiti, weeds, and broken glass, when national economies swirled in ragged strands around the drain, I prospered. I searched.

And I found.

When you scour the globe for a rare treasure, you don't expect to find it close to home without fanfare. I had wandered under the mahogany arches of Trinity College and the frescoes of El Escorial, Spain. I had hunted among the marble pillars of monasteries and the steel columns of technical institutes, and had long ago ceased anticipating a tingle of intuition upon entering a library, a feeling that this could be the one. And so it took me utterly by surprise when at last I found *The White Door* in Newburyport, Massachusetts where I had settled to enjoy an early retirement in my fifties.

On the fateful occasion, I hadn't even entered the library with the book on my mind. It was my weekend to take the children, and after a morning spent bickering with my ex-wife about what to do with them, I had settled on taking them to the library. Only after dropping my daughters off for Story & Craft Hour, did I find myself ascending the stairs to the quiet of the third floor, passing the nonfiction stacks and empty study cubicles and arriving at the small occult section.

I knew I'd found it before I was close enough to read the title—a black leather volume with raised bands standing out among the tattered New Age paperbacks like a Masonic officer in a tuxedo and white gloves amid a crowd of hippies. I walked toward it as if in a dream, not quite believing what I saw, not knowing what I felt. And I realized in that moment that I no longer knew why I wanted to read this book, that I hadn't known for years, had maybe *never* known.

Had I embarked on this quest to find proof of a single piece of magic in a mundane world? Well, here at last was my proof, long after

I'd mastered the spells of mathematics and accounting to conquer that mundane world.

Did I really want to know what awaited me beyond death's door? I'd seen what that knowledge had done to others.

As I slid the book off the shelf I thought of Professor Nourse. He was an old man nearing retirement when I'd paid my last visit to the academy, but his opinion of me still carried weight, and I feared he would think me foolish to still be chasing a phantom he had entertained me with as a boy. And yet, in his company it was all I could think of. My research had proven to me that most of what he'd told us had at least some basis in fact, but had he ever read the book?

I had to know.

After a few drinks and the sort of disclaimer adults make before inquiring about magic, I asked him flat out, "Did you ever find *The White Door?*"

Nourse held my gaze in silence as tears welled up in his raw pink eyelids.

"*Yes,*" he said at last, with a tone that conveyed how odd he found it that I'd never asked him before.

"What did you find when you opened it?"

He looked through me, beyond me, and said, "It's so close now. So close." And I wondered if he spoke to himself when he said, "It's not so bad, not so bad. Better than ceasing to exist, I suppose."

Deciding that whatever vision the book had granted him was his alone, I simply asked, "Where did you find it?"

"Right here at the school. One day there it was. Knocked the wind out of me." He laughed.

"And do you *still* look for it?"

"No. I don't need to see it again. Once was enough."

Emboldened by his admission, I confessed to having done a little research of my own after college. "No two accounts of the contents ever match. It's enough to make you doubt the whole business. And of the few who claim to have seen it twice, some—*but not all*—visited different realms on each occasion. What do you make of that?"

"Maybe ..." he began, and paused to formulate the sentence in his mind before continuing, reminding me of his manner in the classroom. "Maybe a man's final destination can change over the course of a lifetime. Remember, one of the oldest bits of lore about *The White Door,* one of the first things I ever told you boys about it, is that it's the only book in the world that reads the reader. Maybe if you get a second look, it behaves like a GPS and ... what do they say? *Recalculates.*"

The notion chilled me for some reason I could not explain.

It was the last time I saw my mentor. I'd left him on that occasion expecting him to have more years, but he'd been right. When I last saw him, what lay beyond the white door was close.

Driving east on 101 and leaving the academy behind, I contemplated the blank screen of my GPS and wondered what cosmic intelligence could be responsible for the recalculation of a man's soul and its trajectory.

I've never been a gambling man—except at work where the house always won—but I feel I am becoming one now; a man down and hoping for redemption before the clock runs out. I know the location of every library within a sixty-mile radius of my home, and I visit a new one every time I have reason to travel outside that radius. I have also become a charitable man recently.

My children knew where to look for me when I didn't appear with the other parents at the end of the story hour. They climbed the stairs, ran to my favorite aisle, and found me splayed on the floor regaining consciousness.

The book was gone.

The lawyer I'd met in Providence had it right. *The White Door* was illustrated. At least, for me it was. A woodblock print of a long corridor lined with bookshelves constituted the first page. The drawing reminded me of a tarot card, and I felt a cold unease spreading in my belly as I brought my nose closer to the page, the leather clammy in my hands, the paper redolent of sandalwood.

The illustration was suddenly infused with a wash of colors: walnut in the shelving, navy in the carpet, and a mosaic of green, purple, and gold where the steep-angled perspective lines converged on a stained-glass window at the end of the row. I caught my breath, and then, for a moment, for a brief eternity, I was *in* the picture, in a library that felt familiar, though I was unable to place it. I walked toward the stained-glass window, passing stack upon stack, and yet, it remained too distant for me to discern the pattern. I felt certain I would recognize which library this was, if only I could see the details of that one distinguishing feature. And then it struck me what a cosmic joke it was to spend one's life searching libraries for a clue to a personal afterlife only to learn at last that one's designated dominion was to be an infinity of bookshelves.

It couldn't be true. The others would have told me, the ones who had found *The White Door* would have told me if this had been their lot. I felt anger rising, heat flushing my face and sweat prickling at my collar. The vision wasn't personal in the least. And yet, nagging at me was the indubitable sense that I *knew* this place, had been here before in life or in dream, and then I realized that I could at least learn the name of the library from the stamp on one of the books before the vision ended.

The spines were bare of call stickers, quelling my hopes before I'd even laid a hand on a random volume. Turning it over in my hands, the edging bore no stamp, and flipping it open to the title page, I found no label. The title read *TRESEDER*. I fanned the pages and found a black-and-white photograph of a two-story clapboard starter home with a single-car garage, the front door boarded up and posted with a notice, a rusting bicycle with tattered streamers hanging from the handlebars abandoned in the overgrown front yard. The name from the title page rang a bell in the back of my mind: a name on a junk mortgage package I'd prepared. I've always prided myself on a sharp memory, and now the first names came to me: Rodney and Tamara. I flipped through the pages, scanning, and caught fragments of scenes from the domestic life of the Treseders— snippets of dialogue, heated words about bills, childcare, and name-brand medicines. More pages, more photos, and then one that made me drop the book: a forensic photo of Rodney Treseder slumped against the steering wheel of his Toyota Camry with a garden hose snaking from the exhaust through the cracked window.

I took a lurching step away from the fallen book and put a hand out to steady myself. My mind was reeling. I could make no sense of my physical state, but felt that I might be sick. My hand settled on another random spine, and I drew it from the shelf. Title: *COSTA.* I opened it and found more transcripts of despair; more photos of the abused abusing each other as their worth was stripped away and sucked into a whirlpool of debt. I tried to return the book to the shelf but my numbing fingers knocked an adjacent volume to the floor where it fell open on another forensic photo: a man in a lawn chair cradling a shotgun, an indecipherable chaos of bloody meat where his head should have been.

I gazed down the aisle and read the gilt titles stretching away from where I stood: *FOWLER, WRIGHT, HOLOROYD, GROHMAN, MENENDEZ,* and on, and on. Names I recognized. Forms I'd filed, lives I'd gambled, souls I'd bargained to line my pockets and bankroll my quest for a glimpse of something true, something transcendent beyond the white door.

Story Notes and Acknowledgments

I've always thought that short stories are like songs—the first dozen or so you write don't necessarily make an album, but the first dozen with a shared theme or style might. I'm a slow short story writer. The two oldest tales presented here were published in 2013, the year after my first novel was released. I've now published six novels and a couple of novellas ahead of this, my first short-fiction collection, and yeah, I know, I'm doing it backward. Because three of those novels were a trilogy of Lovecraftian thrillers, I started getting invited to write stories for Lovecraftian anthologies. Typically one or two per year, but eventually they added up. Funny thing about Mythos fiction: it seems to never go out of fashion and once you've published some, people tend to keep asking you to write more of it.

The stories in this book all have connections to other stories and books, whether to my own novels, the mythos of H. P. Lovecraft, or both. I'm guessing if you picked this volume up, you have at least a passing familiarity with those tales, but we all start somewhere with what's become known as the Cthulhu Mythos, so on the off chance that you've first encountered it here—or on the more likely chance that you're already acquainted with the work of Lovecraft, his influences and the early writers who took the torch from him, but you haven't yet checked out my novels—this seems like a good place to point out some of those connecting threads.

I wrote these stories in the hope that each would entertain without the need for a larger context, but half the fun of playing with a mythology that's been growing new tentacles (sorry) for a century is riffing on references that will tip off your fellow cultists like a secret handshake. And for the uninitiated, if one of these tales piques your interest in a particular monster, character or theme, you'll have a signpost pointing to where you can take a deeper dive.

Rattled
This one takes the legend of Yig, the Father of Serpents, from the story by H. P. Lovecraft and Zealia Bishop. Like most of my short

227

stories, it came out of a juxtaposition of unrelated ideas that I felt had some chemistry between them. Part coming-of-age story, part horror, and part commentary on the inherent sins of colonialism, it took shape when I was asked to write a story about the serpent god for an anthology in which each invited author was assigned a different god from the Lovecraftian pantheon. Having recently visited Valley of Fire State Park in Nevada, I knew it would be the perfect setting for a snake story with Native American associations.

Something in the Water

I was a writer before I was a musician, but songwriting seduced me away from fiction long enough for me to go to music school, play in a rock band, and work as a recording engineer. So it's not surprising that the power of music keeps surfacing in my stories. It's a major theme in the SPECTRA Files books, where we also find a mystical choir using sound waves to commune with Cthulhu. "Something in the Water" was partly inspired by a weird nature documentary I saw about *Cymothoa exigua,* an isopod fish parasite that eats its host's tongue and then digs itself into the roots, effectively replacing it. What could be more Lovecraftian than that?

The Last Chord

I wrote this story for the Rock and Roll Horror issue of *Dark Discoveries* magazine after reading an article about Bob Dylan's famous lost Stratocaster being rediscovered and sold at auction for almost a million dollars. This was the same guitar the folk hero sparked controversy with when he went electric at the Newport Folk Festival in 1965. Guitarists sometimes talk about how a well-loved instrument might have some songs kicking around in it from the previous owner, which is itself a kind of ghost story. From there it wasn't much of a leap to imagine a sixties mystic rock star whose dabbling with cosmic forces might survive him in his favorite axe. The recording engineer in the story, Jake Campbell, is one of the main characters of my first novel, *The Devil of Echo Lake,* which takes place before the events of "The Last Chord."

Good Bones
Here we have a sequel to Lovecraft's "Dreams in the Witch House" that upends some of the conclusions of that story and, in true horror-sequel fashion, brings back a couple of characters (including the house itself) that we thought were killed off in the original. Who needs linear causality when you've thrown out the Euclidean baby with the bath water, anyway? The title was inspired by the devastating poem about parenthood by Maggie Smith. Thanks to Nick Nafpliotis for last-minute renovations.

The Voyager
Agent Jason Brooks plays a major role in the SPECTRA Files novels. This story, set years before the events of *Red Equinox,* is about one of his first assignments for the agency. Ever since reading Bradbury as a teen, I've always felt that carnivals are places where anything can happen.

The Mouth of the Merrimack
A trip Lovecraft took to Newburyport in the early 1920s famously influenced his story, "The Shadow Over Insmouth," with its freaky fish people and their sunken city off the coast of Massachusetts. In those days the town was little more than a huddle of derelict fishermens' shacks rotting into the sea. Now it's a cute, cosmopolitan tourist destination. My wife was born and raised in Newburyport when it was something in between, and around the turn of the century we settled in the area where most of her family still lives. In the Lovecraft story, the protagonist does research at the Newburyport Public Library and examines strange artifacts of the cult of Dagon at the Newburyport Historical Society. As a fan, moving here excited my sense of trivia, and living here has influenced much of the mythos fiction I've written over the years. Kayaking around the mouth of the Merrimack River or watching the moonrise over the iconic pink house on Plum Island takes on a different flavor for a Lovecraft fan. I guess it was inevitable that I would eventually get around to writing a Deep Ones story.

Douglas Wynne

No Mask
One of the four new stories I wrote to complete this collection during the long, dark winter of 2020–21, here we have my only COVID-19 story. Weird fiction aficionados will know just from the title that it's an ode to Robert W. Chambers' mythic play, *The King In Yellow,* from his classic collection of the same name.

The Enigma Signal
Another take on the power of sound, music, and art as channels for communication with cosmic forces. Here we encounter the Shoggoths of Lovecraft's novella, *At the Mountains of Madness.* That story is set in Antarctica, where the Pabodie Expedition discovers evidence of an ancient alien civilization. After reading about how climate change is opening up the Northwest Passage and exposing geographic features long covered by ice around the North Pole, I found myself speculating about how these changes might awaken Lovecraft's monsters on the opposite side of the globe. Other news items about the flipping of Earth's magnetic poles led to the idea that such a civilization might use the planet as a kind of battery with stations at both poles for transmitting and receiving signals and even manifestations from their distant home.

Contact
Earlier this year I published a stand-alone techno-thriller called *His Own Devices.* That novel breaks away from traditional Lovecraftian elements but does flirt with cosmic and occult horror in a somewhat ambiguous way. This story fills in a missing piece by showing us what happened to Sgt. Matt Ritter when he went missing in action after an ambush on his team in Afghanistan in 2016. Of course, his encounter with occult forces in Central Asia turns out to have a connection to the mythos. Thanks to Andrew Bobo and Erik Amstutz for generously answering my questions about Army equipment and tactics.

Tracking the Black Book
One of the first Lovecraftian stories I ever wrote and the first to see publication. Like the newest story in this collection ("Contact"), this

230

take on the dread *Necronomicon* explores the idea that our military ventures abroad may stir up ancient evils where it would be better to let sleeping dogs lie.

Time Out of Mind

Fans of the SPECTRA books have occasionally asked if I will ever write about Becca Philips and Jason Brooks again. I always say, "Never say never," and here we are. These two characters have a special place in my heart, so it was nice to hear their voices again, even if it was for another bleak encounter with terrible powers.

The White Door

Tales about magical books with the power to transport their readers to other dimensions are a staple of the genre, and it seems fitting to end this book with one. I always hung out in the parapsychology section of the library as a kid, which led to the idea for "The White Door." Never entirely forgotten, the idea collected dust at the back of the Things I'll Write Someday drawer until the right submission call came along in the form of *Tales From the Miskatonic Library* from PS Publishing. The story had a unique voice of its own from the moment I put pen to paper, which I think is a cool thing about short stories: they can feel like a moment of possession that has very little to do with the author's own voice or worldview. Lovecraft's librarian Henry Armitage from "The Dunwich Horror" plays a role in the backstory. In the process of acquiring the story for its first publication, editors Darrel Schweitzer and John Ashmead suggested that I try writing an alternate ending. I took their advice and felt that it improved the tale, but a file mix-up resulted in the first version going to press. Readers of the anthology seemed satisfied with the original ending, but I'm happy to have the opportunity to present that other version here at last.

◆

This book wouldn't exist without the imagination and ingenuity of the editors who first published most of the stories herein: Mike Davis, Aaron French, Christopher C. Payne, Doug Murano and

Douglas Wynne

D. Alexander Ward, Jennifer Brozek, Kenneth W. Cain, Darrel Schweitzer, and John Ashmead. My sincere thanks also to Joe Morey of Weird House for the guidance, encouragement, and faith necessary to bring the project to fruition and the hard work to make it something special, to my friend Curtis Lawson for introducing us, and to M. Wayne Miller for the fantastic artwork. And thank *you*, dear reader and fellow traveller who, like me, took the wrong fork at the junction of the Aylesbury pike and came upon this curious country. You've made the journey less lonely.

About the Author

DOUGLAS WYNNE is the author of the novels *The Devil of Echo Lake,* *His Own Devices,* and the SPECTRA Files trilogy (*Red Equinox,* *Black January,* and *Cthulhu Blues*). His short fiction has appeared in numerous anthologies, and his writing workshops have been featured at genre conventions and schools throughout New England. He lives in Massachusetts with his wife and son and a houseful of animals. You can find him on the web at www.douglaswynne.com.

About the Artist

ENnie Award-winning illustrator **M. WAYNE MILLER** still continues his quest to synthesize the perfect blend of science fiction, fantasy, and horror with his work. Primarily focusing on science-fiction and horror imagery for limited-edition book covers, lavish interiors, and numerous role-playing games, Wayne strives for constant improvement as an artist and illustrator through continuous education, training, and pushing the boundaries of his skill set.

A primary goal for 2021 is to gain work for Magic: The Gathering, a client that has proven as elusive as it is prestigious. His list of clients include Weird House Press, Thunderstorm Books, Chaosium, Modiphius Entertainment, and Pinnacle Entertainment Group.

Made in the USA
Columbia, SC
10 February 2023

11581563R00150